Discovery

Book One of the
Council of Powers Trilogy

Lisa White, author of *The Laws of Love*

CRIMSON ROMANCE

F+W Media, Inc.

This edition published by
Crimson Romance
an imprint of F+W Media, Inc.
10151 Carver Road, Suite 200
Blue Ash, Ohio 45242
www.crimsonromance.com

For Collin and Christopher,
whose powers are immeasurable.

Acknowledgments

Thank you, thank you, thank you again to editor extraordinaire, Jennifer Lawler. You continue to make happily-ever-afters and dreams come true.

Thank you to Meredith O'Hayre, Jessica Verdi, and all the other Ladies in Red at Crimson Romance. You are a kind, talented, and supportive group and I am grateful to be on this journey with you.

Thank you to Sarah Blevins, Morghan Clark, and Sarah Luther who took the time to read Discovery and reminded me how to be young again.

Thank you to Lori Byington, my "sista" cousin and mistress of the English language. Your continued insight, guidance, support, and love are gifts from above. Udooo!

Thank you to my family whose power of love is consistent and unconditional.

And most importantly, thank you to my husband and our two wonderful children whose powers bring me joy. You are true blessings from God and I thank you all for loving me.

Best Wishes,
Lisa

Prologue: *And Then There Was One*...

The highway patrolman wrote "Unknown" on the blank line across from the word "Cause." He hated using that word, especially when death was involved, but the seasoned officer did not know what else to write in his report.

The weather was clear. The road was dry. No other cars were involved. But here he was, staring at a crushed wad of metal in the middle of the road while the sun glimmered brightly off the van's chrome accents. The chrome accents that had adorned the van only a few hours earlier. The shiny chrome ribbons contrasted sharply against the black tar of the hot pavement underneath and it seemed strange to the patrolman that, despite the acrid smell of burnt metal lofting around the van, there was no evidence of fire. None of the chrome pieces were burned or even scratched. They were dented and twisted, sure, but no burn marks could be seen anywhere.

Looking closer at what used to be the family's minivan, the patrolman noticed that the same was true for the van's paint. It was a metallic light blue that matched the color of today's clear sky, but the van's blue parts, while wadded up together like one large piece of notebook paper, were as clean as the day the car rolled off the assembly line. There were no scratches crossing through the blue, no burned spots dirtying up the paint's glitter. Instead, it looked as if the parts were originally molded in their present contorted form and then sprayed with the shiny blue paint like some modern-day sculpture on display in the latest hip art gallery.

The patrolman stopped writing his report, placed his pen in its usual spot on his clipboard, and peered down through the shattered window into what was left of the van's interior. In all his years on the job, he had never seen anything like this. Except for the dark red blood stains running through the beige leather and the copious used gauze pads left behind by the paramedics, the van's crushed interior was pristine, as clean as the new models sitting on the showroom floor at an auto mall. It was as if someone had picked up the minivan, dunked it in bath water and, while still holding it under the water, crushed the van and its occupants, ending the massacre by delicately placing the washed metal mess back in the middle of the road from whence it came.

The patrolman took a deep breath, kicked at a stray gauze pad, and began writing his report again. Four of the van's five occupants died that day and the patrolman reasoned that the van's unusual pristine interior somehow helped protect the surviving, slender, four–year–old girl from the other occupants' fate. He had dealt with dozens of crashes during his years on the force, but those involving children never failed to affect him, especially those that produced orphans. The young girl's wide eyes frantically darting around the scene as the paramedics loaded her into the ambulance left another scar on the patrolman's memory and he knew her blue eyes would haunt his dreams for quite a few nights going forward. He was so captivated by the girl's eyes he never saw the man standing on the high ridge overlooking the crash site.

The man who smelled of burnt metal.

The man who did not understand why the girl was still alive.

Chapter One: The Meeting

Almost eighteen years later…

Her hands were tingling.

Again.

From her wrists to her fingertips, each hand shook and pulsed with tiny electric shocks. The minute Grace felt the tremors return, she shoved her vibrating hands into her pants pockets. How in the world was she supposed to work today? She could not even carry one plate, let alone a whole tray of them. But while the shaking made it difficult to use her hands, the sensation itself wasn't really painful. Most of the time, her hands felt more like they had fallen asleep. Unfortunately, Grace had not figured out how to make the shaking sensation go away so she just stood to the side of the stainless steel serving counter with her hands in her pockets, hoping this episode would be a short one.

There. Almost gone. Only her fingertips shook now.

"Order up!" the cook's assistant said.

Grace slowly pulled her hands out of her pockets and gave them one last squeeze.

"Gracie? I said order up!" Grace's best friend, Annie, shoved a martini glass filled with shrimp cocktail in her face. "Lady Covington is waiting."

Grace glanced down at her hands. They were no longer shaking, not even her fingertips. Surely she could carry one simple glass. She smiled at her friend and reached across the serving counter for the shrimp cocktail. "Annie, this isn't a diner. You know you're not supposed to yell 'Order up' like that. What if Julian heard you?" Grace stood at the serving counter until she was certain she could hang on to the glass full of shrimp.

"Oh, calm down. He can't hear me." Annie peered over at the banquet manager on the other side of the kitchen. "Besides, I just do that to bug him. You know how snobby he is over this place."

Grace sighed and shook her head as she gripped the shrimp cocktail with both hands and headed into the formal dining room. It was a packed house at the Southern Pines Country Club that spring afternoon, so even the waitresses were pulling double duty in the kitchen. Luckily for Grace, however, Lady Covington had dropped by for lunch. The elderly woman preferred to have Grace wait on her, so Julian, the banquet manager, had chosen his nemesis Annie to abandon her waitress duties and play first mate to the club's cook.

As Grace expertly weaved in and out of the crowded dining room tables toward Lady Covington, another club member seated nearby waved to the young waitress. "Gretchen, over here."

"Yes, Mr. Williamson." Grace smiled without bothering to correct him on her name. Even though she had waited on Mr. Williamson a hundred times, he had yet to get it right. He was one of the club's regular golfers and his penchant for hideously bright plaid golf knickers made him a well-known figure at the club. In return, he knew just about everyone working there, even down to the deliveryman who restocked his Dewar's Scotch each week. But for some reason Mr. Williamson had a mental block on Grace's name. The other day she was Gwen, today it's Gretchen, but he never could remember to call her Grace. His consistent memory loss didn't really upset her, however, because being anonymous made it easier to blend in.

"Can you ask Ben to bring me another Scotch? He knows how I like it." Mr. Williamson half-smiled, swirling his ice cubes as he tipped up the almost empty glass to Grace.

"Of course, sir," Grace nodded before continuing on her way. She finally made it over to Lady Covington seated at a corner table and, using both hands, carefully placed the shrimp cocktail in front of her discerning diner. "Here you are, Lady Covington. Your salad should be out in a minute. Can I get you anything else?"

"No, dear. I'm fine. Just trying to get back to my mahjong game in the ladies lounge so this will be a quick lunch today." Lady Covington smiled up at Grace. The matriarch of the country club was a large woman who, despite her size, carried an air of sophistication around her in the same way other women wore perfume. Grace did not know why she was called "Lady." In fact, her Chanel suits and Jackie Kennedy triple-strand pearl necklace made her look more like a 1960s New York socialite rather than some titled English matron. The rumor around the club was that Lady Covington had actually run in the same circles as Mrs. Kennedy when she lived in New York City, but no one had ever figured out why she was a "Lady" or how the elderly New Yorker ended up all the way down here in Southern Pines, South Carolina. Normally grouchy with other wait staff, Lady Covington was more tolerant of Grace for some reason and, so, by default, Grace had become her private servant at Southern Pines. Despite the incessant teasing from her coworkers for being Lady Covington's favorite, it was not a bad deal for Grace considering the tips the elderly patron left her. That and she was one of the few club members who actually remembered Grace's name.

"Well, I'll be back to check on you in a bit," said Grace as she turned to head back to the kitchen. Her hands were back to normal now so she took the long way around the dining room, discretely checking on her other tables and even on some that did not belong to her. She eventually made her way back to the kitchen's swinging doors but almost plowed down another waiter in the process.

"Hey! Gracie, watch it!" The waiter, Ben, reached down and caught a falling wine glass just before it hit the marble floor. He moved so fast, Grace almost did not see the glass until it was already placed back on Ben's tray. "What's the rush?"

"Sorry. I'm just trying to get it all done." Grace stood to the side and held the door open for Ben with her foot as she reached behind her head and adjusted the hairclip holding her long, brown hair back from her face. Julian liked all his waitresses to be perfectly coiffed but Grace's wispy tendrils would never stay in the required ponytail. She spent most of her time between orders unsuccessfully fussing with her hair.

"Well, slow down a little and try to remember how clumsy you are. You've got to give the rest of us a little room to maneuver." Ben smiled at Grace with a contagious mixture of amusement and mischievousness. He was one of those people who smiled with their eyes more than their mouth and Grace liked that about him. She also liked the fact that Julian hated Ben's hair almost as much as he hated Grace's. Ben's thick, dark hair always had that messed up look. The kind of look that male models used gallons of expensive hair product to achieve, but for Ben all he had to do was get out of bed and he had runway hair. Combined with his high cheekbones and aqua eyes, Ben's messy model look often made women stop and stare. But while women liked Ben's look, Julian hated it. He said Ben's hair belonged on some rock star wannabe and not on a member of the Southern Pines Country Club staff. Of course, Julian's comment only ensured that Ben never cleaned up his messy look and Grace envied her friend's silent defiance of Julian.

"More room. Got it." She started for the door again but stopped when she saw a bright red plaid napkin on a nearby tray. It reminded her of Mr. Williamson's golf knickers and his present need for another Scotch. She turned back to Ben. "Before I forget, Mr. Williamson wants another drink."

"Mr. Williamson?" Ben grinned. "Who were you today?"

"Today I'm Gretchen." Grace winked as she tightened her ponytail again and reentered the kitchen.

The club was unusually busy for such an early spring day, and the kitchen's bustle left no room for mistakes. Workers were all over the place, and Grace had to push her way through the crowded kitchen to get to Annie who was still in the back helping the cook and probably thinking of new ways to annoy Julian. Just as Grace had almost reached her friend, the banquet manager abruptly appeared out of the kitchen crowd and stepped directly into Grace's path.

"And how is Lady Covington today, Miss MacKay?" Julian looked down at Grace over his wire-rimmed glasses. He seemed to be purposefully ignoring the mocking faces Annie made at him just three feet away.

"She's fine, Julian. Don't worry. I've got her covered," Grace assured her boss. She bit the inside of her cheek and held her breath, trying to suppress the laughs bubbling inside her. Annie's facial expressions got her every time.

"Very good. Please let me know immediately if there are any problems. And get that silly hair out of your face. You know how I feel about that." Julian wagged a finger at Grace's flyaway hair and then turned up his pointy nose, put his hands behind his perfectly straight back, and strode over to his office as if he were a captain on a ship. When he reached his office door, he stopped without turning around and, enunciating each word with his British precision, added, "Miss Anne, if you put as much effort into your job as you do mocking me, you might actually make something of yourself." He then disappeared into his office without looking back.

The minute the office door closed, the entire kitchen erupted in stifled laughter.

"You're going to get fired," Grace said to Annie. Sometimes she could not believe how far Annie pushed it with Julian.

"No, she won't," Ben said as he reentered the kitchen with a new tray of dirty dishes. "Julian loves the attention he gets from Annie. Doesn't everyone?" he teased as he emptied the tray on the counter near the sink.

Annie blushed, causing her long, blonde hair to look even lighter against her rosy skin. "Oh, shut up. You're just jealous because I'm more into your brother's hot bod than whatever that thing is you have going on," she teased back as she finished preparing Lady Covington's salad.

"Too bad my brother's not into blondes with smart mouths," Ben smirked. "I can promise you *that* will never happen."

"Enough, you two." Grace grabbed the finished salad from Annie. "Let's just get this shift over with so we can get out of here." Grace shook her head and smiled at her two best friends as she left the kitchen to dote on Lady Covington. She was still smiling after depositing the salad as she thought of the constant banter between Ben and Annie and how work was a little more tolerable with their back and forth mock hostility. Ben's family had lived next door to Grace's foster family as long as she could remember, and Annie had joined their close duet when she moved to their small South Carolina town their senior year in high school. Since then, the Three Amigos, as they called themselves, had been inseparable and, with none of them having any money to speak of, they had accepted jobs at the local country club after graduation. Grace wanted to take the college route but no money and no parents backing her left her with few options. She had hoped serving the Southern Pines elite would open other doors for employment but so far it had only led to free food and use of the club gym after hours. College was looking like an unrealistic goal.

"What time do you all get off work today?" Grace asked them when she returned to the kitchen.

"I've got another hour or so," said Ben.

"Me too," sighed Annie. "I really think this shift would go by faster if I was working the tables instead of being stuck back here in the kitchen." She had left her post with the cook and was staring into the dining room through the small window at the top of the swinging kitchen door. Suddenly, she gasped and her tired posture stood erect. "Wow. Talk about beautiful."

"What?" Grace rushed over and pushed her face against Annie's in order to share the window's narrow view. The second she peered through the window, Grace knew who had caught Annie's eye. Entering the dining room was the most gorgeous family she had ever seen. Dressed in their tennis whites, they glowed like angels sitting down for a heavenly meeting. The man's commanding presence and Arian features matched those of his wife's with her long, thick, blonde hair swishing around her shoulders as she gracefully took her seat. Two fair-haired young men sauntered behind and assumed their obviously pre-appointed places in between their parents at the center dining table. Every eye in the dining room was soon focused on the luminous family whose brightness resembled a crystal chandelier floating in the middle of a church sanctuary.

"Dibs," Annie quickly called.

"But you're on kitchen duty today," whispered Grace, unable to take her eyes off the family.

"Okay, then you go." Annie playfully pushed her friend through the swinging door and into the crowded dining room. Grace's abrupt eruption through the kitchen door as she stumbled into the dining room caused a few nearby diners to look her way in surprise. Not wanting to attract any more attention than she already had, Grace nonchalantly returned their awkward smiles as she tightened her ponytail again and tucked a few stray hairs behind her ears. She then headed straight for the center table, ignoring any other table that got in her way, including Lady Covington's. As she moved closer to the family, one of the young men, in particular, rendered her breathless. He had blonde hair that shimmered like a light beaming down across his tan body and taut muscles that screamed beneath a white Izod tennis shirt. He looked like the Abercrombie & Fitch models Grace lusted after from the *In Style* magazines that cluttered her bedroom floor and she thought for a minute that she might actually be waiting on a real live celebrity.

"Hello," she said, still unable to catch her breath and almost panting as if she had just run a marathon. "Welcome to Southern Pines. I'm Grace and will be waiting on you today. Are you all new members?" She focused on the father because looking at the young man caused her knees to tremble.

"Well, hello Grace. Yes, we are new members. I'm Jamison Reich," the perfectly poised man said. He then gestured to the others seated at his table. "This is my wife, Ava, and these are my sons, Gregory and Andrew. We just moved here and this is our first day taking advantage of your club's amenities. Do you have anything you would recommend for lunch?"

Mr. Reich's formal diction matched the refined exterior he projected and Grace was almost embarrassed to speak with her heavy South Carolinian accent. Trying to enunciate more than usual, she replied, "Almost anything we offer should meet your approval." She smiled directly at Mr. Reich, pleased with herself for succeeding at sounding slightly less than southern in her response.

"Fine, fine," Mr. Reich said. "I would like a vodka tonic and the grilled salmon salad, please. Darling, what would you like?" He directed his gaze to his luminous wife.

"The same," said Mrs. Reich without looking up from her menu, her voice almost a purr, but with a slight edge. Elegance dripped off her like Chanel No. 5 and she wore large, black Dolce & Gabbana sunglasses as if her family's glow hurt her eyes.

"Gregory, do you know what you want?" Mr. Reich directed his question to the son who had previously impacted Grace's ability to stand.

Gregory looked up from his menu and smiled directly at Grace. His dark green eyes and long, thick eyelashes forced the young waitress to grab the back of Mrs. Reich's chair in order to keep from falling down. Grace's legs were beyond wobbly and the intensity of his eyes sucked her breath away again.

"Yes." Gregory's voice was smooth. "I know what I want." His eyes bored into Grace along with his smile. "I'll have iced tea and the shrimp and grits, please."

Grace continued to grip the back of Mrs. Reich's chair while the other son, Andrew, ordered, but her eyes never left Gregory's chiseled features.

"I...I'll be right back," she said as she turned toward the kitchen.

She wound through the dining room, trying to remember the entire family's order but shrimp and grits was the only item of which she was absolutely certain.

"So who are they?" Annie pounced on Grace the minute she hit the kitchen's swinging doors.

"The Reichs. Jamison Reich and his family," Grace said as she looked up the family on the kitchen's computer. After a few keystrokes she found what she needed.

"Here they are. They just joined last month. They live here in The Pines and the sons are close to our age."

"Does it give their weight and eye color too?" Ben smirked as he unloaded another tray from the dining room.

"Green," Grace responded without looking up from the computer screen. "Gregory's eyes are green."

"Gregory?" Ben's voice took on a slightly more serious tone. "So you are already on a first name basis with them?"

"Good gosh, Ben. Jealous much?" Annie pushed past him to see what Grace was reading. The two girls studied the computer screen, seemingly oblivious to anything else around them.

"They look like college guys. Where do you think they go to school?" asked Grace, her eyes still glued to the screen.

"Who cares as long as they are at least here for the summer? We should invite them to your party," offered Annie.

"Oh, no, that's okay." Grace blushed. "You're doing way too much already." There was no way that gorgeous guy was coming to her birthday party and see her make a fool of herself.

"I am not," said Annie. "Besides, they're good-looking. They should come. We want everyone who is anyone coming to your party and, as hot as they look, they obviously meet that criteria."

Grace just half-smiled back at her. Why wouldn't Annie ever listen to her? She was dreading this party like the plague and Annie knew it. Grace's primary goal in life was to avoid being the center of anyone's attention and she was well practiced in the art of blending in. So the thought of a party in honor of her twenty-second birthday actually made her physically ill. It's not like this year was some major milestone like a sixteenth birthday or anything. Even then Grace hadn't had a party and she had been fine with that. But Annie wanted a party and, since Annie usually got what she wanted, Grace had resigned herself to the next few weeks of constant nausea until it was all over.

"You…you're going to invite total strangers to Grace's party?" Ben asked Annie.

"No. Gracie and I are going to get to know them first and then invite them. They won't be strangers for long if I have anything to do with it." Annie stuck out her tongue at Ben and returned to the back of the kitchen to help the cook.

Ben turned to Grace who had left the computer and was again staring at the Reich family through the narrow window in the kitchen's swinging door. "You're not really going to invite those guys are you?" Ben asked as if Grace had any control over Annie's party plans. "You don't even know them."

"What am I supposed to do? You know Annie's more into this party than I am. Besides, they probably won't even come. I doubt coming to a birthday party for some random club waitress is high on their list." Grace continued to stare out the window. "But that one on the left, Gregory, is awfully cute," she said almost to herself.

"Give me a break." Ben rolled his eyes and stepped closer to Grace. "I just think your party will be more…special if we keep it to close friends, that's all."

Grace allowed her gaze to leave Gregory's glowing face and turned from the window to face Ben. "Annie's right. You do sound jealous today. What's with you? Afraid I might actually have a date for once? Maybe you should try it too sometime."

"Don't you worry about me. I get my share. You don't know everything about me, you know."

"Promises. Promises." Grace playfully nudged him with her elbow. "Besides, it might be kind of fun watching Annie try to flirt with your brother and keep up with her date all in the same night? That may be too much even for a professional like Annie."

"Yeah. Too much." Ben snickered without any humor in his eyes. "Uh…speaking of Tom, I need to give him a quick call. Can you cover for me with Julian for a sec?"

"Sure," Grace said absently. She was already staring at Gregory Reich again through the kitchen door's narrow window.

• • •

Ben needed to get away from Grace. He needed to get away from Grace and those intensely blue eyes of hers. Her eyes that held so many secrets and so much power.

Her eyes that were now interested in someone new.

Ben headed out the back door of the kitchen and walked right into a wall of cigarette smoke. The outside area near the large, metal dumpsters was the chosen spot for the kitchen staff to catch a smoke and the stress of today's busyness had forced more than the normal number of employees outside to calm their nerves with nicotine.

Not being a smoker, Ben held his breath through the crowd until he reached the other side of the dumpsters and found a secluded spot. He looked around to make sure he was alone before he discretely, but effortlessly, pushed the last heavy dumpster aside and slid into the newly made narrow opening. Crouching down, Ben barely had enough room to reach into his pocket and retrieve his cell phone, so he used his elbow and superhuman strength to easily nudge the full dumpster a few more inches. He had his older brother on speed dial so one press of a button and the phone made its connection. It only rang once before Tom picked up, as if he knew Ben would be calling.

"Hey," Ben whispered into the phone. "I think we've got a situation brewing with Grace."

Chapter Two: Flash of Light

Years ago, way before the age of telephones and video conferences, face-to-face meetings were a requirement of Council members. In fact, most Council members enjoyed the camaraderie of their fellow legislators while they established the laws by which those born with superhuman abilities would live, governing over the Powers' secret world as protectors of the human race.

But that was before the rebellious Anti-Powers came into existence and knowledge of a Council member's identity and secret powers became so risky. Risky for the Council members, the Powers they governed, and the humans they all protected.

Now, the Council rarely met in person and today was no exception. Everyone had agreed such a minor detail could be resolved with a quick conference call.

"Well, I don't think this is anything to worry about right now. The family seems to be harmless," one of the more conservative Council members said. "Let's find out more about them before we take action."

"But it's so close to her birthday and she is almost ripe," stated his polar opposite on the Council. "We really don't have time for mistaken assumptions now. If the Anti-Powers take her when she is fully ripe, her life—"

"They won't take her," the Council leader sternly interrupted, enunciating each word as if it was more a directive than a statement. She looked to her lieutenant seated beside her. "And Grace still doesn't know anything?"

"No, Madam," her lieutenant confirmed. "Nothing at all. We are definite about that."

"Then let's trust the brothers for now and let them handle it. If we need to step in, we will." And with those final words from their leader, the Council meeting adjourned with no record of it ever having taken place.

• • •

"Man, I *love* Mondays." Annie closed her eyes and leaned back in her chair with the midday sun on her face and her long blonde curls falling like silk waves behind her.

"Yeah. Good thing the club's closed on Mondays. It's the only day I can get someone to serve *me* instead of the other way around," said Ben, munching on an onion ring. The Three Amigos sat outside their favorite downtown restaurant, enjoying the first really warm spring day they had off work in a while.

"Okay. Who else do you want to invite?" Annie asked Grace. Despite Grace's innate self-consciousness, the guest list in front of Annie was growing with no end in sight.

"Annie, I told you, this is your thing. I really don't want a party. Turning twenty-two is not that big of a deal. Besides, you two are the only friends I want to hang out with on my birthday," replied Grace before she took a bite of her Caesar salad. With her party nerves revving up her stomach again, she now wished she had ordered the chicken noodle soup instead.

"No. This may be your birthday party but I'm the party planner and I say let's make this thing big. You're going to love it." Annie glanced up from her party notes and nodded toward the street. "Hey, how about Old Man Hillary? Do you want to add him?"

Grace looked up from her salad to see Carleton Hillary crossing the street toward them. Mr. Hillary was one of the older golfers from the club and a favorite member for all of the staff.

The wisdom of his age allowed him to treat everyone as his equal since the years had granted him more tolerance than most people. He was distinguished looking, still boasting a full head of hair, and carried himself with the stature of a man half his age. If Lady Covington was the club's matriarch, Mr. Hillary was the staff's grandfather.

"Well now, who do we have here on this fine spring day?" Mr. Hillary asked as he nimbly stepped up the curb onto the sidewalk near the trio's table. He spent an inordinate amount of time playing golf at the club so he almost seemed out of place in his khaki pants and white button-down oxford cloth shirt today. He looked more like the retired businessman he actually was rather than the professional golfer he pretended to be.

"Hey, Mr. Hillary. Taking a break from golf today?" Ben asked.

"Monday's the only day I don't tee off," said Mr. Hillary with a mischievous grin. "But if I was able to play the club today, you all would not get the day off now, would you?"

"No sir," said Annie. "And we certainly thank you for that!"

Mr. Hillary tossed his head back with a deep–throated laugh. "Enjoy your day off!" The old golfer then scooted along the sidewalk and into his favorite men's clothing store two doors down.

"Okay. He is definitely invited. That man is a hoot!" Ben said.

"If we invite him, we better invite Lady Covington. You know how that old bag loves our Gracie," said Annie. "Okay, who else?"

"Guys, enough already!" said Grace. This party was officially getting out of hand.

"Nope, not enough. The Cavern Café is huge and they told us to invite as many people as we want. That guy who owns the place really loves you, Grace, so we are going to take full advantage of his hospitality," Annie said.

"Oh, he just likes me because I give him the kitchen's leftovers for his dogs."

"Well, who cares *why* he likes you? I'm just glad he does." Ben laughed and looked over at Annie's list. "Hey, what about Will Crenshaw?"

"Nah, I doubt he'll come," said Grace. "Broke his leg and fractured his elbow when he crashed his motorcycle last weekend. You can invite him but I don't think he'll be going anywhere anytime soon."

"Man, broken bones are the worst," Annie said as she took a bite of her rare cheeseburger.

"Yeah." Ben nodded in agreement.

"I wouldn't know. I've never broken anything," said Grace without meaning to sound impertinent.

"We know, we know," said Annie. "And you never get sick either. How do you manage that?"

"Just lucky I guess. My foster parents told me I barely scraped a knee when I was little." Grace folded her legs up into her chair, pulled them close to her chest, and began examining the smooth, flawless skin covering her knees.

"You weren't even hurt in that car crash when your parents and brothers died, were you?" asked Annie as she continued to study the guest list in front of her.

"Nope. They told me not a scratch. But I was only four. You know I don't remember much about that," said Grace matter-of-factly as she took another bite of her salad. As she lifted the fork to her mouth, her hands began tingling and shaking again, starting at her wrists and pulsating right down to her fingertips. Having never been sick or hurt, Grace had avoided doctors her entire life, but this latest thing with her hands was making her rethink her position on the medical profession. When the tingling and shaking first started a few weeks ago, she had assumed it was a side effect of the fatigue brought on by her extra shifts at the club. But the episodes were becoming more frequent now so she might have to give in and find a cheap doctor who would treat a waitress with no health insurance. Grace put her fork down and discreetly wriggled her fingers under the table until the sensation began to disappear.

"Okay. Enough talk of injuries and death. We're supposed to be planning a party here, remember?" said Ben. After a long pause, he asked, "Are you…uh…are you all still inviting those Reich guys?"

"Working on it." Annie seemed to ignore Ben's tone as she looked over at Grace. "I was able to get their court schedule for this week from the tennis pro and am trying to rearrange some shifts so you and I can work the lunch crowd when they play."

"Annie! You are shameless!" Grace could not believe her friend's boldness. "What if they find out?"

"They won't. I promised the tennis pro an invitation to your party if he keeps his mouth shut."

"Oh." Grace clutched her stomach under the table. Her nausea was definitely returning now and no doctor could cure that. If only Annie would get off this party kick, Grace could stop drowning in Pepto–Bismol.

"I still think it is a bad idea to invite a bunch of strangers to the party. They could be a couple of crazies or something. What if they ruin it?" Ben looked hard at Grace.

"Oh, give it a rest, Ben. They're cute and they're coming, so get over it. Besides, you had your shot at Grace a long time ago and didn't take it," said Annie. "She needs a date to her birthday party and she likes Gregory Reich, so I am going to make this happen. End of discussion."

At the mention of her failed attempt with Ben, Grace started intensely examining her knees again, avoiding the inevitable sympathetic look she knew he was giving her across the table. With his piercing aqua blue eyes and broad shoulders, Grace had developed a crush on Ben their senior year of high school but he had made it painfully obvious that the feeling was not mutual. So, after more than a few excruciating months of unrequited love, Grace had placed Ben back into her "friends bucket" and there he had stayed ever since. He had never given her a reason for his rejection, but now, years later, the reason did not matter as much as the lingering effect his rejection had on her psyche. Since then, her mind had placed each of the Three Amigos in what she assumed to be their proper places: Ben was the good-looking, funny one, Annie was the gorgeous one who got all the guys, and she was, well, she was just Grace. While Ben occasionally dropped hints that he thought she was just as much a beauty as Annie, Grace knew he was only being nice because he felt guilty after denying her affections in high school.

"Okay. Now let's talk theme." Annie interrupted Grace's silent memories. "I'm thinking Senior Prom."

"What?" said Grace and Ben in unison. They both looked at Annie with eyebrows raised and jaws wide open.

"Oh, come on. Think about it. There will be all age groups there and think how fun it will be to get dressed up in our prom clothes again. People will have a blast pulling that stuff out of their closets." Annie's decision appeared to be final.

"Whatever." Ben rolled his eyes. He caught Grace's glance and winked at her.

Ben's wink eased her sick stomach. He always seemed to know what she needed and when she needed it. "I give up." Grace threw her hands in the air. "I guess there's no reeling Annie in now."

"Yeah!" squealed Annie clapping her hands like a little girl. "Then it's all settled. Just leave the rest to me."

"Are we done here? I need to go meet Tom." Ben stood up to leave. "Annie, it's your turn to get the check."

"Grace is going to have to cover me." Annie did not look up as she gathered together the guest list and her notes on the party. She then leaned over to Ben and batted her eyelashes. "Oh, and tell that hot older brother of yours 'hello' for me," she said in a singsong voice.

"Good gosh, Annie. Give it a rest." Ben pushed her away with his elbow. "Grace, you got this?" he asked as he ceremonially waved the check in Annie's face.

"Yeah. I'll just add it to the rent she still owes me." Grace grinned as she shook her head and looked up to see Ben give her a knowing look and an eye roll. "At this rate, I'll never make it to college. Annie spends my tuition faster than I can save it."

• • •

All three were laughing as they stood up to cross the street in front of the restaurant, however what happened next was not the least bit funny to Ben.

Because to say Grace did not see the truck coming would be an understatement.

She had stayed to pay the check and was several feet behind Ben and Annie in the crosswalk when an old pickup truck screeched around the corner and barreled straight for her. Its speed caused the white paint of the truck to appear like a flash lighting the middle of the street, but that one flash was all Ben needed to see out of the corner of his well-trained eye. With his undetectable speed, Ben spun around, scooped up Grace and whisked her back to the sidewalk from which she had just stepped, all at the exact same moment the truck raced past, barely missing Ben and its intended victim. As the white pickup sped past Ben, he could see the driver was an older man with long gray hair and wire-rimmed glasses.

While all this excitement was happening, Annie remained safely on the sidewalk on the opposite side of the street. She was browsing a downtown store window, twirling her fingers in her long, blonde hair, and seemingly oblivious to the action behind her.

"What the…?" breathed Grace as she looked up into Ben's eyes.

His arms cradled her like a shielding blanket and he could feel her heart pounding through her chest. With his speed facilitating the imperceptible rescue, Ben knew Grace had no idea how she got back on the sidewalk or how she ended up in his arms. He also knew being this close to him, cradled in his arms, probably made her feel a little weird. And as unsettling as that was to him, deep down Ben hoped her feeling was a good weird.

"Ben?" Grace prodded but she made no effort to leave his embrace.

But Ben did not answer her. He was watching the truck move on down the street and memorizing its license plate number when the driver stuck his head out the window and sneered back at him. Chills ran all over Ben when the face looking at him from the truck's driver side window no longer had long gray hair and glasses. Instead, the face looking at Ben now belonged to a blonde teenage girl.

"Shape shifter," whispered Ben under his nervous breathing.

"What?" gasped Grace still wrapped in Ben's arms. "What did you say?"

"Nothing," Ben replied with an absent stare at the pickup truck as he gently set Grace back on the sidewalk. When her feet hit the ground, he still held her tight, protecting her from everything and nothing. He didn't release her immediately even though he knew he should. Then, as if someone had called to him in silence, Ben suddenly turned around to see Mr. Hillary standing outside the men's clothing store, expressionless and still.

• • •

Sunlight streamed thought the study's large windows like a spotlight on the soldier's disappointment. "I don't understand why we can't just take her now. I almost had her out there!" His empty drinking glass crumbled into tiny shards in his fist. He absently brushed the glass onto the floor like dust without a drop of blood staining his massive hands.

"Because *I* told you not to. She is not ripe yet," the elder leader said firmly. He stood up from behind his antique mahogany desk and walked over to place a hand on his soldier's shoulder. "You must be patient like your brother. The Council is no closer than we are and, I promise you, we *will* capture her first. Let's just wait until she is ready. By that time our troops will be fully prepared to take on the Council." The leader of the Anti-Powers looked at his soldier with pride, hoping all his warriors had the same passion as this one. "Your grandfather would have been proud of your enthusiasm," he said squeezing his son's shoulder a little harder than necessary. "But do not ever disobey me again." He then glanced down and pointed to the glass shards sparkling on the thick Oriental rug below. "Now, clean up this mess before your mother sees it."

"Yes, sir," the young soldier sighed.

Chapter Three: Frustration

"What were you thinking?" Tom yelled. His voice bounced off their small apartment's beige walls.

"I wasn't." Ben clenched his teeth and ran both hands through his thick hair.

"That's obvious." Tom knew his sarcasm was justified.

"Look, I don't know what I was thinking. I just knew I had to get to Grace before that truck did." Ben stared at his older brother with pleading eyes. "You weren't there. You don't know. What was I supposed to do? Let the truck hit her?"

"No. But this is a huge Council violation. You know you aren't supposed to use your powers out in the open like that." Tom sat staring at Ben seated on the other side of their worn couch for what seemed like a long time before he finally succumbed to his younger brother's pleas. He sighed and pursed his lips. "What did Grace say?"

"Nothing. I moved so fast I don't think it even registered to her what was happening. If she had suspected anything, she would have said something to me by now, so I think we're okay."

"But we're not okay. Old Man Hillary saw you, remember? Not cool, little brother. Not cool at all." Tom felt himself getting riled up again so he took a deep breath to calm down and think for a moment. "Maybe Mr. Hillary won't say anything about your speed. Even if he does, everyone thinks he's a little crazy anyway so who would believe him?" Tom closed his eyes and rubbed his temples. "Did anyone else see you other than that old man?"

"I…I don't think so." Ben shook his head. "I don't know."

"Well, you better hope no one else saw you or you'll have more than me to deal with. Trust me, I'm being a lot easier on you than the Council will be if they ever find out about your public display of powers today," Tom softly scolded. He knew Ben was under more pressure than he himself would ever be and that, for now, Ben's job as Grace's Guardian and head of her secret protection team was critical for the Council's continued existence. He needed Ben to get his head back in the game. Knowing food usually helped his younger brother focus, Tom decided dinner was next on tonight's agenda. "Okay. Enough fussing. I know you were only doing your job. Just please be more discreet next time." He stood up and ruffled the top of Ben's dark hair before he crossed their small living room to enter the adjoining kitchen. "Now let's eat."

Ben scowled and followed his brother into the kitchen. He jerked open the refrigerator door and accidentally bent its thick handle as he grabbed a can of soda. "I'd swear that was an Anti-Power driving that truck. And a shape shifter of all things! If they're already here, I don't understand why we can't take Grace away to the mountains or somewhere to keep her safe. Why do we just have to sit here and wait?"

"Because we do what we're told and, Anti-Powers or not, the Council wants us here in Southern Pines. Have some patience little brother." Tom glanced at the bent door handle. "And stop taking your frustrations out on our kitchen appliances. That strength of yours has caused enough damage around here. I still haven't fixed that table you broke." His eyes then focused on Ben's drink which instantly flew out of his brother's hand, crossed the kitchen, and smacked into his own open palm. Tom took a swig and winked at Ben.

"I hate it when you do that. Practice levitation on your own time." Ben reached over and grabbed his drink out of Tom's hand before taking a seat at the kitchen's serving bar. "I just don't like

Grace sitting out there like she's bait when it's so close to her birthday."

"Bro, let it go. Everything will be fine. The Council knows what they're doing. And you of all people should know they would never use her as bait. Besides, they know Grace has the best Guardian around." Tom playfully pushed Ben off his bar stool. "You can handle her."

"Yeah. Right." Ben grabbed the stool to settle back at the serving bar, but the stool's thick wooden seat crumbled in his grip.

Tom looked down at the splintered stool seat scattered on the kitchen's tile floor. "Just make sure you handle her better than you handle our furniture."

• • •

"I can't believe you arranged all this," gushed Grace a few days later as she and Annie primped in the ladies locker room at the club before their shift. She finished putting on her lipstick and dabbed her blush brush on her cheeks for a little extra color. Grace did not normally wear a lot of make-up, especially for work, but Annie was wearing more than her usual palette so Grace thought she should do the same. She had even bought some expensive hair product from one of the home shopping networks to try to control her ponytail's flyaway strands, but, of course, it was not working. Grace stepped back from the mirror and scrutinized her reflection. "Do I look okay?"

"You look great. Hair perfect. Make-up perfect. Ready to flirt," replied Annie without even glancing at Grace. "I just wish we didn't have to wear these uniforms. They aren't exactly sexy." Annie looked down at her black pants and white Oxford shirt and proceeded to unbutton the top two buttons of her blouse. "There. That's a little better." She was revealing more skin than Julian liked for his waitresses but she didn't seem to care. Everyone knew Annie found pleasure in annoying her uptight boss. She flounced her intentionally loose long blonde hair and did her best supermodel pose for Grace.

"You are such a tease," Grace shook her head. "And I cannot believe you talked me into this. What time is their tennis match?"

"Pete in the pro shop said they should be finished by noon or so. He's going to try to steer them our way for lunch and all it cost us is another invitation to your party. This one is for Pete's girlfriend." Annie applied her usual red lipstick and leaned in to kiss her reflection in the mirror, leaving red lips on the glass for all of the lady club members to see. "Voila."

"Looks good." But then Grace thought Annie looked good under any circumstances. "Um, by the way, are you sure you don't mind taking Andrew?"

"Honey, I don't mind at all. The way you've been rambling on about Gregory these past few days, I wouldn't dare get in your way. Besides, it'll be fun. Two best friends dating two brothers. This is going to be a great summer."

"But what if Gregory doesn't want me? What if he is more into…blondes?" Grace sheepishly asked as she reexamined her long dark ponytail in the mirror. She knew from experience that Annie usually got her first choice when it came to guys and Grace took whatever was left over. To assume Gregory would choose her instead of Annie was really asking too much.

Annie finally diverted her eyes away from her own reflection in the mirror and looked hard at Grace. She placed one hand over her heart and held her other hand up as if taking an oath in court. "I, Annie Phillips, do solemnly swear that I will not flirt, talk to, look at, or even think about Gregory Reich for as long as I live." She ended with a wink.

"Okay, okay, good enough. I get the picture. Thanks." Grace glanced down at her watch. "Come on. Time to get to work."

They left the quietness of the locker room and headed to the kitchen. The bustle and busyness of the other day still pervaded the room and the friends quickly fell back into their serving roles. Today, however, Grace's tables did not receive her usual attentiveness because she kept her eyes glued to the dining room entrance in between orders. She was nervous and the butterflies in her stomach combined with the smells of the kitchen to add to her now ever-present birthday party nausea. She did not really know how to flirt, especially with someone as gorgeous as Gregory, and she had no idea what she was going to do if he did show up today. She usually didn't go for blondes but something about Gregory made her absolutely crazy so she really hoped Annie's plan worked.

Noon came and went and, as more time passed, Grace was beginning to think the brothers were never going to show up. Just when her stomach had almost returned to normal, Andrew Reich walked into the dining room. He stood at the entrance as if surveying the room but his roving eyes stopped when he spotted Grace and Annie standing at the far corner waitress station. He had a massive muscular physique with biceps that implied steroid use and legs that were almost as thick as they were long. The sweat dripping from his brow evidenced a hard-fought tennis match as he strode straight over to the waitresses huddled in the corner, casually swinging his tennis racquet back and forth as he walked.

"Hello," Andrew said with a voice as strong as his biceps. "It's not too late to grab some lunch, is it?"

"Of course not," Annie said in the smooth sexy voice she had practiced with Grace in the locker room. "Just sit wherever you want and we'll be right with you." She smiled up at the large man with the wavy blonde hair towering over her and batted her eyelashes just for good measure.

"Thanks." Andrew winked at Annie and headed toward a nearby table overlooking the golf course.

"Take it," Annie whispered to Grace as she watched her flirt target walk away.

"No. You take it," Grace whispered back. "He's yours, remember?"

"Yeah, I know. I was just offering you the table to be nice." Annie did not take her eyes off Andrew's posterior end. "I'll go find out where his brother is."

Annie sashayed more than usual as she made her way to Andrew's table.

"Is it just one today?" she asked nonchalantly. Even seated, Andrew's face was still tall enough to be the same height as Annie's was while standing and their eyes met intensely on the same level plane.

"No. My bro—Oh, there he is," said Andrew pointing to the dining room entrance.

Annie turned in the direction of Andrew's point and Grace's eyes followed her friend's quick head turn. Grace actually gasped out loud as she gazed once more on the gorgeous boy who literally made her knees weak.

There stood Gregory Reich in all his tightly–fitted tennis white glory. He smiled when he spotted Andrew on the other side of the room and the shine of his smile made Grace's butterflies flit nervously in her nauseated stomach. She forced her eyes to leave Gregory's glowing face and work their way down his well-developed body. While his physique was not as bulky as Andrew's, he was still muscular enough to grab the attention of all the ladies in the room. He seemed oblivious to this fact as he floated between the dining tables toward his brother. Grace could not stop staring at Gregory's toned body and when her eyes finally made their way back up to his face, Gregory's dark green eyes were staring straight at her. Like an emerald knife, his gaze tore through her heart and stole her breath. She quickly turned around, embarrassed by her own ogling, and tried to busy herself by pretending to organize the condiments on the waitress station. As she reached for a ketchup bottle, her fingers started tingling again, so she ended up just standing there with her hands thrust in her pockets until the sensation went away.

"What's wrong with you?" asked Annie coming up behind her.

"He caught me staring at him," whispered Grace.

"So? At least now he knows you're interested in him." When it came to guys, Annie could turn any situation into a positive one. "Now get over there and start flirting." She gave Grace a hard elbow toward the Reich brothers' table.

Grace was getting really tired of Annie shoving her around the club's dining room.

But once again, Annie's push was obvious enough that Grace was forced away from her waitress station safety zone and ended up halfway into the dining room facing the brothers. Both boys quickly looked up from their menus, but Gregory's eyes were the ones that drank in Grace.

"Hi," she quietly said when she reached their table. "What can I get you all today?" Grace kept her eyes on Andrew.

"Hey, Grace. Good to see you again." Gregory flashed her a smile.

Grace's brain screamed, *Oh my gosh! He remembers my name!*

"Uh, hi. Gregory, right?" Grace tried to act cool but acting cool was in direct contradiction to her blending in persona.

"Yeah," he laughed, gesturing across the table, "and you remember my brother Andrew." Gregory's cheeks were flushed but not one drop of sweat could be found on his face. He looked down at his menu. "How about some iced tea and the Club Cheeseburger – rare."

"I'll have the same," said Andrew.

"Are you all making it easy on me today so I don't have to remember much?" Did she just try to make a joke? Why did she feel so comfortable? Just because the most gorgeous guy in the world remembered her name? What was happening to her?

"Wish he had made it easy on me on the court," said Andrew nodding to his brother.

"Yeah. Looks like you had a rough time today. You definitely have Gregory beat on the sweat factor." Grace was amazed at how easy she felt standing there despite her embarrassment a few minutes earlier. She knew it was unnatural for her to feel this relaxed in front of someone as beautiful as Gregory but, for some reason, her whole body felt like Jell-O.

"I…uh…have strange sweat glands," stuttered Gregory with a sideways glance toward his brother. He then looked up at Grace and changed the subject, "How about some fries, too?"

The intensity of Gregory's green eyes boring into her began to cloud Grace's mind and her easy feeling left as quickly as it came. "S—Sure. Be right back."

She turned and headed back toward the waitress station with her stomach's butterflies moving into overdrive again. She had read in some fashion magazine that a good posture improved the back view of a woman's figure so Grace stood a little straighter as she walked, cognizant that Gregory might be watching her backside and uncharacteristically immune to her own self-consciousness. So much for blending in.

"Well?" Annie pounced the minute Grace reached the waitress station.

"He remembered my name!" Grace excitedly whispered.

"So what's your next move?"

"I don't know. You know I don't have any moves," answered Grace as she placed the boys' order in the club computer. "But it's your turn now. Take them some iced tea."

Annie grabbed the two teas while Grace printed out the checks for the only other table lingering after the busy lunch rush. It was a group of lady golfers who were obviously ready for their tee time but instead sat and ogled the Reich boys like cougars at a downtown singles bar. Grace placed the ladies' checks on their table and stood to the side waiting for their signatures, intentionally blocking their view of Gregory. Eventually, the lady golfers picked up on Grace's hint and paid their checks, leaving Grace to clear their table while sneaking her own glances at the Reich brothers.

After delivering the brothers' lunch, and with no other patrons remaining in the room, Annie had set up residence in the chair directly across from Andrew and beside Gregory, apparently taking full advantage of the empty room to exhibit her famous flirting skills. Grace had seen Annie work her magic with boys before and, after clearing the cougars' table, she decided to hang back at the waitress station while her friend worked the brothers over.

"Hey Grace!" Gregory's voice glided across the room toward her. "Why don't you join us?" He smiled and pointed to the seat directly across from him.

Mission accomplished. Annie had done her job. Grace sucked in her stomach, suppressed her butterflies, and quickly moved to sit down across from the most gorgeous guy in the world.

"Hey," was all Grace could mutter when her eyes met Gregory's. The white tablecloth stretched wide between them and made his tan look even deeper up close.

Annie seemed to recognize that Gregory's presence impacted her friend's ability to speak. "We were just talking about the fitness benefits of tennis versus other sports. What's your take, Gracie?"

"Uh, I don't know. I haven't played tennis in a while." Grace sheepishly smiled at Gregory.

"Well, let's change that. Do you all want to play after work today?" Andrew asked Annie.

"Sure," Annie said without even glancing at Grace.

"Grace, what do you think? You and me against Andrew and Annie?" Gregory's long eyelashes melted Grace's brain. "It should be a pretty fair match even if you haven't played in a while. I can carry us. I beat Andrew almost every time so this won't be much of a challenge, even with Annie helping him." Gregory's smooth voice coaxed Grace, "Come on. You won't have to do anything but stand there and smile. I promise you'll have fun." His face lit up the entire table.

Grace's train of thought was lost in between Gregory's dark green eyes and the silk of his voice. No matter how badly she knew she would play today, she also knew she was not about to say 'no' to anything involving Gregory.

"I would lo—," Grace started when a familiar voice abruptly came up behind her.

"Grace doesn't play tennis," Ben sternly interrupted. He appeared out of nowhere and his tone indicated he wasn't leaving anytime soon.

Grace visibly jumped in her chair and turned around. "Ben! I didn't even see you come in. How long have you been standing there?" She gave him the subtle 'go away' look without it being seen by the others seated at the table. He was not on today's work schedule and was violating club policy wearing jeans in the dining room. Ben's hair was especially messy today and, while his afternoon facial stubble gave him a certain bad-boy hotness, Julian would blow a gasket if he saw Ben looking like he did. Grace did not need this complication while she was trying to flirt with Gregory.

Ben didn't answer and overtly ignored Grace's subtle look. He just stood behind her chair and stared at the two brothers.

Gregory stood up and held out his hand. "Ben, is it? Nice to meet you. I'm Gregory Reich and this is my older brother Andrew." Gregory smiled as he gestured toward his brother.

Ben crossed his arms and refused Gregory's handshake. He stood a little straighter and, without smiling back, said, "Hello."

"You'll have to excuse Ben. He has no manners." Annie glared at Ben across the table. "Just ignore *it* and *it* will go away."

Andrew chuckled but did not say anything. He just stared right back at Ben.

"Well, Ben, we were just trying to get Grace and Annie out on the courts with us today. Perhaps you could also join us as our guest." Gregory's smooth voice invaded the stare-off between his brother and Ben.

"I don't play either." Ben's eyes never left Andrew. Apparently, Gregory's voice had no effect on Ben.

Grace turned around in her chair again and looked up at Ben. She had had enough of his attitude. "Well, that's too bad because we are playing." Grace glared at Ben and gritted her teeth. "*Today.*" She then turned back to Gregory and, without thinking, said, "We get off work in half an hour so we'll meet you at the courts right after that. Is that okay?"

"Sure. Can't wait." Gregory smiled. His eyes moved from Grace to Ben to Andrew and back again.

"Great. See you then." Grace suddenly stood up from her chair. "Let's go Annie." She pushed her way past Ben without saying another word and headed into the kitchen with Annie close behind. Neither girl looked back at the guys still in the middle of their stare-off.

•••

Once the girls were in the kitchen and out of earshot, Gregory's eyes took on a menacing reddish-green glare as he leaned toward Ben, cocked his head and whispered, "What's the matter, Benny-Boy? Don't like that Miss Gracie is going to be spending time with a *real* man today?" He then stood back and smiled with what could only be described as smug sarcasm.

"Come on, Gregory. Cool it." Andrew's bulkiness rose up from the table. "Let's not waste our time on this weakling."

The brothers headed out the door toward the tennis courts, nonchalantly swinging their racquets again. Ben was left standing there alone, his face red with anger.

Weakling, Ben thought. *If they only knew who they were dealing with.*

He was mad at the Reich brothers' arrogance but he was even madder at himself for allowing them to get into his head. He had always been jealous of Grace's boyfriends but had never let it show as much as he had just now. Ben felt a hatred growing inside him and he didn't like it. Despite their green eyes, he couldn't really think of any specific reason to *hate* those boys. No reason other than they had Grace's attention for the moment. That and there was something familiar about Andrew's eyes that made Ben particularly uneasy. The thought of those eyes notched up Ben's anger another level and, without thinking, he cleanly snapped the back of the heavy oak dining chair he was gripping into two pieces.

• • •

"Ugh! Sometimes that boy makes me so mad!" Grace paced back and forth in the ladies locker room, her fists clenched.

"Oh, Ben's just being overly protective Ben. You know how he is." Annie sat on the locker room bench filing her nails. She had obviously moved past Ben's rude behavior in the dining room. "Just forget about it. We have more important things to worry about, like what to wear this afternoon."

"But why does he do stupid stuff like that? He knows I'm interested in Gregory."

"Maybe that's why," Annie said with a raise of her eyebrows.

"Oh, please." Grace brushed off Annie's implication.

Suddenly, Annie jumped up. "Wait. I'll be right back." She ran out the door of the ladies locker room without another word, leaving Grace to stew all by herself in the dressing area.

Grace knew she needed to get over Ben's behavior if she was going to enjoy her afternoon with Gregory but some things were easier said than done. Ben had never been overly friendly with any of Grace's boyfriends but she could not remember him ever being so openly rude to any of them. It couldn't be blamed on Ben's jealousy as Annie implied because he didn't feel that way about her. This fact had been proven in high school. So what was his problem with the Reich brothers?

"Ta-dah!" Annie bounded back into the locker room a few minutes later and interrupted Grace's contemplative puzzling over Ben. She was holding two tennis racquets, a tennis dress, and a tennis skort and shirt set, with price tags boldly dangling from both outfits.

"What did you do?" Grace had seen that look in Annie's eyes before and knew from experience to be suspicious.

"I borrowed a few things from the pro shop," Annie coyly replied.

"What do you mean 'borrowed'?"

"Oh calm down. Pete said it was okay and all it cost us is another invitation to your party. This one's for Pete's girlfriend's sister."

"Oh, good gosh." Grace rolled her eyes. Annie's antics began to take Grace's mind off Ben.

"We just need to figure out a way to hide these price tags. Oh, and you can't sweat. Pete wants these returned tonight, so take it easy on the court and try to stay dry this afternoon."

Grace knew Annie was serious even though she sounded ridiculous.

"No sweating. Got it. I haven't played in such a long time, I'll have no problem taking it easy. I won't know what I'm doing."

Grace looked over the clothes Annie had spread across the locker room bench. "Which outfit do you want?"

"Whichever one you don't. I think I have Andrew about reeled in so you pick first." Annie's ever-present self-confidence appeared to be in overdrive.

"I'll take the shirt and skort set," Grace said.

"Great. The blue matches your eyes." Annie threw the set to Grace and then began changing into the tennis dress. She stopped with the dress halfway over her head. "Uh-oh. I need tennis panties with this."

Grace had already put on the tennis skort and was working on the shirt. "What are you going to do? Do you want to switch?"

"Do *you* have any tennis panties?" Annie giggled.

"No." Grace smiled.

"Then how would switching outfits help the situation?" Annie burst out in a full-blown cackle.

"I guess it wouldn't." Grace was now laughing too and her thoughts of Ben had completely disappeared.

"I suppose I can just wear my own underwear and try not to bend over the rest of the afternoon." Annie grinned as she finished putting on the tennis dress. She examined herself in the locker room's full-length mirror. "There. Problem solved."

Grace smiled and continued getting dressed without saying anything more on the subject. She knew from experience that Annie would have no problem wearing her own underwear in place of tennis panties out on the court today. She also knew Annie would do her best not to bend over while they played. Grace just wished Annie had worn something other than a thong to work today.

• • •

The late spring day felt more like midsummer and Grace began to stress over the tennis pro's no-sweat rule as she and Annie walked over to the club's tennis courts. Gregory and Andrew were already there warming up on the courts and the minute Grace saw Gregory's agile body in action, she forgot all about her own sweating and Annie's choice of underwear.

"Hey," Gregory waved and motioned for them to come over. "Are you ready to kick some butt, Grace?" he asked as he held the gate open for the girls to enter the courts.

Grace could not remember the last time that a guy other than Ben had held open a door for her. She added 'gentlemanly' to her mental list of Gregory's attributes and noted that elegant Mrs. Reich had obviously taught her boys some manners.

"In your dreams, little brother," Andrew yelled to them from the other side of the net.

Annie skipped over to side up with Andrew and was already in full flirt mode. Luckily for Annie, Andrew was no dummy and obviously receptive to her advances. He placed his large arm around her tiny waist and guided her to her place on the court near the net before he headed to the back line to receive the first serve. He crouched down into his tennis stance, racquet ready.

"Bring it on!" Annie yelled to Gregory before smiling back at Andrew. She bent slightly at the waist preparing to receive Gregory's serve. Grace knew Annie had not forgotten her choice of underwear. Her stance was simply enhancing Andrew's view.

Gregory looked over at Grace and his green eyes blindingly twinkled. "Come on. We can take them."

Grace smiled and followed him onto the court. Even though she was absolutely positive she was getting ready to make a total fool of herself, she again felt unnaturally calm, as if someone had placed a protective blanket around her nerves.

Gregory aced every serve of the first game so Grace simply walked from one side of the court to the other side until their score reflected an official win. With Gregory's expertise on the court, Grace would not have to worry about the no-sweat rule in her tennis outfit. As Gregory had said, all she had to do was stand there and smile. Her hands started tingling in the middle of the third game but Grace bent down and pretended to tie her shoe until the feeling subsided. It passed quickly and Grace was grateful this episode was brief.

The serves went back and forth with Gregory and Grace winning almost every game. They were in their last game of the first set when Grace spotted Ben lurking behind an old oak tree near the court fence. His hands were shoved deep down into his jeans pockets and his face scowled as he watched the foursome play. When Grace's eyes met his, Ben quickly looked away toward Annie, but he did not otherwise move. He stayed behind that tree, watching the two couples out on the tennis court without saying a word to any of them.

Grace had hoped they could finish their set without anyone else seeing Ben spying but she soon realized it was too late for that. Gregory was getting ready to serve when he caught Grace looking over at the tree. His eyes followed hers and the minute he saw Ben, Gregory threw down his racquet and started to cross the court toward him.

"What *is* your problem, dude?" Gregory exclaimed.

Ben did not say a word. He just continued to stand there with his hands in his pockets.

"Hey! I'm talking to you!" Gregory's pace quickened across the court.

"Gregory, just don't pay any attention to Ben. Let's finish our set and then go get something to drink," Grace said trying to diffuse Gregory's ire.

For the first time since meeting her, Gregory completely ignored Grace and walked right past her, his eyes focused on Ben and the tree.

Still, Ben did not move.

By this time, Andrew had caught up with Gregory and both brothers seemed intent on reaching the tree before Ben could get away. Annie glared at Ben and rushed around the net to stand near Grace. She was clearly not happy that Ben had interrupted their tennis game.

"I said I'm talking to you. Are you deaf?" Gregory yelled at Ben.

Ben did not say a word. His eyes just moved back and forth from the boys to Grace and Annie.

"Fine. You're not talking! I'll make you talk," Gregory jerked the tennis racquet out of Andrew's hand. "Why don't you just get out of here?" He swung the racquet back and threw it directly at Ben and the tree.

But the racquet did not hit Ben or the tree.

Instead, the racquet slammed into the side of a large Range Rover sitting over fifty yards away in a parking lot on the other side of the Clubhouse. The force of Gregory's throw buried the steel racquet six inches deep into the Rover's thick metal, ripping a large gash in the front passenger door. The racquet now stuck out of the vehicle's side like a toothpick in an appetizer meatball.

Ben just stood at the tree, glaring at Gregory.

"How did you do that?" Grace came up behind Gregory. "How did you throw that racquet so far? And how could it rip into the side of that car?" She stood directly in front of Gregory, dumbfounded at his ability to violate the basic laws of physics.

Gregory's eyes widened at the site of the racquet stuck in the Range Rover. "I guess your friend Ben acting all weird like that pumped up my adrenaline." He looked over at his brother and then back toward Ben who had now disappeared from view.

"Well, he's gone now so how about that drink you mentioned, Grace?" Andrew asked as he herded the group toward the gate in the fence. "It'll be our treat, girls."

"Sure." Annie put her arm through Andrew's and made her claim on him official.

Grace did not respond. She was still reeling. First Ben's strange behavior this afternoon in the dining room and now Gregory seemed to have a superhuman ability to turn tennis racquets into hacksaws. The boys in her life were driving her crazy.

But her craziness did not last long. Out of nowhere, Grace had that same unnaturally relaxed feeling she had earlier. Her nerves' protective blanket fell over her again just as Gregory's arm fell across her shoulders.

"Do you mind?" he asked nodding to his arm, his face so close she could feel his breath on her cheek. His eyes that were previously so angry with Ben had transformed back into the green twinkles that melted Grace's brain.

"No, not at all." Grace smiled and nuzzled her head in the crook of his neck just as they reached the tennis gate. Her thoughts of Ben and the tennis racquet had already melted away with her brain.

...

"Answer me!" Ben was hidden in a cluster of pine trees near the Club's fourteenth green. "Have I been replaced?" Ben tried not to grip his cell phone too hard for fear of breaking the contraption in two.

"No." Tom's voice boomed over his cell phone. "What are you talking about?"

"I just need to know. Would the Council replace me as Grace's Guardian without me knowing?" Ben nervously paced from one pine tree to the next, knowing his speed prevented anyone from seeing him in this state. His heart pounded so hard it hurt.

"Of course not. You're her Guardian. You're the only one in charge of Grace's protection team right now."

"Well then, they're here," Ben sighed in resignation. He stopped pacing to rub his temples. "Tell the Council to get ready because the Anti-Powers are definitely here and they're close to Grace. Real close."

Chapter Four: Apologies

Grace burst into Ben's apartment like a hurricane. "We need to talk." She pointed directly at Ben and threw her large purse on the floor with a thud.

Tom placed the book he was reading on the coffee table and slowly stood up from the couch. "Hey, Gracie. Good to see you too." He nodded to her and then glanced over at his brother. "I was just leaving anyway." Tom grabbed his car keys and exited the front door without waiting for a response from either of them.

Ben sat up straighter in the recliner where he had been napping only a few seconds earlier and took a deep breath. "Look, Gracie—"

"Don't you 'look Gracie' me." Her eyes glared. "What *is* your problem lately?"

Ben should have seen Hurricane Grace coming. He had not taken any of Grace's calls after the tennis court incident so he knew she had been stewing for a couple of days. Apparently, she was now up to a full–blown boil. She stood in the middle of the apartment's small living room with both hands on her waist and her feet firmly planted in the worn shag carpet.

By the looks of her stance, Ben could tell he was in for a long afternoon.

"I don't have a problem. I…I'm just not too crazy about those Reich brothers, that's all." Ben nervously fidgeted with a hole in the recliner's upholstery, diverting his eyes away from Grace's glare.

"Why? What business is it of yours who I date?"

Ben's focus immediately flipped back to Grace. He bolted up from the recliner, his voice cracking with incredulousness, "So now you are *dating* him?" His heart beat faster as each word left his lips.

Grace did not answer. The two friends silently stood in the middle of the living room, eyes locked on each other as if they were muted strangers. Neither moved. They were at an impasse and did not even know it.

Finally, Grace broke the awkward silence. "Dating. Hanging out. Whatever it is that Gregory and I are doing. You still have no right to act the way you're acting. I mean, what was with you at the tennis courts the other day? You looked like some creepy stalker standing there behind that stupid tree. And why haven't you returned any of my calls?"

Ben took another deep breath and stepped toward her. His eyes never left her face. He desperately wanted to put his arms around her and protect her from everything he knew was coming. From the hurt she would experience soon. From the truth that would overshadow all the anger she was feeling right now. He wanted so much to be the one to tell her everything. To tell her of her destiny, of her true place in this world.

To tell her how he really felt about her.

But to tell her all that would risk the Council taking Grace away from him forever.

And that was the one thing he could not let happen.

So he just stood there and said, "I'm sorry."

"You're sorry?"

"Yeah. I'm sorry."

"That's all you have to say after the way you've been acting?"

"I'm not sure what else I can say other than…I'm sorry." Ben's cracking voice almost sounded like a whisper now and he tried to focus on the carpet below in order to escape Grace's eyes. Her big, blue, beautifully intense eyes.

Grace seemed to soften a little at the tone of Ben's voice. She sighed and relaxed her arms down at her side. "Are you going to explain why you've been so crazy?" she asked, now slightly calmer than before.

"No. I can't…I mean I…I don't know." Ben finally looked up at her. "Can't we just agree to disagree on that Gregory guy?"

"Will you promise to behave in front of 'that Gregory guy' from now on?"

"Maybe." Ben did not know how to answer that one.

"Well, can you at least try?" Grace stepped closer to him. "Look. For the first time in a long time I really like a guy. I mean *really* like him. But you are my best friend and I kind of need to keep you around too." Grace reached over and closed up the now small space between them with a hug, flinging her arms carelessly around his neck. "I hate it when we fight," she whispered in his ear, "so you stop acting crazy and I'll stop getting mad at you and then we won't fight anymore. Okay?"

Knowing her lips were close, almost touching him, Ben lost his train of thought. He shouldn't be this close to her. As he reluctantly leaned out of Grace's embrace, their faces brushed against each other and he could feel her warm breath on his cheek. He closed his eyes and inhaled deeply, savoring her familiar scent before he finally stepped out of her arms completely. He looked down into her eyes again and knew what he had to do. "I'll try," was all he said.

Grace smiled up at him. "Thanks. I really think once you get to know Gregory, you'll like him." She leaned over to pick her purse up off the floor. "Okay. Now that we have that settled, let's go eat."

Ben looked at Grace and shook his head. One minute she was full of fire and brimstone, the next minute painfully self-conscious, and then the next minute playful and ready for her next social engagement. Her mood swings would drive anyone crazy.

But sometimes Ben liked feeling a little crazy.

"Where are you going?" he asked.

"*We're* going to the Cavern Café to meet Annie." Grace began pushing Ben out the front door. "It's Wing Night and I'm in the mood for something spicy."

"Of course you are." Ben smiled and turned to lock the door of his apartment. "Is Gregory going to be there?" he asked with his back still to Grace.

"No. He has some meeting with his father." Grace stopped in her tracks and turned around to face Ben who was now walking toward her. "But so what if he was going to be there. That's not going to be a problem now, remember?"

"Just getting myself prepared. I need to take baby steps with this guy. Okay?"

"Okay. Baby steps. But you won't have to start tonight. Tonight it will just be the Three Amigos. I promise." Grace took Ben's hand and pulled him toward her car. But she didn't have to pull too hard.

• • •

"Well, boys. What do you think?" Jamison Reich sat behind his massive antique mahogany desk, the fingertips of each hand pressed together in contemplative habit. He looked at his sons seated in front of him with a mixture of pride and impatience. "Do you think you made a mistake? Answer me that one question." He enunciated each word with razor-sharp precision.

Neither son replied. Both stared at the floor, avoiding their father's glare. Mr. Reich knew they weren't ignoring him. They were just too afraid to speak.

But Jamison Reich did not accept fear from his sons.

"I…said…answer…me!" Mr. Reich bellowed and slammed his fist on the desk. The entire room shook with his words and several books actually flew off the floor-to-ceiling bookshelves that covered the walls of the large room.

The stereotypical wooden paneling and shelving found in the classic lawyer's office surrounded Mr. Reich's study. This abundance of wood was a good thing considering one of his many powers was the ability to maneuver metal with his mind. A power he found difficult to control when he was angry. The few items in the study that did contain metal met Mr. Reich's wrath that afternoon and melted quickly as his frustration filled the room. Staples, paperclips, misplaced knick-knacks, all distorted into little, individual liquid messes throughout the study. Before the boys could answer their father, the stench of burnt metal flavored the air and Mr. Reich's anger escalated even more.

"Now look what you made me do!" he roared pointing to a melted pile of paper clips on the corner of his desk. He looked around the room and then carelessly waved his hand. Instantly, the melted metal objects and pieces around the study transformed back into their original state.

But the burnt metal smell lingered on. There was nothing Mr. Reich could do about that.

Without looking up, Gregory finally spoke, "Father, I made the mistake with the tennis racquet, not Andrew. It will not happen again. I promise."

Jamison Reich eyed his sons sternly and stood up from behind his desk. "It better not. I told you both just like I've told every other soldier. We cannot tip off the Council before our troops are ready so there can be no public display of your powers until the girl's birthday party. Then you will have your chance to show the Council and the world your greatness."

"Yes sir," both boys replied in unison, finally looking up at their father.

"Good." Mr. Reich was now pacing behind his desk to calm himself down. "I don't have to tell you what's at stake here. Our years of hiding will be over soon. We have eliminated everyone else in the girl's family line, albeit sometimes a little messier than

I liked, but as soon as we have her under our control, our rise to power will be complete. I knew when she survived her parent's car crash, she was the key to regaining our place in the world. By doing away with every other member of her family, we have left the Council with no one else to harvest. The girl and whatever enabled her to survive the crash belongs to us alone and those goody-two-shoes on the Council will finally disappear forever. Once she is ripe, I will at last have the authority that is rightfully mine." He stopped pacing and turned to look at his sons. "Is everything set for the girl's party?"

"Yes sir," said Andrew. "We have been able to place Anti-Power troops both inside the party and also at strategic locations surrounding the Cavern Café."

"And of course, I'll have Grace with me the entire time," asserted Gregory. "We will take her the minute you give the signal."

"Don't wait for my signal. Just take her after she dances her first dance. We should let her enjoy her party a little before we ruin her life," said Mr. Reich.

"Yes, sir." Gregory smiled, his green eyes tinged with red anticipation.

"Good. Good." Mr. Reich nodded. "Everything appears to be finally coming together. Your grandfather's dream will soon be our reality and those do-gooders on the Council won't even know what hit them."

Chapter Five: An Unexpected Kiss

Grace stood in her bedroom, examining this evening's shoe choice in her full-length mirror, and had to pinch herself to make sure she was not dreaming. With tonight being the fourth night in a row that she was seeing Gregory, she believed she could honestly now say she and Gregory Reich were dating. Exclusively. The gorgeous, blonde-haired, emerald-eyed, muscular guy who made all the ladies at the club swoon was actually, totally, fully and without question *hers*. At least that's what Annie had told her and Annie was usually right when it came to guys.

Grace had not believed it in the beginning when they had their official first date. How could she? He was so beautiful and totally out of her league. She had not really considered their tennis match a date at all. But, when Gregory actually called and asked her to go to dinner a few days later, she was so stunned she just about dropped the phone. Of course, it had been a double date with Annie and Andrew, but the brothers had actually come to their front door to pick them up and had paid for everything, so, according to Grace's standards, that was an official first date.

And to top it off, Gregory had actually picked her over Annie. What were the odds of that?

But tonight was going to be different. Tonight was *the* night. She and Gregory were actually going out by themselves. They had been spending so much time with Annie and Andrew, they had not been alone once. Not that she minded that. She loved Annie. But not having any alone time with Gregory meant there had not been any kissing time either.

However, tonight would change that.

Tonight Grace was getting her first kiss from Gregory. She just knew, deep down in her heart she knew, she was going to be kissed tonight.

"Hey." Annie bounded into the room and sprawled across Grace's bed, leaving black combat boot prints all over the flowered lavender comforter. "Is that what you're wearing tonight?"

Grace's eyebrows knitted together as she continued to study herself in her full-length mirror. Just today, she had purchased a new blue sundress and ballet flats for tonight and she thought she looked pretty good. At least she thought she did until Annie came into her room. "Yeah. I just got this dress. What's wrong with it?"

"Nothing. If you're going to church. You are going on a date. With Gregory. The man of your dreams, remember? Maybe we should be going for sexy. Not saintly."

"Annie, you know I'm not a 'sexy' kind of girl. I'd rather be… comfortable." Grace tilted her head and continued to look at herself in the mirror.

"Well, comfortable isn't going to cut it tonight," Annie asserted. "Come on to my room."

Grace followed her down their small apartment's hallway and plopped down on Annie's bed. Looking around her roommate's bedroom, Grace was reminded how different the two girls were in style and taste. Annie's painted black ceiling and red walls contrasted against the lavender and mint green motif in Grace's room down the hall and the red dragons painted on the black ceiling above Annie's bed looked more disturbing than mythical.

"How do you sleep with those things staring at you each night?" Grace asked, pointing to the ceiling.

"You don't like my dragons?" Annie did not sound interested in Grace's response. "I love them. Their voyeuristic qualities make it a little more exciting when I entertain in here if you know what I mean."

"You're gross," smirked Grace.

"Oh, you love me and you know it." Annie rummaged through her messy closet and eventually pulled out a short, red halter dress. "Here. Try this."

"I don't know," said Grace, feeling the smooth, silky material. "This may be a little much."

"A little much?" Annie scoffed. "This dress shows more skin than a spa wrap."

"No. I meant it may be a little over the top. A little too dressy."

"Try it on. Now," Annie playfully demanded as she threw the dress at Grace.

Grace reluctantly changed out of her new blue sundress and pulled Annie's silky red dress over her head. It fell over her shoulders effortlessly, hugging her body in all the right places. Grace looked in the full-length mirror on the back of Annie's bedroom door. "Wow," she said, almost to herself. Now this was a kissing dress.

"I knew it would be perfect," Annie said. She then dug down further into the bottom of her closet. "Here, try these." She held up a pair of red, strappy, high-heeled sandals.

"You know I can't wear heels very well and these are at least three inches tall," said Grace.

"You also said you're not a 'sexy' kind of girl and now look at you. Put these on. You need them," said Annie, shoving the shoes in Grace's face.

Grace slipped on the sandals and looked at herself in the mirror. Annie was right. Grace *needed* these shoes.

At that very moment, the doorbell rang.

"He is always right on time," said Annie. "I'll get it while you go in the bathroom and grab my red lipstick. It should be right next to my contact solution. You really need a little more lip color with that dress." Annie paused at the doorway and looked back at Grace. "Hey, roomie. You really do look good."

Annie then bounded out of the room leaving Grace staring at herself in the mirror. "I hope Gregory thinks so," she said to herself. "Maybe even good enough for a kiss…"

After taking Annie's lipstick advice, Grace found her roommate and Gregory talking in the living room.

"You look fantastic." Gregory smiled at Grace. "Red is my favorite color."

"Thanks," she blushed. *Note to self. Wear more red.*

Gregory put his arm around Grace's waist and guided her to the front door of the apartment. "Don't wait up, Annie," he called back to her roommate.

"Of course not." Annie winked at Grace.

Grace silently blushed.

Just like the three previous nights, Gregory opened Grace's car door for her but tonight they were not riding in Gregory's Chevy Tahoe as they had before. No, tonight Gregory had brought out the big guns and had his father's silver Mercedes SL63 AMG convertible.

"I love your car," Grace gushed after Gregory slid into the driver's seat beside her.

"Thanks." Gregory smiled. "I love your dress." He reached over and held her hand all the way to the restaurant. At first, his touch felt like tiny electric shocks bouncing between his palm and her palm. Remarkably, despite the electricity, his touch made her stomach's butterflies disappear and Grace relaxed down deep into the Mercedes' soft leather seat.

They ate by candlelight at a local downtown restaurant that Grace had never heard of before. But her ignorance of the restaurant stemmed more from the menu's prices than anything else. Her budget would never have allowed her to eat here and she was almost uncomfortable ordering something that was nearly equivalent to a day's salary for her.

But Gregory had no problem with the menu's prices and must have been a regular because everyone in the place knew him. The whole night it was "Mr. Reich this" and "Mr. Reich that" and at one point she even thought she heard their waiter call Gregory "Prince."

But that was ridiculous so she must have heard him wrong.

"Do you want dessert?" Gregory asked after the waiter had cleared their dinner plates.

"No. I'm fine." Grace sat with her elbows on the table and chin in hand, staring at Gregory's face. She could not take her eyes off him in the candlelight.

"Something else to drink?"

"No," sighed Grace dreamily. With her stares and sighs, Grace knew she looked and sounded like a lovesick teenager but she could not help the way she felt when she was around Gregory. She was drugged and woozy as if Gregory was her personal anti-depressant prescription and she liked feeling that way.

"Then I guess it's time for me to get you home," Gregory said.

Home? thought Grace. *Where there's a front door and possibly a kiss?*

Gregory paid the check and again opened her car door for her. Before she knew it, they were pulling into her apartment's parking lot and walking to her front door holding hands. The electric pulses started up again with his touch.

"Thanks for tonight," Grace said when they reached her door. Her heart was pounding and her chest moved with deep nervous breaths.

"No. Thank you. It was nice to finally spend some time alone with you." Gregory's voice glided through the night air as he turned to take her other hand. He stepped toward her, inches away from her heaving chest.

"Yeah. Alone." Grace nervously sighed as Gregory leaned down and placed his lips millimeters from hers.

"Do you mind?" he whispered.

"No." She held her breath, afraid to move.

And so, with her consent, he took her lips and made them his own. His kisses were soft at first, massaging her lips with his. Small dainty kisses, but each one becoming slightly more intense than the previous until his lips fully engulfed hers, and his hands gripped her shoulders so tightly she had to hold on to his arms in order to remain standing upright. Grace had not been kissed this forcefully in so long she was not exactly sure what to do. So when he pushed his tongue into her mouth, she took it, allowing her own tongue to explore Gregory's taste.

They stood at her front door, arms wrapped tightly, tongues flitting, and lips eating each other apart, for what seemed like forever. Grace was totally lost in Gregory's kiss and even with her eyes closed, psychedelic colors ran through her brain and she was unable to think. Her mind went blank and the only parts of her body that felt alive were her lips and the parts of her back and shoulders that Gregory's hands and arms had taken over. Each place his skin touched hers felt like an electric shock. Her lips, hands, arms, shoulders. Every inch he touched was energized.

Without warning, in the midst of awakening her passion that had hibernated for so very long, two things happened.

The first was the fact that Grace suddenly felt like she was being watched. Despite the relaxed feeling she had in Gregory's arms, with his lips and tongue discovering parts of her mouth she did not even know existed, she suddenly felt as if she were the target of some CIA investigation. The hair on the back of her neck stood up and she knew, without a doubt, that she and Gregory were not alone.

The second thing that happened was more within the realm of plausibility but was much more upsetting to a girl of Grace's moral values. Without notice, Gregory's right hand released its grip on Grace's shoulder and abruptly moved down the nape of her neck and under the front of her halter dress to grab her breast. At first she did not realize what had happened, her mind clouded by Gregory touching her in a place that had been sheltered for so long. But then, as if waking from a trance, feeling Gregory's hand roughly groping her breast's delicate skin caused her to stiffen and she tried to push him away. Her immediate thought was to escape. Escape his lips, his arms, his everything.

But he was too strong.

She opened her eyes and turned her head, trying to hide her lips from his mouth's grasp and in that instant she felt fear. Not because Gregory was roughly grabbing her and would not stop. But because Gregory's eyes were wide open in the middle of his kisses, wide open and wickedly red.

She tried to push him away again and, when her mouth was finally free, she screamed, "No!"

But Gregory was in his own trance and was not listening to her. He kept coming at her, groping her.

Grace pushed him harder. "I said no!" she screamed even louder and pushed both hands against his chest with all her might.

Her screams must have torn through Gregory's trance because his hand fell down leaving the top of her dress pushed to one side, her naked breast exposed to the night. He released her finally and stepped back as the redness of his eyes disappeared, replaced once again by his green twinkles.

"I guess I got carried away," he said without emotion.

"Yeah. I'm not ready for that right now," Grace replied, still panting from the force of her push out of Gregory's arms.

"Of course," Gregory said, his emerald eyes unashamed. "I'll call you tomorrow." He abruptly turned and disappeared into the night.

Grace stood there in shock, her breast hanging out of her halter dress and tears falling on her nakedness. How could her first kiss with Gregory have gone so wrong?

•••

Ben sat in his dark car and covertly watched the scene at Grace's front door play out like some B–grade horror movie. The Council had specifically told him not to interfere, that they did not want the Anti-Powers knowing how close they actually were to Grace. They instructed him only to watch her discreetly from a distance, unless her safety was at risk. But that was like asking a mother rabbit to watch a fox attack her baby. When he saw Gregory's hand move down Grace's neck, Ben gripped the steering wheel tighter, his strength inadvertently bending it into a narrow upright oval. From Ben's viewpoint, he could not see where Gregory's hand landed on the front of Grace's dress, but his assumptions were confirmed when he saw her struggling out of Gregory's grasp.

"Forget the Council and their stupid instructions," Ben said to himself as he started to get out of his car. His fist grabbed the door handle just as Gregory stepped back from Grace and walked away. With Gregory gone, Ben released his clutch on the now-mangled door handle and decided to remain in his car. He sat in the dark, watching Grace's tears fall down her face and land on her naked breast, until she turned and was safely in her apartment.

"I can't take this anymore," Ben sighed as he bent the steering wheel back into its original form.

•••

Jamison and Andrew Reich were in the study when they heard the front door open and close.

"Gregory?" Mr. Reich called.

"Yes, sir." Gregory entered the study and sat down across from his father.

"Well? How did her test go?" Mr. Reich leaned back against his desk and crossed his arms.

"She's got more willpower than we expected."

"Really?" Mr. Reich raised his eyebrows.

"Yes, sir. I was able to manipulate her emotions the whole night. You know, one minute I made her nervous, the next minute totally calm. But when I went in to cop a feel, she fell out of my control and tried to push me away."

"You copped a feel?" Andrew interrupted, quickly tossing aside the book he was reading. "Way to go little brother."

"Yeah. I was having a good time until her stupid willpower got in the way."

"How was it?" Andrew pressed.

"Great breast," Gregory smirked. "Best mission I've been on in a while."

"Boys," Mr. Reich interrupted. "Can we get back to the task at hand?"

Both boys grinned and looked at their father.

"Gregory," Mr. Reich continued. "I'm glad you enjoyed yourself tonight but do you think Grace passed your test?"

"No, sir," Gregory sat up straighter. "I don't understand it. I am able to control her emotions but it looks like when I get close to challenging her goodie-two-shoes principles, she has some pretty intense pushback. Her willpower is unreal. I've never seen anything like it."

"Good to know." Mr. Reich smiled and turned to Andrew. "Call Doc tomorrow and have him put together a little birthday drink for Grace. Tell him we just need her dazed at her party. We don't want her dead – at least not yet."

"Yes, sir," replied Andrew.

"Father," Gregory said. "I really don't think that will be necessary. I can handle her. I just need a little more practice before her party. I promise. I can do this."

Mr. Reich looked hard at his youngest son. "Gregory, like me, you have many powers but your ability to manipulate the mind will be one of your greatest when it is fully developed. If you think more practice will get it to the level we need for the party, well then, you better start practicing." He then turned back to Andrew. "But you still need to call Doc. I am leaving nothing to chance that night."

Chapter Six: Purpose

Tom was still up when Ben returned home.

"Is your shift over already?" he asked. Tom sounded more concerned than surprised.

"I got someone else from the team to cover for me the rest of tonight. I had to get out of there." Ben purposefully avoided Tom's eyes as he fell down into his recliner.

Tom turned off the television and shifted around on the couch to face Ben. "What happened?"

"Nothing." Ben did not look up.

"Ben, did something go wrong?" Tom pressed.

"No. I said nothing happened. Grace is fine. Safe and sound in her apartment."

"And?"

"And nothing. I'm just sick of spying on her and her boyfriend. That's all. All that kissing and stuff. It's disgusting." Ben stared down at his jacket's zipper.

"But that's your job. You are Grace's Guardian and part of that job means you have to take a shift or two to watch her, even when she is with her boyfriend." Tom's voice grew stern. "You're not falling for her again, are you? Because we've been over this a thousand times. You are not the Chosen One. I am. When the time comes, it's my job to be with Grace, not yours. So no feelings for her, remember?"

"Yeah. I remember." Ben's fingers were now nervously fumbling with his jacket zipper. If Ben looked up, Tom's powers might allow him to see his younger brother's true feelings reflected in Ben's eyes. Tom's reading gift was one of his stronger powers and had always been a pain in the butt for Ben. One strategic look into someone's eyes and Tom knew a person's soul and the source of their emotions. Ben knew his propensity for breaking furniture had always bugged Tom, but it was nothing compared to living with someone who could discover all your secrets. Through the years, Ben had learned to fake his emotions when he needed to around Tom. But faking took more self-control than Ben had right now so he continued to stare down at his hands when he said, "I think Grace really likes this Gregory guy."

"Why do you say that?"

"I don't know. The way she kissed him. The way she didn't slap his face off when he groped her. She just pushed him away."

"He groped her? Where were they?"

"At her front door. Gregory went in for a little more than a good night kiss. Luckily, Grace stopped him."

"How could she stop him? I thought he was some Anti-Power with all this strength." Tom's eyes narrowed. "Did you interfere?"

"No. Grace's willpower must be getting stronger than we thought. All I know is he just left her standing alone at her front door." Ben was finally in control enough to look up at his older brother. "She was crying."

"So. Remember she's just a job. If she cries, that's part of being human and you can't worry about her feelings. You just need to keep her alive until her twenty-second birthday. The Council will take it from there."

"The Council? What do they know?" Ben was tired of listening to the Council.

"Everything," reminded Tom.

"No, really, Tom. What do they know? We don't even know who is on the Council. To be honest, I really don't think we know anything at all! All we know is that we have to live by their rules just because they are the governing body of the Powers, the so-called old superheroes."

"I hate that term," Tom interrupted.

"Whatever. Okay, instead of superheroes, let's just say those of us with *special powers*," Ben smirked.

"Better," Tom inserted.

"Anyway, this great, all-knowing Council determines how those of us with special powers can live our lives and yet we don't know anything about them. We just get these random messages about discharging our duty and how do we know it's real? How do we know the Council is real, Tom?"

"Because Mom and Dad told us."

"Mom and Dad are dead because of the Council." Ben's words were coming out of his mouth faster than his brain could filter them.

"No, they're dead because of the Anti-Powers. The Council tried to save them. You know that. You and I would be dead too if not for the Council."

"Right," said Ben, rolling his eyes. "Sometimes I think I'd rather be dead."

"Ben, calm down."

"No," Ben vented at his brother. "This is too much. The Council groomed me to be Grace's Guardian just like they groomed you to be the Chosen One. Did anyone ask us if we wanted these jobs? No. They just threw them to us and told us to handle it. Well, what if I don't want to *handle it* anymore?"

"Then the Council will assign someone else to protect Grace and you'll never see her again," Tom stated bluntly.

Those words immediately silenced Ben's rage. He already knew them to be true but he had never felt their reality more than he felt them at that moment. In the middle of his madness, Ben knew one thing. He could not lose Grace. He loved her too much. He just hoped no one else knew how he felt or he really would never see her again.

"If that's my only option, to stay or to quit, I better shut up and suck it up because I'm not quitting this job. I have too much time invested in it." Ben tried to sound firm on the subject and hoped Tom bought his bogus excuse.

"Good," said Tom. "You just need to hold it together a little longer. Once Grace turns twenty-two, the Council will take her in and your job will be over."

"And your job will begin," mumbled Ben.

"Look, Bro. I'm sorry I'm the Chosen One. Like you said, I didn't ask for this. The Council decided this a long time ago. And I'm sorry Grace is the last survivor of the Family. It's not my fault your best friend is the only human remaining on earth with the DNA needed by the Council to survive."

"Needed by the Council *and* the Anti-Powers," said Ben.

"Exactly," said Tom. "And once she turns twenty-two, if the Anti-Powers get her, Grace's life is over."

"Her life, our lives, the Council—"

"But you won't let that happen, right?" reminded Tom.

"Right," sighed Ben.

"So let's just keep her alive until she turns twenty-two and her DNA is ready for the Council and then you can take a nice, long vacation."

"Sure," replied Ben. *A nice, long, miserable vacation without Grace*, he thought.

Chapter Seven: Making Up

"Thanks for agreeing to see me," said Gregory.

"You need to be thanking Annie. She's the one who convinced me to give you a second chance," Grace said. They sat on the couch in Grace's living room. Annie had quickly exited the apartment upon Gregory's arrival so Grace could be alone with him. Annie said she and Gregory needed to hash out the front door incident, as they were now calling it, but the minute Gregory appeared at the door, Grace knew there would be no "hashing" tonight. Grace's memory of the incident started fading as soon as he sat down beside her.

"So?" Grace was trying to stand her ground but her faux tough girl act was hard to maintain with Gregory's green twinkles staring back at her.

"So…I'm sorry." Gregory reached over and took Grace's hand. The electricity was back. "I'm really sorry. I would never take advantage of you like that. I guess kissing you was a little more than I anticipated and my hands had a mind of their own. Do you forgive me? Can we start over?"

Once again, Grace felt an unnatural calmness fall over her. Her head felt woozy and Gregory's words sailed around her mind and enveloped it just as Gregory's fingers intertwined with hers. He pulled her hand to his lips and began kissing each finger.

"Please?" asked Gregory, looking at her over his kisses.

Grace sighed. "Don't let that happen again." She paused. "At least not until I'm ready."

"I promise." Gregory smiled. "Perhaps we could try another kiss now that I promise to be a good boy?" Gregory moved closer to Grace on the couch.

"Sure," said Grace hesitantly. She had not asked Gregory about his red eyes from the front door incident but she had earlier rationalized it must have been her porch light playing tricks on her mind. Her nerves' protective blanket returned with Gregory's presence tonight and the minute she felt his breath on her cheek any remaining fear she had over Gregory's red pupils disappeared completely.

"I promise to be good," Gregory whispered just as he drew her face toward him. His lips lightly brushed hers as his hands held Grace's face in place against his. His kisses were delicate but Grace felt a need for more than Gregory's delicacy. For some reason, her confidence was in overdrive and she reached up to place both arms around his neck, pulling him against her. His hands immediately left her face and wrapped around her body. Electric tingles flew over her skin as they clutched each other on the couch and pressed their lips together in coercive motion. They kissed for what seemed like a long while until Grace finally had to come up for air.

"Wow," she said, pulling her lips away from Gregory's grasp.

"Was that better?"

"You could say that." Grace was lightheaded and Gregory's kiss confirmed what she thought all along. He was her own personal drug. And Grace was addicted.

"How about something to drink?" Grace tried to stand up from the couch. But standing up was not an option in her dizzy state and she almost fell over just as Gregory caught her.

"Do you need me to get it?" Gregory smiled at Grace's unsteadiness. "I didn't know I had that effect on you. Perhaps we need a little more practice in the kissing arena. My father always says practice makes perfect."

"No. I'm fine." Grace giggled as she pulled herself out of Gregory's arms and headed to the kitchen. She grabbed two beers out of the refrigerator and was grabbing two cocktail napkins out of a drawer when she glanced out the kitchen window and spotted Ben's car parked across the street.

"Great," she said to herself.

"What?" Gregory called from the other room.

"Nothing," replied Grace as she returned to the living room and placed the drinks on the coffee table. She crossed to the front window and drew the blinds. *That will stop Ben's weirdo spying game*, she thought.

"Now, where were we?" Grace asked as she settled back onto the couch and into Gregory's arms.

Gregory smiled. "I believe we were practicing."

• • •

"I think I like the red satin dress on you best," said Annie as she stood outside Grace's dressing room. "Now, what do you think about this one with my skin tone?"

Grace exited her dressing room and evaluated Annie standing in front of the boutique's three-way mirror. "The green looks good with your eyes. Besides that one is on sale and you don't have any money so you better get it before someone else does." Grace turned to look at herself in the mirror. "I really like this blue one on me. Plus it's on sale."

"But Gregory likes red and he is your date so go with the red. Trust me." Annie stood next to Grace in front of the mirror, her black combat boots sticking out from the chiffon folds of her long green dress.

"We'd look like a Christmas tree with all that green and red," said Grace.

"Oh, who cares?" said Annie. "It's your birthday party. We can paint our faces purple and no one can say a word about it that night."

"I really can't believe the party is almost here. You know I'm actually having fun shopping for a new dress, but I still feel weird about having this huge party." Grace's stomach had been nauseated all day.

"Weird, shmeird, get over it. As for the dress, forget what's on sale. Get what will make Gregory happy. As guest of honor, you have to have something new for your party and you need to feel pretty that night. Who knows? You might get lucky," stated Annie matter-of-factly.

"Annie! What if someone heard you?" Grace whispered as she looked around the dressing room area. "Besides, I don't think Gregory and I are ready for that yet." The image of Gregory's red eyes from the front porch incident flashed to the front of Grace's mind and the fear she felt that night briefly passed through her heart again.

"You never know—"

"No. I know. It's not time for that even if it is my birthday," said Grace.

"Oh, for Pete's sake. You are as prudish as Ben," said Annie, rolling her eyes.

At the mention of Ben, Grace's discomfort switched gears. "Speaking of Ben, have you seen him lately?"

"No. Pete in the pro shop said he heard from his girlfriend that Ben asked Julian if he could work different shifts from us. Guess he's really mad at you."

"At me? What did I do?" exclaimed Grace.

"Started dating Gregory," said Annie.

"So."

"So. Our Ben apparently doesn't like that."

"But he said he would try—"

"Try. Shmy. If I were you, I would tell Ben not to come to the party unless he gets an attitude adjustment toward Gregory," Annie declared as she reentered her dressing room to change clothes. "It would make the party run a little smoother if you didn't have to worry about Ben weirding out on you that night," Annie said over her dressing room door. "I'm just saying…if I were you."

"I can't disinvite him," said Grace. "He's one of my best friends, remember? That would be like disinviting you. Maybe I should just go talk to him before the party."

"Whatever," said Annie, emerging from the dressing room, green dress in hand. "Do what you want but I don't think talking to Ben is going to do any good. He really hates Gregory and if I had to choose between my boyfriend and my best friend to be at my birthday party, I'd choose my boyfriend. Gregory is hot and rich and you could forget all about college being married to someone like that."

"But I don't want to forget about college. And marriage is not even on my radar." The memory of Gregory's red eyes was now burning Grace's brain.

Annie rolled her eyes. "Yeah, right. Now give me your wallet so I can go pay for my dress."

• • •

Grace stood outside the men's locker room feeling like a stalker. She had stayed long after her shift at the club was over, hoping to run into Ben when he came in for work that night. She was hot and tired after a long day and not in the mood for any heavy discussion right now, but with the party only days away, she needed to resolve her issues with Ben tonight. After seeing his car in the club parking lot and looking everywhere else she could think of, the men's locker room was her last resort.

An eternity passed, but Ben finally emerged and the minute she saw him, all her rehearsed words flew out of her head. She just stood there and said, "Hey."

Ben took a few steps back and looked around before he said hesitantly, "Hey yourself. What are you doing here?"

"I…I was hoping we could talk," said Grace, an unexpected softness falling over her. Except for catching him spying from his car the other night, she had not seen Ben at all lately and had forgotten how blue his eyes were. Blue, beautiful and intense.

"About what?" feigned Ben.

"You know what. You've been avoiding me and I think it has to do with Gregory."

"I'm not avoiding you. I've just been busy, that's all."

Ben's mock ignorance of their situation erased the brief softness she had just felt and, in its place, left full-blown anger. Her rapid mood swings were often a handicap, both for Grace and those around her. And right now was no exception.

"Busy. Right. Busy spying on me and Gregory," Grace said as she crossed her arms and took a defensive stance in the hallway outside the locker room.

A strange look crossed Ben's face. "I don't know what you are talking about." He turned to walk away.

Grace grabbed his arm and spun him around. "Don't you walk away from me. What is your problem?"

"I don't have a problem." Ben jerked his arm out of Grace's grasp. "Now let me get to work."

"Fine," Grace said through gritted teeth. "You don't want to resolve our issues? That is just fine with me. Some best friend you are. But you can forget about coming to my birthday party. Annie's right. I'll have a lot more fun without you and your attitude there so consider yourself officially uninvited. Don't even think about coming to the Cavern Café that night. I don't need you!" Grace fumed. She turned and stormed down the hallway and out the door without looking back.

Chapter Eight: The Party

The doorbell rang just as Grace was taking one last look at herself and the red dress in her bedroom mirror. Annie had left hours ago with Andrew to finish setting up for the party so Grace grabbed her matching red satin purse and headed for the front door to answer it herself. She was a bundle of nerves, still dreading the party, and the thought of being the center of attention for a night was making her palms sweat even with the now constant tingling in her fingers. Having avoided it all her life, she could not remember ever being the center of attention before, not even when her parents died. But then all she remembered about that time of her life was the smell of burnt metal.

As usual, Gregory was precise with his arrival time. She took a deep breath, sucked her stomach in and smoothed out the long, red satin that clung tightly to her curves. She gave her loose, long dark hair one more fluff before opening her apartment's front door.

And there he stood. His tuxedo made him look a little older, a little James Bondish, but it was the boyish grin that said it all. Gregory looked hot and Grace's nerves again turned to butterflies at the sight of him.

"Wow," he said, looking her up and down, obviously evaluating every curvy detail of Grace's body beneath the red satin. "Are you ready to go?"

"I think so," Grace replied with a hesitant smile.

"Trust me. You're ready." Gregory grinned and took her arm to lead her out the front door.

Grace's satin dress swished rhythmically as they walked to Gregory's car and the noise made her even more self-conscious. She didn't want to listen to that all night. She had enough to deal with. When she saw they were riding in Gregory's Tahoe, her tight dress caused her even more consternation. She struggled with it as she climbed up onto the cloth seat of the Tahoe and would have preferred sliding into the soft leather of Mr. Reich's low-riding Mercedes.

"Sorry about the ride," Gregory said as if reading her mind when he entered the car. "Dad has his car tonight to take Mom to your party. They really appreciated being invited."

"Oh, no problem. I'm glad they can come," said Grace as she shifted in the seat trying to get comfortable. Even with her stomach sucked in, the dress was still a little tight and the satin clung to the Tahoe's cloth seat like Velcro.

Gregory grabbed Grace's hand and the minute she felt his electric touch, she took a deep breath and relaxed. His touch always calmed her as if he knew just when she needed him. She was drugged and she was grateful.

They soon pulled up to the front door of the Cavern Café and it was easy to see how the restaurant got its name. Looking like a cabin in the Ozarks, gray stacked stone covered the building's entire façade and thick, rough log columns marked the front entrance. Pine trees lined the front stone walkway leading from the parking lot to the front porch, and Grace knew from talking to the Café's owner that each of these pines had once been a Christmas tree in his family's home.

Grace had hoped that the combination of the restaurant's familiarity and the owner's familial quaintness would alleviate some of her nervousness tonight but this hope was quashed when a valet parking attendant abruptly opened her car door. Having valet parking at the Cavern Café tonight meant her party was a bigger deal than she had anticipated or wanted.

Grace did not recognize the valet but he obviously knew Gregory because he said, "Good evening, Mr. Reich. Nice to see you again," when he took the keys from her date.

"Since when does the Cavern Café have valet parking?" Grace whispered to Gregory as they walked beneath the pines leading to the restaurant's front door.

"Since I hired them for your party. The Café's lot is a little small so I thought it would help with the parking tonight." Gregory smiled at Grace and placed his arm around her waist.

"Thanks, I think," said Grace relaxing unnaturally into Gregory's arm.

"No problem. I just want to do all I can to make tonight memorable." Gregory squeezed Grace's waist a little tighter just as they reached the front door.

"Wait." Grace stopped abruptly, took a deep breath, and stared at the heavy wooden door. She was not prepared to be the center of attention just yet.

"Grace, darling, I promise not to leave your side all night." Gregory looked down at her and his voice seemed to hold a hint of frustration and impatience.

Grace looked up into Gregory's green eyes and fell closer into his tight embrace. Her nerves' protective blanket returned. "Okay. Let's get this over with."

"I promise you. This will be a night you will never forget." Gregory smiled as he opened the front door leading into the Cavern Café.

The restaurant was decorated like a fairy wonderland with tiny white lights and waves of natural pine garland hanging from every nook and cranny of the room's large wooden ceiling beams. Fresh flowers overflowed the white-clothed tables, with Grace's favorite flowers, lilacs, enveloping the room with spring's sweet smell. Grace could not have been more surprised if Tinkerbell herself flew down and landed on her shoulder.

"Do you like it?" Annie came bounding up with her green chiffon dress flowing over her black combat boots. Andrew followed close behind seemingly tied to the long, green satin sash streaming from Annie's waist. In his tuxedo, he looked like an overgrown emperor penguin.

"Annie, it's beautiful! I love it," said Grace. "When did you do all this?"

"Off and on today. I had tons of help. Pretty much everyone here helped out with your party in one way or another," Annie said, pointing to the other party attendees scattered around the room.

Grace looked around at the packed restaurant and her stomach turned when she realized how many people had showed up for her party. Julian was in the back directing the wait staff and wearing a black waistcoat and bowtie that Grace assumed to be some sort of British fashion thing. Lady Covington, with her triple-strand pearl necklace and more sequins than a woman that size should be allowed to wear, was sitting with Old Man Hillary and some of the other senior club members who routinely remembered Grace's name. Pete, the tennis pro, was at another table and, noting the large size of his entourage, Grace wondered how many favors he had promised Annie to get them all here tonight. Even Will Crenshaw was sitting with his girlfriend and crutches at a far corner table.

"Okay. Here is the plan," said Annie moving into cruise director mode. "You go mingle while I go help Julian the jackass get your cake ready. Then we can sing, you blow out your candles, you and Gregory dance the first dance, and then we party the rest of the night. Got it? Good." And with that, Annie rushed back to Julian who, by the look on Annie's face, was not doing whatever he was doing the way Annie wanted it done.

Grace smiled at Gregory and took his hand, intending to speak to Lady Covington and Old Man Hillary before the elderly patrons made an early night of it. As she worked her way over to their table, timidly smiling and thanking the other guests she encountered, out of nowhere Mr. and Mrs. Reich appeared in front of her and stopped Grace dead in her tracks.

"Grace, dear. Happy birthday and thank you so much for inviting us." Mr. Reich looked dashing in his tailored black tuxedo and diamond cufflinks.

Mrs. Reich just stood there and purred a smile at Grace. She looked spectacular as always in a tight black strapless gown that proved her body had not aged in years. Large diamonds covered her ears and neckline and she appeared to belong more at the Oscars than a birthday party for some random club waitress. Despite her fashion sense however, Mrs. Reich did look a little out of place with her large, black Dolce & Gabbana sunglasses hiding her eyes. It was night, the room's light was dimmed, and yet here she was, still wearing those sunglasses like she had every other time Grace had seen her. Grace thought there must be something very wrong with Mrs. Reich's eyes.

"So when will we get to see you and my son show off your dancing skills?" Mr. Reich interrupted Grace's silent critique.

"Oh, I don't know. Annie has this whole night planned so I'm just going to do what she tells me to do."

"Grace, dear." Lady Covington's voice rose up behind Mr. Reich like a song and her large body soon followed, wedging in between Mr. and Mrs. Reich without an invitation. She pulled Grace toward the elder club members' table and never acknowledged the Reichs' presence.

"It was nice talking to you," Grace called back to the Reichs whose facial expressions now reflected resentment rather than the smiles they had had earlier. Mr. Reich glared at Gregory and then walked away with Mrs. Reich who still wore her ridiculous sunglasses.

"Look who I found," Lady Covington exclaimed to her table as she pulled Grace along like an aunt showing off her favorite niece. Lady Covington dragged her from guest to guest around the large round table with each one fawning over Grace like she was a celebrity.

"There's the birthday girl!" Mr. Hillary smiled as he rose from his seat to take Grace's hand. He bowed and kissed it lightly as if she were royalty. In his black dinner tuxedo, Grace could see why all the older ladies at the club doted on him.

"Thank you so much for coming." Grace held both Mr. Hillary's hands in hers.

"I am truly honored to be invited," he replied with another deep bow.

As if on cue, Gregory came up behind Grace and handed her a drink. "Here you go. Thought you could use this."

"Thanks." Grace took a long sip of vodka and cranberry juice.

Mr. Hillary eyeballed Gregory as he continued, "And where is our Ben tonight?"

"I…I'm not sure." Grace motioned to Gregory who was now standing beside her. "Mr. Hillary, have you met Gregory Reich? He and his family are new members at the club."

Gregory stuck his hand out. "Mr. Hillary, it's so very nice to meet you. I hear you have quite a mean golf game."

Mr. Hillary took Gregory's hand but pain immediately fell over the elderly gentleman's face. He quickly pulled his hand out of Gregory's grasp and shook it. "And you have quite a mean handshake, son," replied Mr. Hillary as he placed his still shaking hand in his trouser pocket. Turning to Grace he said, "Now, you should run along Gracie. I'm sure your other guests want to see you too."

Grace smiled and said her goodbyes to the rest of the table before Gregory pulled her toward Annie, who was still bickering with Julian at the back of the room.

"Julian, you are not in charge here. I am," Annie was saying to her nemesis as Grace walked up.

"Hey Julian." Grace intentionally did not give him a chance to respond to Annie's rebuke. She took another drink and its coolness calmed her nervous breathing.

"Hello, Grace. Happy birthday," he said matter-of-factly. "Thank you for allowing me to be a part of your celebration."

Annie rolled her eyes. "Whatever. Just get the cake ready, you British freak," she said before turning to Grace and Gregory.

Julian narrowed his eyes but then simply shook his head and silently walked back toward the kitchen.

"Annie! Be nice," Grace scolded. She took another sip of her drink and realized she had already finished off her first one of the night.

"Oh, he'll get over it," Annie said. "Besides, he just hates not having any control over me or your party tonight."

Gregory laughed. "You do like your control Annie, don't you?"

"Absolutely. Now you all run along and go get us some more drinks," she commanded.

"Aye, aye, Captain." Gregory saluted Annie before taking Grace's empty glass and heading over to the drink table.

Grace was feeling a little looser and wondered if her drink might have something to do with it. Maybe she should lay off the alcohol for now. She surveyed the room's faces, smiling at those she recognized and at those she did not.

"He's not here," said Annie, watching Grace's face.

"Who?"

"Ben."

Grace felt blood rush to her cheeks. "I know he's not here. I asked him not to come remember."

"Yeah, well, then stop looking for him. Concentrate on Gregory, who looks hot by the way."

The two girls looked over at the drink table where the Reich brothers were gathering their next round of libations.

"I told you this was going to be a great summer," Annie said as Gregory and Andrew started heading back their way.

"Here you are birthday girl," said Gregory, handing Grace her drink and kissing her lightly on the cheek. The touch of Gregory's lips sent prickly sparks down Grace's spine and she leaned in to him as if magnetized to his side.

"There sure are a lot of people here," said Grace looking around the room. "Some of these people I don't even recognize."

"Maybe the owner invited some people as well," Andrew quickly responded.

"I'm sure we have some party crashers. This *is* the party of the year from what I hear," said Gregory. "Do you want me to ask them to leave?" He placed his arm around Grace's waist and pulled her closer to him.

"No." Grace smiled. "It's all good. The more the merrier." Gregory's touch once again put Grace at ease and her wooziness returned with his presence. Either that or her drink was stronger than she thought. "How much alcohol did you put in this?" she asked, leaning face forward into Gregory's arms.

"Enough. Is it okay?"

"It's fine." Grace's words began to slur out of her mouth. After a few more sips of her drink, she felt totally relaxed despite the fact that the room's details were beginning to disappear into a blur of colors. She could no longer see the guests at the far side of the room, and even up close Gregory's face had a slight haziness to it. The decorative foliage hanging from the ceiling's wooden beams transformed into vague ripples of green and the tiny white lights now glared instead of twinkled. Even the flower centerpieces melted into one round blob of color floating in front of Grace's eyes. Nothing was distinct anymore.

"Happy birthday, Grace." Tom's voice floated through the room's colors as they swirled around and eventually came together to form his face.

"Tom!" Grace exclaimed when his face was close enough to be a little clearer. She leaned further into Gregory's arms and slurred, "Your brother didn't show."

"You asked him not to, remember?" Tom looked into Grace's eyes. "Uh, are you okay?"

"Couldn't be peachier." Grace now smiled with only one side of her face and she was having a hard time focusing.

"She's fine," Gregory interrupted. "She's just a little excited."

"Are you sure you're okay Gracie?" Tom pressed, ignoring Gregory.

"Yes. I'm fine!" Grace hissed. "My gosh! You're worse than your brother." Grace swayed a little before she slurred over her shoulder, "Annie! I believe it's time for cake!"

"Okay." Annie winked at Tom. "Whatever you say, Birthday Girl." Annie turned and headed back to the kitchen, leaving Grace weaving between Gregory and Andrew.

Tom silently stared at Gregory and Andrew, both of whom stood on either side of Grace to control her balance. The Reich brothers returned his stare.

"Nice talking to you, Grace." Tom leaned in to kiss her cheek and then abruptly walked away.

"You too," Grace called after him with a wave of her hand. Tom disappeared back into the room's colors again and the only detail she could see now were the red eyes of Gregory and Andrew who still stood on either side of her, holding her up by each arm. She turned her head, casting her hazy gaze back and forth from Gregory to Andrew. "I think you put too much vodka in this drink. Cause I see red eyes and I don't like red eyes," she slurred.

"Boys, calm down. It's not time yet," Grace heard Mr. Reich's perfect voice rumble through the room's swirling colors at the same moment the brothers' red eyes disappeared.

"Shhh, dear," Mrs. Reich's voice purred behind Grace's ear. "Everything's going to be fine."

Grace did not ever remember feeling so happy and relaxed. She was sure her drink was helping but she did not care. It was her birthday party and she was with Gregory. The room's colors continued to swirl and she still felt Gregory and Andrew holding her arms, but her right arm began to sting from Gregory's touch. Out of the color swirl a light began to emerge and she heard a familiar song ring in her ears. This was the moment she had dreaded. Grace knew all eyes were on her as the party guests sang "Happy Birthday" but for some reason she did not mind being the center of attention. All she saw was the emerging light coming toward her.

By the time Grace realized the light belonged to the candles on her cake, Annie was standing there nudging her, "Come on, Gracie. Everyone's waiting. Blow out your candles."

Grace blew, unsuccessfully aiming at the light and missing the candles entirely, so Gregory and Annie leaned over to help.

"It's time for our dance now," Gregory whispered in Grace's ear after Annie took the cake back into the kitchen for cutting.

Peter Gabriel began singing Grace's favorite old song, "In Your Eyes", over the Café sound system and Gregory guided Grace toward the dance floor in the middle of the room. Grace's mind was drugged with the tornado of colors swirling around her and her arm still stung from Gregory's touch. They were almost to the center of the dance floor when suddenly Grace felt sick.

Very sick.

Beyond nauseated sick.

She pulled out of Gregory's grasp and groped her way through the room's swirling colors toward the bathroom in the far back corner. She heard Mr. Reich and Gregory calling her name but all she could think about was reaching the bathroom in time. She hurled herself through the door and locked it behind her just before she fell on the floor and threw up in the toilet. She could not believe she was this sick, this suddenly. She had heard of people throwing up before but had never experienced it herself. She never got sick. Everyone knew that. But feeling her body convulse uncontrollably confirmed her diagnosis and that fact frightened Grace, even in her dazed state.

After a few more heaves, and when she was finally and totally empty of her stomach's contents, she stood up and made her way over to the sink. Splashing cold water in her mouth and on her face oddly sparked a rare memory of her parents. Grace looked up at her blurred reflection in the mirror over the sink and saw their faces clearly emerge out of the room's swirling colors. But in the instant this memory flashed, she realized it wasn't the cold-water splash that triggered her memory bank.

It was a smell.

The smell of burnt metal.

The smell that took her back to her parent's car crash.

The bathroom's colors were still too hazy to register anything recognizable but as she leaned over the sink to steady herself, she felt an urgent need to get out of there. Her memory pushed her to unlock the door and leave the bathroom. Something about that smell.

Just as she found enough strength to stand upright and head for the door, two hands came from behind her head and grabbed her shoulders. In that instant, the room's swirling colors disappeared and she was pulled into complete and total darkness.

Chapter Nine: Darkness and Movement

The Council leader leaned forward in her chair at the head of the long rectangular wooden table. "Tom, I am sure you appreciate the seriousness of this situation," she said sternly.

"Yes, Madam." Tom stood straight as a stick facing their Council leader at the opposite end of the large boardroom. She had eyes of blue stone. The other Council members flanked their leader on both sides of the table, each one staring back at Tom. Blue stone eyes were everywhere. Tom had never been called into a Council meeting before and standing there, in the large Southern mansion, in their sacred boardroom, finally meeting the Council's infamous members face-to-face, he felt abnormally weak. He knew Ben's team had messed up. He just never imagined he would be the one called in for it. He wasn't Grace's Guardian. He was the Chosen One. His job had not even begun yet.

"Have you spoken to your brother?" the Council Lieutenant asked.

"No, sir. Not yet." He'd tried repeatedly, but Ben wasn't answering his cell phone.

"You know this is a serious dereliction of duty, young man," another Council member stressed.

"Yes, sir."

"Your brother will be severely punished."

"Yes, sir." Even as the Chosen One, Tom had no power to stop the Council from making an example of Ben. For an instant, he was glad Ben was not there. He did not want to be present when the Council handed down his younger brother's punishment.

"For years, we have watched over Grace and when her time finally comes, we lose her," the Council leader's voice slowly escalated. "With all our vast resources, we can't find one tiny girl!" The Council leader was now standing at her seat, her eyes cutting into Tom like scalpels. "If you don't want the Anti-Powers taking control, if you don't want human life to end as we know it, I suggest you and your brother…go…find…her!" she bellowed.

The room shook and Tom could almost see her anger rolling through the air, across the long table and slapping him right in the face.

"Yes, Madam," Tom whispered, unable to take his eyes off his leader.

"You are excused." She harshly dismissed Tom with a wave of her hand.

Tom bowed and quickly strode to the large wooden double doors leading to the hallway.

"And Tom," the Council leader called after him.

Tom stopped and slowly turned around. "Yes, Madam."

"Tell your brother we want to see him. Now!"

•••

It was dark. And she was moving. As Grace slowly regained consciousness, she was only certain of these two things: darkness and movement. She was lying on her side curled up in the fetal position, her back against something pliable. Her head pounded and she could not think. Where was she? Where was she going?

She tried to focus her eyes out of the darkness but it was too hard.

Try harder.

She blinked a few times but all she could see in front of her was black. Nothingness.

She turned her head slightly upward. Instant pain. Why did she hurt so much? It even hurt to breathe, much less turn her head. But she needed to see. There was something up there.

Slowly squinting upward, past the pain, she saw sparkles. What was sparkling? What were those lights over her?

Focus, Grace. Focus.

Stars. The lights were stars.

Blink. Blink. *Focus. Focus.*

It was a sunroof. She saw the stars through a sunroof.

Focus. Focus on the stars.

The stars ripped through Grace's darkness. She knew these stars. And these stars were moving with her. These were the same stars she saw last night and the night before and the night before that. But tonight was different. Tonight she needed these stars. Tonight, these stars, these familiar stars moving with her, would keep her sane.

So focus on the stars, Grace. Focus on the stars.

Too afraid to move, Grace forced her mind to process as she stared at the stars. She was in a car, more specifically the back seat of a car. And the car was moving. And it was night.

Process your thoughts, Gracie. Process. Look at the stars. Focus.

She could not see over the front seat. Who was driving? Who else was in the car?

Quietly, she slid her hands down her body. She was not tied up, her feet were not bound. She was still wearing her red satin dress from the birthday party, but she was barefoot.

She silently felt around the back seat. Her hand brushed against something hard. Her shoes. She found her shoes on the floorboard. She continued to silently search. There. Her purse. Slowly, she eased the small satin purse along the floorboard, closer to her. When it was right below her head, she used one hand to open the clasp while the other hand cupped over the purse, muffling the clasp's sound.

Where were they? Grace's fingers silently weaved through the purse's contents.

There. Her keys. She found her keys. Her keys with the novelty keychain Ben had given her. The keychain with the monkey on it. The monkey with the LED lighted nose.

Grace softly placed her purse back down on the floorboard and held one hand over the monkey's nose while she pushed the 'on' button with the other. She aimed the monkey's LED nose toward the floorboard and faintly made out a Mercedes symbol. It was either that or a peace sign. Grace always got the two confused. No, it was the Mercedes symbol. Grace was in the backseat of a Mercedes.

Grace scanned the rest of the floorboard with the monkey's nose. Nothing else. Her shoes. Her purse. And the Mercedes floor mats. That was it.

Grace was afraid to shine the light any higher. The car's other occupants might see it. As she tried to place her keys back into her purse, her hands started their mysterious tingling again and, in the darkness, she clumsily missed the purse opening. The keys fell down onto the Mercedes floor mat, their tinkling sound breaking the car's dark silence.

The car slowed down.

Grace frantically fumbled around the dark floorboard. The keys. She needed her keys.

The car stopped.

Where were the keys? Panic amplified the tingling in her hands and almost rendered them useless.

The driver's door opened and closed.

Grace's shaking fingers finally found the keys. She remembered from her high school self-defense class that she could use her keys as a weapon by entwining her fingers between each key and making a fist with the keys sticking out between her knuckles like spikes. There. She did it. Fist and weapon ready.

The backdoor opened and the car's interior light glowed over the back seat.

The cool night breeze rushed in, temporarily clearing her head. She took her makeshift weapon and forcefully plunged her shaking fist toward the breeze and outside into the darkness.

But the darkness sharply seized her wrist. Her fingers sprang open and her weapon fell apart. The keys rattled back down to the floorboard of the Mercedes and out of Grace's reach.

Her hand went limp and she started to cry. Then the darkness clutching her wrist fell soft and moved up to caress her hand.

Grace looked out toward the darkness.

"Shhh," the darkness said. "Gracie, don't cry. It's me. Ben."

Chapter Ten: Awakening

"Ben?" It was still too dark to see outside the car.

"Yes. I'm here. Everything's going to be okay." Ben bent down into the car's interior light. "Come on, Gracie. Can you sit up?"

Grace pushed herself to sit up, but even that small movement caused her head to split right open. The pain combined with her confusion to make her nauseatingly dizzy. She swayed on the seat. "Ooh," she said as she leaned her head forward into her hands and closed her eyes.

"What's wrong?"

Grace pointed to her head.

"Your head hurts?" Ben leaned in and softly put his arm around her drooping shoulders.

Grace tried to nod but the pain was too much so she simply whispered, "Yes."

"Okay, Gracie." Ben looked around. "Sweetie, we really need to get going again. I promise to make this right. Just lie down and sleep some more. Maybe your head will feel better in the morning." Ben gently lay Grace down on her side and she curled back into the fetal position on the back seat of the Mercedes.

The last thing Grace remembered was the car moving again through the night. More movement. More darkness.

• • •

Grace woke early the next morning to the thump-thump-thump of the car's tires on a concrete bridge. She was still moving but the darkness was gone. She slowly turned her head and was blinded by the sun's rays trying to tear through the tinted sunroof.

Blink. Blink. *Focus. Focus.*

It was all coming back to her now.

Gregory. Her birthday party. The room's swirling colors. The darkness. And Ben.

"Ben?" Grace whispered as she slowly sat up in the back seat of the Mercedes.

"Hey, sleepy head. How are you feeling?" Ben's tired eyes smiled at her through the rearview mirror. His hands gripped the steering wheel at the ten o'clock and two o'clock positions.

"Head hurts." Grace rubbed her temples and closed her eyes. The bright sunlight was not helping her pain.

"Are you hungry?" Ben's eyes flickered back and forth from the road in front of him to Grace in the backseat.

On any other day that would have been such a simple question to answer but Grace's mind was cloudy. Something was not right and it had nothing to do with her hunger.

"Wait," Grace whispered. Her mind struggled. "Where are we? What's going on?"

Ben stared at the road in front of him.

"Ben?" Grace pressed. "What happened? Did I drink too much at the party? Please tell me I did not embarrass myself. Where's Annie? Where's Gregory?"

"Whoa," interrupted Ben. "For someone with a headache, you sure are asking a lot of questions."

"Just please tell me I did not embarrass myself in front of Gregory."

"No," snapped Ben. "You did not embarrass yourself in front of your precious Gregory. Geesh, Gracie. Is that all you care about? If you'd look around, you'd see we have more important things to worry about."

For the first time since she woke up, Grace looked outside at the scenery flying past her back seat window. Gone were the pine trees of the flat South Carolina landscape and in their place were lush, green, rolling hills filled with maples and oaks, trees as wide as they were tall. There were no landmarks. No signs of civilization. Just trees and a two–lane road stretching between them, weaving in and out of the rolling hills. Nothing looked familiar. Not the hills. Not the car. Just Ben. Ben was the only thing she knew.

"Where are we? Where are we going?" Grace asked again. She was now sitting straight up in the back seat of the Mercedes. She looked down at her red satin dress. It had ripped at the side seam sometime during the night, revealing a right leg covered in scratches and bruises. "Ben, answer me. What's going on?" she asked, anxiety replacing the confusion she experienced earlier.

Ben just looked at her with a strange look in his eyes.

"Ben!" Grace beat her fist hard against the back of his seat. "I said, answer me!" Her aching head pounded with her fist's thrust.

Ben stared straight ahead and did not answer.

"Ben!" Her anxiety was now replaced by anger.

"Gracie." Ben talked to her as if she were a child. "You need to calm down now."

"Calm down?" Grace punched the back of Ben's seat again. "I'll calm down when you tell me what's going on."

"I'll tell you what's going on when you calm down!" Ben replied.

Grace sat back, slamming herself and her aching head against the back seat with her arms crossed. She glared at Ben with unmoving eyes.

Ben continued to stare at the road ahead.

Grace looked out her window. The car behind them had moved into the oncoming lane and was accelerating to pass the Mercedes. The car sped by and reentered the lane in front of them, its speed rapidly creating distance between their front bumper and its back bumper. Soon the car had sped over the horizon, but not before Grace had read its license plate.

"North Carolina?" Grace yelled. "We're in North Carolina?"

"What?"

"That car. That car had a North Carolina license plate! Are we in North Carolina?"

"I told you to calm down, Grace."

"Hmph." Grace slammed back against the seat again. Her head was still pounding, numbed only slightly by her anger.

The silence seemed to last forever, but the car's clock had only counted out sixteen minutes when Grace said, "Okay."

"Okay what?"

"Okay, I'm calmer. Now will you tell me what's going on?"

Ben smiled. "For once, I'm glad for your rapid mood swings."

"Well?" she said impatiently.

"Well," Ben said. "I'm not sure where to start."

"How about you start in the bathroom at the Cavern Café because that's the last thing I remember." Memories of the throw-up session she had endured prompted Grace to reach for her purse and search for a piece of gum. Plopping a piece in her mouth, she continued, "Well?"

"Gracie," began Ben slowly, "do you trust me?"

"I did until I woke up in stupid North Carolina with you driving this stupid Mercedes." Grace smacked her gum and looked around the car. "And since when do you drive a Mercedes?"

"I have…resources." He glanced at Grace through the rearview mirror. "Grace, do you trust me?" Ben repeated.

Grace saw the seriousness in his eyes. "Yes."

"Well, I really need you to trust me now."

"What does me trusting you have to do with where we are going and what happened last night?" Grace's voice began escalating again.

Ben shifted in his seat. "Because, honestly, I really can't tell you everything going on. You just have to trust me."

"Are you kidding me?" Grace shook her head. "You tell me what's going on right this instant or…or," Grace looked around the car and grabbed the nearest door handle, "I swear, I will open this door and jump out of this car. I mean it, Ben! You know I'll do it."

Ben's eyes widened. "What if I told you that I can't tell you?"

"Can't tell me what?"

"Can't tell you…anything."

"Ben, you are making no sense whatsoever. Now, you tell me what's going on or I'm jumping." Grace's hand was still on the door handle.

Ben pushed a button and locked the doors.

Grace unlocked her door.

Ben locked the doors again.

Grace unlocked her door again. She pulled the door handle slightly, all the while staring at Ben's eyes in the rearview mirror.

"Wait," Ben said. "You don't understand. If I tell you, they'll take you away. I'll never see you again. Please Gracie, you have to trust me."

"Who're *they*?" Grace released the door handle.

"The Council," Ben sighed, his eyes staring at the road ahead.

"Who's the Council?"

Ben glanced at Grace through the rearview mirror and gripped the steering wheel tighter.

"Ben, who's the Council?" Grace pressed.

"You wouldn't believe me if I told you," he replied.

"Ben," Grace glared.

"Grace, if I tell you, the Council will make sure I'll never see you again."

"If you don't tell me, I'll make sure you *won't want* to see me again," she hissed. "Now you tell me what's going on right now. Now, Ben!"

Ben took a deep breath.

"Ben?" Grace glared and placed her hand back on the door handle. "Your mouth better start moving."

Ben gripped the steering wheel tighter.

Grace even thought she saw it bend slightly. "Ben, who's the Council?"

Ben glanced at Grace in his rearview mirror and then focused on the road ahead. "Okay." He took a deep breath. "Here goes. Let's start with the premise that there are two kinds of beings in this world. There are those that are normal and those that are special. Follow me?"

"No."

"Okay…well…the Council governs those beings that are special."

"What do you mean special?"

"Special…like they have special powers. Special like they can do some stuff normal humans can't."

Grace's brow knitted together. "You're still not making any sense."

"This is harder than I thought," Ben muttered to himself. "No wonder this is a huge code violation."

"Ben," Grace prodded him.

"Okay, let's start over. You are human."

"Yes…?"

"Some people are…more than human."

Grace looked at Ben like he had lost his mind. "How can someone be more than human?"

"Some people are born with special powers." Ben shook his head. "Geesh, this hard."

"What kind of special powers?"

"All kinds. Some have super strength or speed. Some can read minds. Some have super intelligence."

Grace glared at Ben. "Stop messing with me. Tell me the truth."

"I am."

"No. You've read too many comic books and have seen too many movies."

"Grace, this is serious. There *are* beings in this world that have special powers. And the Council is the group of beings that govern those with special powers. They make the laws that these special beings have to live by."

"Like Congress for your comic book characters?" smirked Grace.

"Sort of," Ben said.

"Get real, Ben." Grace rolled her eyes.

"I am. Please Grace, you have to believe me. These special beings call themselves the Powers. The Council tries to maintain order between the world of the Powers and your world, the human world."

Grace didn't know whether to jump from the car because she was mad at Ben her friend for taking her to North Carolina or because she needed to get away from Ben the crazy person. She placed her hand on the door handle.

"There's more," Ben continued, eyeing Grace's hand on the door.

Grace stayed still.

"You see, the Council has existed for thousands of years," Ben continued. "It ensures that those of us with special powers, the Powers, can live peacefully among you humans. Members are appointed for life. When one Council member dies, the remaining members choose the replacement and so on and so forth. With me so far?"

"No. Wait. Back up. What do you mean those of *us* with special powers?" Grace gripped the door handle tighter.

Ben glanced at Grace through the rearview mirror and then turned back to the road again. "Anyway, like I said, the Council has been around for thousands of years. A long time ago, the Powers didn't have to hide their super human abilities. They didn't flaunt their powers, but if a human happened to discover a Power's ability, it was no big deal. Everything was explained away with magic or divine intervention or some other lame excuse that the humans believed. But then came the Salem witch trials beginning in 1692. So many of the Powers were murdered because of those trials. They were accused of the vilest things, but there were really no witches in Salem. Just a bunch of Powers who practiced their abilities a little too openly."

"Uh-huh…" Grace's fingers wrapped tighter around the door handle.

Ben eyed Grace and then returned his focus to the road. "Anyway," he continued, "after the Salem murders, as we call them, the Council had to choose between allowing the Powers to take over the humans or forcing the Powers to hide forever. Because the Powers had always prided themselves on being the caretakers of the human race, the Council chose the latter and we have been in hiding ever since."

"Uh-huh." Grace raised her eyebrows. "Tell me more." Grace thought that the longer Ben talked, the more time she would have to figure a way out of this mess.

"Well, the Powers continued to live among the humans from that time on, but they could never openly practice their superhuman abilities after the Salem murders. To do so was a strict Council code violation, in some instances punishable by death. So, for about three hundred years, the Powers and humans lived together somewhat peacefully until the 1960s, when one of the Council members got tired of hiding his powers. He tried to take over the Council, essentially hoping to convert it from a democracy into a dictatorship. The other Council members booted him off but not before he had gathered a ton of support from some of the other Powers. Apparently, this rogue Council member and his son were very persuasive when arguing in favor of the public use of powers. Anyway, this rebel member was eventually killed but this only made him a martyr among his supporters who started calling themselves the Anti-Powers. With me so far?"

"Sure." Grace rolled her eyes. "Go on."

"Well, the Anti-Powers, led by the deceased rebel's son, have been fighting with the Council and the other Powers ever since. The son has never been identified by name or face but we do know that his whole goal in life is to get rid of the Council and take over the human race. Payback for the death of his father or something Shakespearean like that. Anyway, think of the Council and the Powers as the good guys and the Anti-Powers as the bad guys. There is a kind of cold war going on right now between the two groups with the Anti-Powers wanting to control the human race and the Powers, led by the Council, wanting to preserve it." Ben glanced back at Grace. "Is any of this making sense?"

"Sure. Whatever you say." Grace didn't hide her patronizing tone.

"Grace, I'm being serious."

"Ben, what does any of this have to do with me?"

Ben slowed the car slightly when he replied, "Because without you, the Council would eventually disappear and the Anti-Powers know it. If the Anti-Powers get you and your genes, they can take over the Powers and the humans would become nothing more than their slaves. That is, if they allow any humans to survive at all."

At that point, Grace knew Ben was no longer her friend but was instead a certifiable lunatic. She silently watched the trees zoom past her window.

"Grace?" Ben asked. "Are you still with me?"

"Uh-huh," Grace mumbled. "Just processing it all." She had to get out of that car. Seeing a small two-pump gas station emerge at the road's horizon, she said, "Uh…could we stop for a minute? I'm feeling a little car sick."

Ben glanced at the dashboard. They had less than a quarter tank remaining. "Yeah, I guess it couldn't hurt. We need some gas anyway." Ben looked back at Grace. "I'm sorry I've thrown so much at you about the Powers and all. I just want you to understand what we're up against."

"Sure," Grace said, not understanding anything at all except that her best friend had gone completely insane.

Ben pulled into the gas station and started pumping gas. He leaned down into Grace's open window. "Do you want something to drink?"

"Sure."

"Okay, but stay in the car. Don't get out under any circumstances. I don't know who all is around here yet."

"Of course," replied Grace, feigning acceptance of Ben's story.

Ben finished pumping the gas and then headed into the gas station. The minute he was out of sight, Grace reached into her purse and pulled out her cell phone. There were eight missed calls from Annie and six missed calls from Gregory.

"Hello?" Annie's voice sounded like an exasperated angel on the other end of the line.

"Annie?" Grace whispered into her phone.

"Gracie! Where are you? What the hell happened last night? One minute you were there and then you disappeared. Gregory and I were so worried about you. I mean we looked everywhere and—"

"Annie, would you shut up for one second?" Grace interrupted. "I don't have much time. I think Ben is suffering some sort of mental breakdown or something. He has me in the backseat of this random Mercedes I've never seen before, driving through North Carolina, talking about Powers and Anti-Powers and some stupid Council. I really think he's lost his mind."

"Where are you exactly?"

Grace looked out her window at the gas station sign overhead. "I told you. In North Carolina somewhere. I don't know the town but the name of the gas station is Taylor's Gas-n-Go. You've got to help me, please!"

"Who are you talking to?" Ben's voice boomed into the back seat. He reached through the open window, grabbed the phone out of Grace's grasp, disconnecting the call in the process, and hurled it toward an empty field on the other side of the road. The phone flew up into the sky so high, Grace never saw it land.

"What the—" Grace stammered.

"Who were you talking to?"

"Annie. And who do you think you are? That was my brand new phone you just threw out!"

"Look, I'm sorry. But you obviously don't grasp what I'm telling you. You are in danger, Gracie. They can track you with your cell phone. I don't care if you were talking to Annie or the Queen of England. From now on, you don't do a thing without my approval. Got it?"

Grace's shocked eyes just stared back at Ben.

"Here. I got you something to drink. This should last you for a while." Ben handed her two bottles of water. "Now sit back there and be quiet. We have a long ride ahead of us and I need you to do what I say. Okay?"

"Okay," Grace whispered. *So this is what it feels like to be kidnapped*, she thought as she uncomfortably settled down into the back seat of the Mercedes.

• • •

The foyer in the Reich mansion was darker than most. Dark wooden flooring. Dark Turkish Orientals. Wallpaper of deep burgundy leather. Even the lights from the massive chandelier hanging over his head were dimmed to the point of being useless. So Doc thought it only fitting that his last few minutes on this earth would be spent in such a dark, empty-feeling room. Even the ornately carved cherry deacon bench on which he was sitting was pillow-less hard, uncomfortable. But the elderly man assumed Mr. Reich liked his guests to feel that way.

Uncomfortable. So they would not stay long.

Not that he was a guest tonight. Having worked for Mr. Reich's father when he was a member of the Council and thereafter when the older man defected, Doc knew the Reich family well. He only hoped his years of service had earned him a quick death.

Death.

The thought of it made Doc shift slightly on the bench, and his fingers pinched the top of his nose between his eyes to ease his now ever-present headache. He had no power to stop the inevitable. In fact, he had no powers at all. He was just a simple pharmacist who had fallen in with the wrong crowd, as his mother would have said.

The heavy, double doors to the study opened.

"Father is ready for you," Andrew said.

Doc nodded and slowly stood up. His legs felt like lead poles as he shuffled over the thick Oriental toward the study. He stopped in the open doorway, unable to go any further.

"Now, Doc," Andrew prodded him. "Don't make this any harder than it has to be."

Doc looked up at Andrew knowingly and shuffled his lead poles into the room. Seated behind the large antique desk was Mr. Reich with Gregory standing to his left. Mrs. Reich and her sunglasses lounged on a chaise nearby, nonchalantly flipping the pages of a magazine, stopping every now and then to study a fashion ad as if it were any other evening.

"Doc," Mr. Reich began. "You know how it pains me to do this, don't you?"

"Yes, Master," Doc replied without looking up.

"Obviously I hold you responsible for the girl's allergic reaction to your drink, but you have served the Anti-Powers well so I'll make this quick."

"Thank you, Mast-," Doc sighed but before the words could complete their journey from his lips, Mrs. Reich was at his side, her presence placing an unnerving calm over Doc. He relaxed and before he could utter his final words that he had rehearsed so well, Mrs. Reich's glasses were off. The last thing Doc would see on this earth were the beautiful red eyes of Mrs. Reich glaring down on him just before the laser beams escaped her pupils and tore through the middle of his forehead. He collapsed limply on the floor. Instant death. Exactly what he had hoped for.

Mrs. Reich replaced her sunglasses and purred, "Darling, will there be anything else?"

Mr. Reich rose from his desk and crossed over to his wife. "No dear. Thank you." He bent slightly and kissed her cheek.

Mrs. Reich smiled up at him, then turned and silently glided from the room, stepping over Doc without hesitation as she exited.

Mr. Reich turned to Gregory. "You could learn a lot from your stepmother, son. She truly has mastered emotion manipulation. Did you see how calm Doc was? He never even thought of fighting his fate."

"Yes, Father," Gregory stated hesitantly. He warily eyed his father, knowing he and Andrew were next on Mr. Reich's evening agenda. They were prepared for their punishment.

"Boys," Mr. Reich began slowly. "Now, let's review. What do we know?"

Andrew responded from a corner of the study, "We know Grace entered the bathroom at the Café alone. By the time Gregory was able to melt the door's lock and we entered the bathroom, she was gone. We think she escaped through the bathroom window."

"And?" Mr. Reich raised his eyebrows.

"And that's all, Father," Gregory said. "There was no trace of her. None of the troops saw her leave the building. It was like she just vanished into thin air."

"The Council must be involved somehow," Mr. Reich said almost to himself. He then looked hard at his sons. "Find her!" he bellowed.

With Mr. Reich's commanding roar, the library's books flew off their shelves. All the furniture in the room slammed back against the far walls and the smell of burnt metal permeated the room's tension.

Mr. Reich looked around the room, glared at his sons, and stormed out, casually stepping over Doc and leaving the brothers to clean up his mess.

Chapter Eleven: Discovery

The black sedan had been following them for about thirty miles now. It was keeping a safe distance and Ben was certain Grace was still oblivious to its presence. Ben was splitting his concentration between the black sedan behind them and the road in front of them and was grateful for Grace's temporary silence. A silence that filled the Mercedes until they hit the Virginia state line.

"You know crossing state lines makes kidnapping a federal offense, don't you?" Grace leaned up from the back seat and rested her arms on the back of Ben's seat. "So technically you've been a federal fugitive since we left South Carolina."

Her breath brushed the back of his neck, immediately breaking Ben's concentration.

"Enough, Gracie," Ben sighed. "I didn't kidnap you. I rescued you. There's a difference."

"Right." Grace rolled her eyes and leaned back, crossing her arms. "I forgot. You rescued me from the…what were they? The Anti-Powers? And just how did you do that again?"

"Stop being a smart-ass. Just sit back and shut up." Despite the sweet feeling of her breath on his neck, Ben was getting tired of Grace's mouth. He glanced in the rearview mirror. The black sedan was still there.

"No, really. How did you get me out of that bathroom?"

"I carried you," said Ben. He smiled a little at the memory of Grace in his arms.

"You carried me?"

"Yes, Gracie. I picked you up and carried you out the bathroom window and down to the car. I was moving so fast no one saw us."

"Why don't I remember that?"

"Because you were passed out. They must have drugged you or something. All I know is that when I came through the bathroom window you were right in the middle of passing out. I caught you and carried you to the car and took off."

"Why did you do that?" asked Grace.

"Why did I do what?"

"Why did you come through the bathroom window?"

"Grace, I'm your Guardian. It's my job to know exactly what you're doing at all times. I was watching you. I saw you in trouble and stepped in. It's what I do."

"As my…what did you call it? Guardian?"

"Yes."

"If you say so." Grace's hand was on the door handle again.

Ben heard the doubt in Grace's voice but didn't feel like dealing with it anymore.

"Where are we going now?" she asked.

Ben glanced at the black sedan that still maintained an unusually consistent distance behind them. "To the safest place I know. To the mountains."

Grace looked out her side window at the steep wooded mountains flashing by. They were still on the two-lane road without any sign of civilization in sight. "Aren't we already in the mountains?" she asked.

"We're almost there. We just need to get a little deeper into Appalachia. There's a…place…a special place there. People who can help us."

"Look, Ben." Grace took a deep breath. "Enough of this game. You've had your fun. Can't we just go home now?"

"No, Grace. I told you. We need to get you away from the Anti-Powers."

"Oh, yeah. Right. The Anti-Powers. Does Tom know what you're doing?"

"No. We're on our own on this one. If Tom knew, the Council would punish him too." Ben had thought about calling Tom so his older brother wouldn't worry but decided against it. The less Tom knew, the better for Tom. As it was right now, Ben was the only one who had broken any Council laws.

"I bet if we went home, Tom could help us." Grace interrupted Ben's thoughts.

"No, Grace. Tom can't help us. If we go home, the Council will just take you away and punish me for telling you all that I have. There are so many code violations against me, I can't go back right now. I need to make sure you're safe before I go deal with the Council."

"So who are these people in Appalachia?" Grace sounded genuinely interested.

"They're my friends. Some of the Powers call them Misfits but I never liked that name. They aren't human but they aren't full Powers either. They're somewhere in between. They have powers per se but their powers aren't as...developed...or useful as those of us with true Powers." Ben's mood was lightened only slightly by Grace's feigned interest.

"So how can they help you...us?"

"My father's best friend, Dave, is a Misfit. He'll know what to do." In the rearview mirror, Ben saw the black sedan shorten the distance between the two cars.

"So to sum it up, you kidnapped me from my birthday party to take me to the Appalachian Mountains to meet Misfit Dave and save me from the Anti-Powers?" Grace smirked.

"Yeah," Ben paused. "But it sounds kind of stupid when you say it like that."

"Exactly."

"You think I've lost my mind, don't you?"

"Yes," stated Grace matter-of-factly. "Or lying. I haven't decided which yet."

"Look Grace. I don't care if you believe me or not now. I just need to keep you safe."

"Because you are my Guardian?"

"Yes."

Grace glanced out the window then said, "Well, as my Guardian, I am ordering you to take me home."

"It doesn't work that way, sweetie."

"It was worth a shot," Grace said as she rolled her eyes. Just then, a restaurant appeared on the horizon, just at the crest of the road's next hill. "Look, can we at least stop and get something to eat?" Grace began putting her shoes back on.

Ben glanced at the car behind them. "Uh…yeah. Sure. I could use something too." He pulled into the parking lot of Bess's Diner but the black sedan didn't follow them. It sped on down the two-lane highway out of sight.

"Okay. I think we're good," Ben said almost to himself as he got out of the car. He turned to Grace who had already exited the car behind him. "Stay close to me."

"Of course," Grace smarted and walked quickly past Ben and into the restaurant, her red satin dress swishing as she stomped off. She let the restaurant's front door slam behind her, purposefully and directly in Ben's face, and then glared back at him with a fake smile, "Do you mind, oh great Guardian, if I use the restroom?"

"Okay, but let me check it out first." Ben was now ignoring Grace's sudden but constant mood swings.

Ben followed Grace into the ladies restroom and received a distasteful look from an elderly woman washing her hands at the sink. He smiled at her and began opening the door to each stall. The woman hurriedly left and, satisfied they were now alone, Ben said, "Okay. You're good to go. Hurry it up. I'll be right outside the door."

Grace rolled her eyes and locked herself in a stall.

Ben stood outside the ladies restroom like a sentry. Any woman who tried to enter was told it was out of order or closed for cleaning. From his impromptu guard post, Ben could see the front door and parking lot. He had only been standing there a few minutes before the black sedan came back down the road and entered the parking lot. The car parked three spaces down from Ben's Mercedes and two very large men with aviator sunglasses exited and headed into the restaurant.

"Oh, for Pete's sake," Ben said to himself. "How cliché can they be?"

The two large men looked like identical twins trying too hard, both dressed in black slacks, tight black knit mock-turtlenecks, and black tweed sport coats. Their hair was cut military short and they wore the obvious Secret Service grade sunglasses. They glanced at Ben when they entered and sat at a nearby booth directly between Ben and the front door. Ben's instincts immediately went into overdrive.

At that very moment, Grace exited the bathroom. "See. No boogie men or Anti-Powers or whatever you call them in the bathroom. I had a successful and safe pee break. Now can we get something to eat?"

"Change of plans." Ben grabbed Grace's arm, ignoring her sarcasm. He quickly pulled her out the front door, trying to keep a safe distance between Grace and the twins.

"But I'm hungry." Grace tried to twist her arm free but Ben's grasp was too strong.

"Just get in the car, Gracie." Ben yanked her toward the Mercedes.

The twins were already up and out the door following them. With lightning speed, one twin grabbed Grace from behind and forcefully pulled her out of Ben's grasp. Ben spun around just as the other twin threw down his sunglasses. The second twin's red eyes aimed directly and purposefully at Ben's head. Ben ducked to the side of the black sedan just as the twin's lasers missed him by inches, burning two holes in the sedan's front side panel. Ben tried to make his way to Grace who was now on the opposite side of the sedan being shoved toward the back of the car by the other twin, but he was too busy dodging lasers. The red-eyed twin was bearing down on Ben and had him pinned next to the sedan's front passenger door. Ben's mind was as quick as his speed and just as the twin aimed for another shot, Ben tore off the sedan's side mirror and used it to deflect the laser's rays away from his face. The rays bounced off the mirror and hit the attacking twin squarely in the head, leaving two large holes in his forehead. The twin dropped dead instantly onto the parking lot pavement.

"Ben!" Grace screamed from the other side of the sedan. She was fighting the other twin, kicking and punching him with no effect at all.

Without thinking, Ben picked up the sedan and held it over his head. "Drop, Gracie!" he yelled.

Miraculously remembering a dodge ball strategy they had used in elementary school, Grace fell to the ground at the twin's feet. The twin still had a tight hold on Grace's arm but that fact was of little significance to Ben now. With precision aim, Ben hurled the sedan at the twin as if it only weighed two pounds. The car flew through the air like a Frisbee and slammed into the twin's torso, smashing him into a nearby concrete retaining wall. The wall crumbled upon the sedan's impact and buried the twin in a mixture of steel and concrete rubble.

"Aahh! Aahh! Get it off! Get it off!" Grace screamed.

Ben turned his focus back to Grace who had crumpled down in the middle of the sedan's previous parking space. Her eyes were as wild and crazy as her screams as she held her left arm up toward Ben. The twin's hand still held Grace's arm in a tight grip with the rest of his severed arm dangling down at her side, dark blood pouring out all over the red satin folds of her dress. The sedan's slamming force had ripped the twin's arm clean off.

"Ben! Ben! Help me! Help me!" she frantically cried.

Ben ran to her side, pulled the arm off and threw it on top of the concrete rubble at the side of the parking lot. "Shhh. It's okay, Gracie," Ben soothed. "Everything's going to be okay. They're gone now."

Grace looked up into Ben's eyes but it was obvious she couldn't focus. Her wide eyes darted quickly back and forth from Ben to the bloody arm on top of the concrete rubble.

"Come on. We really need to get out of here. We don't want to be around when the cops get here." Seeing diners beginning to congregate at the restaurant windows, Ben quickly picked up Grace and carried her to the Mercedes, buckling her into the front seat beside him.

Grace stared at the pile of concrete rubble as they drove out of the parking lot. "Do you think he's dead?" she whispered.

Ben glanced back at the crushed sedan peeking out of the mound of concrete. "I don't know. They were obviously Anti-Powers. I'm pretty sure Mr. Laserhead is dead but I don't know about the other one. Depends on what kind of powers he had… or has." Ben looked over at Grace seated beside him. "Do you believe me now?"

Grace did not answer. She could not answer. Tears streamed down her face and she started shaking uncontrollably.

Ben reached over and gently caressed her hand. This is what he had wanted to avoid. Her shock. Her pain. He didn't want her to find out like this. Grace's reality had been permanently altered at Bess's Diner that day and Ben knew it was going to take a while for her to get used to his version of the world.

Chapter Twelve: New Reality

For the second time in two days, Tom stood before the Council.

"Are you aware there was an altercation between your brother and the Anti-Powers?" the Council leader asked.

Tom's eyes widened. "No, Madam." He stood very still. He had not heard from Ben in two days and had assumed the worst. The Council's question just confirmed Tom's assumption.

"Well, apparently your brother and Grace had a little incident near the Virginia state line at a little diner called…What was the name of it?" the Council leader asked her Lieutenant.

"Bess's Diner," the Lieutenant replied.

"Yes, that's it. Bess's Diner. Have you ever heard of it?" she asked Tom.

"No, Madam." Tom looked directly at the Council leader. "Grace was with him? Is he okay? Are they…are they okay?" Tom asked without regard to the meeting's protocol.

"Yes, Tom. From what we hear, they escaped unharmed," the Council leader replied. She then smiled. "And I understand Ben destroyed two Anti-Powers in the process."

Tom sighed with relief. "Thank you, Madam. Ben may be younger than most Guardians but he should never be underestimated."

"That we know," another Council member stated. "But what we don't know is why Ben has Grace, and what in the world are they doing in Virginia?" The Council member was obviously directing the question to Tom.

"I do not know, sir. I have not heard from Ben since before the party and I haven't been able to reach him on his cell phone. I had assumed he had gone after whoever took Grace." Tom paused. "I just never imagined he was the one who actually took her." Tom felt like he was on a witness stand.

"Well, regardless of why he has her, we need to find them," the Council leader stated. "Let us know the minute he contacts you."

"Yes, Madam," replied Tom with a bow before he exited the Council chamber.

•••

Grace had not spoken for miles and Ben knew she was still processing today's events. She sat beside him with knees curled up in the front seat, staring out the window. Her shoes were off but she still wore the torn red satin dress from last night. It was getting dark and they had more than a few hours to go before they reached their Appalachian destination. The two-lane highway was winding through the umpteenth backwoods town they had encountered today when Grace finally spoke.

"Do you think we could stop somewhere for the night? I'm really tired of being in this car." She looked down at the now-blood-stained satin. "And of being in this dress."

Hearing a slight resemblance to the Grace of a few days ago, Ben smiled. "Sure. Help me look for someplace to stop."

They drove a little farther and came upon a secondhand store. Ben pulled up to the front door and looked inside. He saw no one other than the sales clerk who was heading toward the door with his keys in hand ready to lock up for the night.

"Stay here and lock the doors behind me," Ben said as he exited the car.

"Wait. Don't leave me in here alone."

"Grace, you'll be fine. I'm going to run right in and right back out. My eyes will be on you the entire time." Without waiting for her response, Ben darted into the store and ran past the clerk, his speed preventing the clerk from seeing him enter. He raced through the store, grabbing clothes, a pair of tennis shoes, and a few other things, and was back at the checkout counter before the clerk had time to even place the keys in the door lock.

"Ahem," Ben cleared his throat.

The sales clerk turned around. "Oh, I'm sorry. I didn't think there was anyone else here. I was just getting ready to close up." He walked behind the counter and rang up Ben's items. Seeing the articles of women's clothing on the counter, he gave Ben a funny look.

"Costume party," Ben said.

"Oh," chuckled the sales clerk. "I really didn't think you looked the type."

Ben smiled but said nothing more as he paid the sales clerk in cash and picked up his bag. He was back in the car and pulling away before the clerk could lock the door behind him.

"Here you go." Ben handed Grace the bag. "I had to guess your size so I hope they fit."

"You're fast," said Grace without looking in the bag. "Is…is that your power?"

"One of them."

"What if that sales clerk had been an Anti-Power?" Grace was still processing what had almost happened to her this afternoon.

"He wasn't."

"How do you know?"

"He had blue eyes. Anti-Powers never have blue eyes. Their eyes are always green."

"But how did you know that until you got in the store?" Grace wasn't understanding.

"Because I saw them from the car. I checked him out before I went in."

"You could see that far?" Grace asked. Then, comprehending what Ben was saying, she answered herself with, "Oh. Another power—"

"Gracie, I promise I will never leave you alone unless I know you're safe."

Grace looked at Ben. "He could have been wearing blue contacts, you know."

"Trust me. He wasn't." Ben drove the car back onto the same two-lane highway that was now heading toward the outskirts of the small town. Ben searched the road, hoping to find a no-name motel away from the town's epicenter. "Now let's get you some place to rest that pretty head." He smiled at Grace but she didn't smile back. She looked at him like he was a stranger.

"Gracie, I'm not some circus freak. I'm still Ben, your best friend, remember?"

Grace just nodded and turned her gaze back out her side window.

They passed the Stardust Motel a few miles outside of town. The one story motel only had ten or so rooms and sat on a large river that ran parallel to the highway. The neon sign in front flashed on and off and Ben could see from the fine dust particles covering it that the "No" in front of the word "Vacancy" was seldom operational, if ever. There were only two cars in the parking lot and Ben assumed one belonged to the night desk clerk.

"Does this look good to you?" he asked.

"Sure." Grace's voice was monotone.

Ben drove past the motel.

"Wait, where are you going?" asked Grace. "I thought we were stopping."

"We are. I just need to get rid of this car first."

"What?"

"Gracie, the Anti-Powers obviously know this car now. We need to ditch it. Don't worry. I've got an idea." Ben drove about ten miles past the motel and pulled over beside the river. He looked around. No other cars were in sight and night covered the road in darkness. "Okay. This looks good. Get your bag of stuff and go stand behind that tree over there."

Obviously no longer questioning Ben's commands, Grace silently did as she was told.

"Stand *behind* the tree, Gracie. Your dress stands out like a sore thumb in this moonlight," Ben directed. On any other night, he might have appreciated the romance of the old oak stretching along the riverbank in the moonlight. Tonight, however, the large tree was just a hiding place.

Grace moved behind the tree, shuffling gingerly over the rocky ground beneath her bare feet.

Ben stood behind the car and winked at Grace. With one hand and a movement that barely amounted to a shove, he easily pushed the large Mercedes sedan toward the wide river.

"Wait!" Grace yelled just as the car coasted down the riverbank and completely disappeared under the water.

"What?"

"Oh, never mind," sighed Grace. "My purse and Annie's shoes were still in the car."

"You don't need your purse anymore and we'll buy Annie some new shoes," said Ben, grabbing Grace's hand and heading toward the motel.

"Ouch," said Grace. "Slow down. I'm barefooted, remember?"

"No problem." Ben scooped up Grace and cradled her close to his chest. She felt soft and warm. The same way she felt when that truck almost hit her. In that moment, Ben realized that the only time he was able to hold Grace was when someone was trying to kill her. Not exactly a romantic way to get close to her. But as Grace's Guardian, romance wasn't in Ben's job description. That part of Grace's life belonged to her Chosen One. That part of Grace belonged to Tom. Ben needed to stop thinking. "Hey, you." He gave Grace a little squeeze. "Want to experience some speed?"

Before Grace could respond, Ben was sprinting to the motel. His speed helped him forget about Tom. At least for a minute or two. Unfortunately for Ben, the ten-mile trip was far too short. Grace didn't even have time to lay her head on Ben's shoulder before they were standing at the motel's double glass doors at the entrance of the small lobby. A stereotypical bell jingled when Ben pushed open the door and the night desk clerk emerged from the back room. Looking to be in her early sixties with bleached blonde hair and a lit cigarette dangling from the corner of her mouth, she narrowed her heavily made-up eyes and gave Grace a once over from behind her counter.

"We don't rent by the hour," she brusquely said to Ben.

Glancing over at Grace's red dress and disheveled appearance, Ben quickly said, "Oh, no. No, it's not like that. We've been driving for a while and need to break up our trip a little. We just need a room for the night."

"One room or two?" The clerk still eyed Grace who was unsuccessfully trying to hide her bare feet beneath the hem of her long red dress.

Without looking at Grace, Ben replied, "One."

"That will be fifty-five dollars. Check out is at ten in the morning. Towels and soap are already in your room. Room seven outside and to your right." The clerk shoved a key and some paperwork across the counter to Ben. "Here. Sign there, initial there and fill in the make and model of your car right here." Her thick red lipstick was more adhesive than flattering and the dangling cigarette never left her lips while she gave Ben his instructions.

"We don't have a car anymore," chuckled Ben as he grabbed the key and pushed Grace back out the front door without waiting to hear the clerk's response. He picked her up again and carried her over the gravel parking lot to a faded blue door denoted with a number seven crookedly hanging by one nail.

"Home sweet home," he said as he carried Grace over the threshold. The motel room smelled musty like a locked-up basement that had flooded years ago and it was filled with relics dating from the seventies. The television didn't even have a remote control and its channel dial looked like something found in the Smithsonian. The pattern of the brown and gold bedding on the full-size bed somewhat disguised its old stains, but even those didn't faze Grace as her eyes went straight to the pillow and mattress with her name on them.

"Let me go. This isn't a honeymoon," she said.

Ben gently put Grace down, double-bolted the door behind him, and started rummaging through the thrift store bag. "Here are some shoes, jeans, and a shirt to sleep in. I did the best I could with the time I had."

"I'm sure it's fine. I just want to sleep." Grace took the bag into the bathroom and closed the door. Seconds later she emerged in an oversized tee shirt that hung to her knees. She crawled into the creaky bed. "Where are you sleeping?" she asked as her head sank deeper into the feather-filled pillow.

Ben smiled. "Don't worry. Your virtue is safe with me. I can hunker down in that chair by the door." Ben glanced at the stained, gold polyester-covered club chair that didn't really look like the hunkering down type.

"Still on guard duty?" she sighed.

"I never stop." Ben closed the curtains on the room's only window. "Do you want something to eat? You have to be starving."

"No." Her voice was soft. "I'm not hungry anymore…not after today…" Her eyes fluttered.

"Then just get some rest now." He bent over Grace and pulled the covers up to her chin. "Everything will be okay, Gracie. I promise." He brushed her hair away from her face, allowing his hand to linger gently on her head.

Grace closed her eyes and, in a matter of seconds, peace finally fell over her face. Ben smiled down at her, grateful to be alone with her even if under these circumstances. He peeked out the closed curtains and quickly surveyed the motel parking lot. Satisfied they were secure for the time being, Ben turned out the light and tried to get comfortable in the chair. He didn't intend to sleep and didn't realize how tired he was until he subsequently woke up at the sound of Grace's stirring a few hours later.

"Gracie?" Ben twisted out of his contorted sleep position caused by the polyester chair. The clock radio on the bedside table glowed and its florescent digits indicated it was two o'clock in the morning.

"Yeah. I'm sorry if I woke you."

Ben sought out Grace's face in the room's darkness. "No. It's okay. What's wrong?"

"I can't get back to sleep." Her voice was soft and childlike.

"Well, can I get you anything?" Ben leaned out of his chair, his tired eyes still trying to focus on Grace's face in the dark.

"Can you…can you make things like they were before?"

"Before?" Ben paused. "Things haven't really changed, Grace."

"Just for me," she sighed.

They sat in silence for a while staring into the musty darkness.

"Ben," Grace whispered. "Why are they after me? I don't have any powers."

Ben's voice almost cracked. She still didn't realize her importance. "Gracie, you have the greatest power of all." He paused. "You have the power of life."

"Life? What do you mean?"

"Your family's DNA, your DNA, is the central component needed for a Power to exist. Every Power has one parent who is a Power and another parent who comes from the Family. Your family."

"I don't understand."

Ben took a deep breath. "If a Power and another Power have a child, that child is born human. If a Power and an ordinary human have a child, that child is human. But if a Power and someone in your family have a child, that child will most definitely be born a Power. The Council discovered this genetic link a very, very long time ago and have been playing matchmaker between the Family and the Powers ever since. Without your family, *the* Family, the Powers would eventually become extinct."

"But why are the Anti-Powers after me?"

Ben had been dreading this question and wished Tom or someone else could be there to answer it. But there was no avoiding it now. Time to face the music. He took a deep breath. "Because, Gracie, six months ago you became the last surviving member of your entire family line. You are the last member of the Family."

Grace whimpered in the darkness, "Why? How?"

"We don't know why but the Anti-Powers murdered the only other known member of your family. He was some distant cousin or something like that from Italy. Anyway, now that you're twenty-two, your DNA is what we call ripe. If they capture you, they can use you to fill the world with Anti-Powers and enslave the human race. You are it, Gracie. You are the beginning and the end of the Powers…and the humans."

Grace was silent. The hum of the clock radio beside the bed provided the soundtrack to her thoughts.

"Gracie, are you okay?" Ben's voice took over the clock radio's hum.

Grace's pain crawled through the darkness. "Can…can you hold me?"

"Uh…sure." Ben freed himself from the binding chair and used his night vision to make his way through the dark room to the other side of the bed. He stretched out on top of the bedcovers beside Grace, trying not to get too close, but not wanting to be too far away. He reached behind her shoulders and her head naturally fell into the crook of his arm. She turned toward him and curled up into a tight ball right next to him, burying her face into his chest. The sudden dampness on Ben's shirt prompted him to wrap his arm tighter around Grace's shaking shoulders.

"Ben," Grace cried. "Gregory has green eyes."

"I know." Ben stared at the ceiling, his heart aching with Grace's tears. "I know."

Chapter Thirteen: Eyes

When Grace woke the next morning, for a fleeting few seconds she felt normal. Back to the way she was. The stereotypical struggling waitress. But then she remembered. Gregory. Her birthday party. The black sedan. The twins. The bloody arm. Being the last living person of her entire family line. She looked up to see Ben staring down at her, his arm still cradling her.

"Hey," he said with a hesitant smile.

"Hey." She slowly sat up. "Did you sleep?"

"Not too much. I'm not really a big sleeper." Ben stood up and gently tossed the bag of clothes from the thrift store to Grace. "Here, Sleeping Beauty. Get dressed. We need to get some food in you before we hit the road again."

Grace carried the bag into the bathroom and closed the door. Crumpled in the corner, behind the bathroom door, lay her red satin dress. The red satin dress that had made her feel pretty. The red satin dress she wore with Gregory. The red satin dress stained with the Anti-Power's blood. For a few minutes she just stood there staring at the dress, her mind reliving the new reality that had invaded her safe normal world. Last night she couldn't wait to get away from that dress. This morning she couldn't take her eyes off it. When she felt the tears welling up again, she closed her eyes tightly and took a deep breath.

Shake it off, Grace. Get it together.

She turned her back to the dress and faced the mirror. For the first time in two days, Grace looked at herself. Really looked at herself. Her smudged mascara and bedhead hair were going to have to go. After taking a long, hot shower and putting on her new–but–used thrift store jeans, fitted tee shirt, and tennis shoes, she threw her long, brown hair back in a ponytail using a rubber band she found in the trash. Of course her flyaway strands fell around her face like they always did and she instinctively started to pull them back again.

But then it hit her.

She was not at the club. Julian was not going to assess her hair today or tomorrow or even the next day. Her flyaway hair, her job, her hopes for college, none of that mattered anymore and Grace briefly wondered if anything from her past life would ever matter again. It was as if the only thing she had left was Ben.

She purposefully pulled the misbehaving strands of hair out of her ponytail and allowed them to wildly fly all over her face. She took one last look at the red satin dress crumpled on the floor before she exited the bathroom.

"Feel better?" Ben asked when Grace emerged from the bathroom.

"A little," she said softly.

"Hop on." Ben bent over and pointed to his back. "I saw an all-night diner across the street from the thrift store last night and everybody knows all-night diners have the best breakfasts. So let's go."

"What do you mean hop on?"

"Grace, we have no car, remember? I'm now your only transportation to breakfast. I've already checked out of this swanky joint so come on. I'm starving."

Grace's brow knitted together but she did as she was told. She hopped onto Ben's back and before she knew it, they were out the door speeding toward the middle of town. She held on tightly to Ben, wrapping her arms around his neck and chest and her legs around his waist. He ran so nimbly, her ride was as smooth as floating on a sailboat. They glided through the air, unseen by all they passed on the road. Grace liked being invisible and was glad that speed was one of Ben's powers.

They arrived at the diner with a swoosh of air at the front door. Ben entered first and paused in the doorway. Grace had never seen him in Guardian mode, or if she had, she had not known it at the time. His face was serious as he quickly scanned the restaurant before allowing Grace to enter. He then chose a booth in the left back corner and sat against the wall, eyes glued to the front door. "How's this?" he asked.

"Fine." Grace finally smiled.

Ben smiled back. "You look better this morning."

"Thanks." She was somewhat energized by the ride and the cool morning air made her cheeks feel flushed as if she had just had a facial.

A young waitress popping a large piece of bubble gum dropped off two waters and their menus and Grace noted she had blue eyes. "Our waitress is not an Anti-Power," she whispered confidently to Ben after the young woman had walked away.

"How do you know she's not wearing contacts?" Ben smarted, repeating back Grace's comment from the day before.

Grace shook her head and sighed, "For Pete's sake, Ben. Why don't you just tell me exactly how this all works?"

Ben hesitated, and then said, "First, you're right, she isn't an Anti-Power. She has blue eyes and isn't wearing contacts."

"See. Told you. But how can you tell who's who?"

Before Ben could answer, the waitress reappeared to take their order. "I'll take the Hearty Farmer's Breakfast with scrambled eggs and a large Coke," said Ben.

"The same but with a Diet Coke," said Grace handing her menu to the waitress.

The young waitress smiled at Grace and blew a huge bubble with her gum. "You sure you can eat all that, honey?"

"I'll try."

"Suit yourself." The waitress shook her head and headed back to the kitchen with their order.

"Okay, go on. Explain," said Grace.

"Well, like I said last night, when a Power and someone in your family, *the* Family, have a child, that child is born with certain superhuman powers. Most of the time, we don't know the extent of the child's powers until they complete training, but at a minimum, we know they're a Power. All Powers are born with blue eyes. The Council says it shows the natural innocence and goodness inside Powers' children. Anyway, once they reach around four or five years old, they're sent away to training camp to develop their powers."

"Wait," interrupted Grace. "They leave their parents at four or five years old? How cruel is that?" Having lost her parents when she was four, Grace spoke from experience.

"Well, it's more of a necessity," replied Ben. "You see, the human parent, the parent from your family, doesn't know anything about the Powers or Anti-Powers or anything like that. They think they've married a normal human and have normal human kids. When the child starts exhibiting powers around age four or five, the Powers parent sends the child to training camp. Unfortunately the human parent has to think the child has disappeared, been abducted, or something like that."

"Ben! That's terrible!"

"I know and I'm sorry. But it's done to protect the child and their human parent. If the child started using their powers without the proper training, the Anti-Powers might find them and try to convert the child, or even worse, kill the child and the parents."

"I'm not sure I want to know anymore. This sounds like a horrible way to live."

"No, Gracie. It's really not. Even though they aren't with their parents, the child is really loved at training camp. There are some really special Powers working there."

"But what about the human parent? The parent from my side of the family?"

"Well, I assume they never really get over it. I mean losing a child is a pretty big deal. But the Council has chosen their Powers mate very carefully so they end up living a pretty good life with someone who eventually grows to love them very much."

"Eventually grows to love them?" Grace was incredulous. "What about true love and all that? What about fate and happiness? Does any of that matter for my family?"

Ben shrugged his shoulders. "It's not a perfect system, Grace. But it's the best we have in place right now. And most of your family has...*had* normal lives. The Council was very selective when picking which members of the Family would be with the Powers. Not all your relatives made the cut."

"Do the parents ever get to see their child again?"

"Yeah. The Powers parent can see their child anytime they want. They can visit training camp, see them when they graduate from camp, there are all kinds of ways to stay in contact with each other. It's part of their training. Tom and I were lucky. We actually got to live with our parents since Dad had essentially the same assignment we did."

"Me? Was I his assignment?"

"Yes, you. Dad was your Guardian until I was old enough to take over," Ben paused, wistful. "Anyway, the human parent normally only sees the child one more time. Right before that parent dies. The Council allows the child, who is usually grown by that time, to visit the human parent on his or her deathbed and the child explains everything. It kind of gives the human parent some peace before going on to the next world."

Grace just sat there, speechless.

The waitress, still popping her bubble gum, brought their breakfasts and drinks. "Need anything else right now?"

Grace looked down at her plate but couldn't really see her food.

Ben glanced at Grace and then at the waitress. "No, we're good. Thanks."

The waitress eyed Grace and then walked off. Grace just continued to stare at her plate but her eyes were still not able to focus.

"Grace," Ben leaned over and pushed her plate closer to her. "Come on. Eat up."

Grace took a small bite of eggs but pushed more food around on her plate than into her mouth.

"Grace, you haven't eaten in two days," Ben prodded. "Eat."

Grace looked up at Ben and put her fork down. "Tell me more," she softly said. "I…I need to know more."

"What do you want to know?" Ben shoved a forkful of scrambled eggs in his mouth.

Grace rubbed her temples and closed her eyes as she spoke. "If all the children are born Powers, how does a Power become an Anti-Power?" She opened her eyes and looked up at Ben. "None of this makes any sense."

"When a Power graduates from training camp, they're assigned to safeguard different parts of the world. They live normal lives among the humans but are always there to protect them, especially from the Anti-Powers. Unfortunately, there are times when a Power doesn't like their designated location or assigned duty. That's when the Anti-Powers come in and, in some instances, have successfully converted the Power."

"How?"

"We don't know. That's one of the problems we have. We haven't been able to really gather enough information on the Anti-Powers to know how they work exactly. We just know we've had some Powers defect to the Anti-Powers and when they did, their eyes changed from blue to green."

"All you know is that they have green eyes? Tons of people have green eyes. Are you trying to tell me they're all Anti-Powers?"

Grace turned around in their booth and started scanning the diner's patrons.

"Turn around here!" whispered Ben as he reached over and quickly pulled Grace back down into their booth. "Of course they're not all Anti-Powers. And no, that's not all we know. But the Anti-Powers are a slippery bunch. They've stayed hidden pretty well so they've been difficult to study. Most of what we know came from the Council members who knew the original Anti-Power, that rogue Council member I told you about who wanted to use his powers out in the open." Ben paused and leaned toward Grace. "But the Council and other Powers have stayed hidden just as well. The Anti-Powers now don't know any more about us than we do about them," he whispered.

"So it's possible that Gregory isn't an Anti-Power? I mean just because he has green eyes doesn't mean…" Grace trailed off, hopeful.

"Gracie. Based on what we've seen, I think we would be stupid to assume he isn't an Anti-Power," Ben stated abruptly.

Grace started picking at the food on her plate again, her eyes pretending to concentrate on her eggs while her heart questioned the absolute certainty of Ben's last statement.

"Is anyone else I know a Power? Is Tom?"

"Tom is a Power. But his powers are mental, more intellectually oriented."

"If you are my Guardian, who does Tom guard?"

"Tom is not a Guardian. He…has another job."

"What?"

"Look, we can get into that later. Now, eat up. We need to get going." Ben took his last bite of eggs and motioned to the waitress to bring their check.

Grace ate a few more bites but her mind was processing too much to concentrate on food. "Are there any Powers near here? Why do we have to drive all the way to the Appalachian Mountains?"

"Grace, there are Powers and Anti-Powers everywhere but we're all in hiding so I don't know who's who. It's not like we have a club directory or anything like that! The Council makes our laws and we live by them and one of the laws is that we cannot reveal we're a Power to anyone without the Council's permission. That's just one of the many laws I've broken by being with you!" Ben finally snapped, obviously exasperated with Grace's questions.

"I'm sorry."

"For what?"

"For putting you in this situation."

Ben took a deep breath and sighed. "Grace, this isn't a situation. It's my job. It's my job to protect you and since every Anti-Power in the world is looking for you right now, I suggest we get going before we run into another one." Ben threw enough cash on the table to cover the check the waitress had not yet delivered and then stood up. "Come on."

Grace glanced at the cash on the table and quickly followed Ben outside. "Now what?" she said looking around at the town's narrow, empty streets.

"Now we need to find a car," Ben replied. "Follow me." He walked across the street toward the thrift store and glanced in the store window. The same clerk from the night before was working. Ben pulled Grace into a small, dark alley that ran along the side of the thrift store building and pointed. "There."

At the end of the narrow alley was an old yellow Jeep Wagoneer that had obviously seen better days. The faux wooden sides were faded and rust dotted the yellow metal like chicken pox scars. Only the tires appeared to be relatively new and the sole parts worth stealing.

"Ben? What are we doing?" asked Grace, her brow now permanently knitted.

"We're buying that Jeep from our friendly clerk." Ben pulled a large wad of cash from his jeans pocket.

"It doesn't look like it's for sale." Grace shook her head, eyeing the wad of cash in Ben's hand.

"It's not, but it will be. Now go hide behind the Jeep while I go inside."

Before Grace could protest, Ben was gone, leaving nothing but a breeze cooling Grace's face. He had disappeared. Grace looked around before squeezing behind the Jeep as Ben had ordered. Before she could even find a comfortable position in which to crouch, Ben had returned and was pushing her forward into the Jeep's front passenger seat.

"What did you do?" Grace asked, buckling her seatbelt with an extra tight tug.

"I bought the Jeep," Ben said nonchalantly as he slid into the driver's seat beside her. "Don't worry. The clerk didn't see me. I ran in there and left enough money on the counter to cover the Jeep and then some."

"How do you know this is his?"

"Because it was here last night parked in the exact same place. That and I saw the Jeep key on his key ring when he was locking up last night. See?" Ben smiled, dangling the key in Grace's face before inserting it into the ignition. "Perfect fit."

Grace's eyes widened. "Your powers…they're…they're…"

"I know, I know," Ben rolled his eyes teasingly. "At least that's what they tell me. My dad was just as powerful. That's why the Council picked us to be your Guardians."

Grace shook her head. "You…you know I have to ask," Grace stammered. "Where did you get all that money?"

"The Powers have been around a long time, Gracie. I told you. I have my resources," said Ben. "Now hang on."

Ben gunned the Jeep out of the alley and down the street back toward the town's outskirts. He drove in silence down the winding two-lane road until the town disappeared in his rearview mirror.

Grace didn't say much either as she processed their discussion from the diner. She still had so many questions but could tell Ben was tired of giving answers. She reached over and turned on the Jeep's radio. The eighties station was playing Peter Gabriel's "In Your Eyes" and the image of Gregory pulling her toward the dance floor at her birthday party flashed through Grace's memory. She immediately turned off the radio.

"Hey," Ben said. "I like that song. I thought it was your favorite."

"It was…it is," Grace said. "I'm just not in the mood for it right now." She looked out her window at the mountains rushing past them. They had past their motel a few miles back and were now officially outside all civilization. "How much longer?"

"Just a few more hours," Ben replied. "We'll be there before you know it."

"What's so special about this mountain place? About the Misfits?" The questions popped out of Grace's mouth before she could stop them. She braced for Ben's expected retort.

"It's a safe place," Ben answered, calmer than Grace expected. "I don't think anyone really knows the Misfits are there. I only know about them because of Dad's best friend, Dave."

"So your father was a Power. That means your mother was related to me?"

"Yes, but distantly. I think you would have to go back a few hundred years to find where my mother and your immediate family connected. Otherwise, they would not have picked Tom to be—" Ben abruptly stopped talking.

"Tom to be what?"

"Nothing. Forget about it," Ben said. He changed the subject quickly. "I think you'll really like Dave. He's a lot of fun."

"Will your father be there or are your parents still in Florida?"

Ben shifted uncomfortably in his seat and gripped the steering wheel tighter. "My father won't be there, Grace. And my parents are not in Florida."

"Where are they?" Grace asked but she was afraid she already knew the obvious answer to her question.

"Gracie, the Anti-Powers killed my parents about a year ago. Tom and I just told everyone they retired to Florida to avoid any weird questions." Ben stared at the road winding in front of them.

"Oh, Ben. I'm…I'm so sorry. So very sorry. I didn't know." Grace shook her head. Ben's parents had always been so kind to her, including her in their family get-togethers, taking her to the beach with them, making sure she was never alone. Then a realization hit her hard right in the middle of her chest. "Ben, were your parents killed because of me? Because of their connection to me?"

Ben didn't reply but his silence was confirmation enough. Overwhelmed, Grace threw her face down into her hands and began to cry. Not just tears, but huge all-out sobs that shook her entire body like an earthquake. She tried to stop but she could not. The tears just kept coming and coming and coming. She did not want to fall apart in front of Ben yet again, but the floodgates were open now and all that had happened the past two days pushed out through her eyes and flowed down her face.

"Gracie," Ben said softly as he placed his hand on her knee and gave it a squeeze. "It's okay. Really. It's okay. It's not your fault."

Grace's head popped up out of her hands, her eyes red with sadness and self-loathing disgust. "How can you say that, Ben? People are dying because of me!"

"No, Gracie, no." Ben shook his head. "You have it all wrong. Can't you understand how important you are? People aren't dying *because* of you. People are dying *for* you."

Chapter Fourteen: Cooper

The Pines was the most exclusive gated community in a hundred mile radius. Lush, green lawns flowed from mansion to mansion, tended with care by workers whose annual salaries barely equaled one month of the residents' monthly association dues. Perfectly poised pink azaleas and crepe myrtles colored the detailed landscapes and dotted the emerald lawns like gemstones. Even the tall southern pine trees that lined the entrance to the Southern Pines Country Club seemed more graceful than their relatives that lived outside The Pines' gates. This rainbow of shrubs, trees, and flowers did more than color the residents' world. This horticulture masterpiece also provided unique sound barriers between the mansions, preventing neighbors from listening in on each other and unmasking the private worlds housed in the individual brick homes. These natural sound barriers ensured the streets winding through The Pines community maintained the high-priced peacefulness that the residents had come to expect.

A peacefulness that was shattered by Mrs. Reich that afternoon.

"Jamison!" she screamed with a pitch that pierced the air and tore through the Reich mansion's walls, rippling out onto the landscape, bending the tall pines like a hurricane's wind. Mrs. Reich burst through the study's heavy wooden double doors without knocking, her eyes a deep crimson red. "Jamison! She killed my brothers!" she shrieked through gritted teeth. "I want that girl dead! I want her head on a platter! And I mean now!"

Seeing his wife without her sunglasses, Mr. Reich rushed from behind his desk to meet her before she burned the whole room down. "Shhh, my darling Ava. Calm down," he said, rubbing her shoulders as he avoided her eyes' glare. "I know, I know. We have it under control."

"Under control?" she fumed. "Under control? If you have it under control then why are my baby brothers dead? My poor precious baby brothers you sent out there. You said they could handle her! Well, apparently you were wrong!" She shoved her husband's hands off her shoulders and stepped back out of his reach. "If you don't take care of this, I'll go out there and kill her myself!"

"Darling." Mr. Reich tried his best to use a soothing voice. "Now you know we can't kill her until our scientists are finished with her. Let them get what they need from her to complete their genetic assessment and then, I promise you, you will have your revenge."

Mrs. Reich seethed, "Have you found her? Where is she?"

"We don't have her exact location but we know the vicinity. Gregory thinks she is traveling with some boy named Ben, possibly a Power. But trust me, every soldier we have is closing in on the area even as we speak. Our sheer numbers alone can handle this Ben person. I promise." Mr. Reich drew his wife into his arms and caressed her long blonde hair. "Shhh, darling. I promise you there is absolutely nothing to worry about."

Mrs. Reich looked up at him, her red eyes on the verge of exploding. "There better not be."

• • •

The woods were denser, the mountains steeper. Even the road seemed narrower.

"How much longer?" Grace asked looking out her side window. She had spent the last few hours avoiding her thoughts by counting the wildflowers on the side of the road. Driving deeper into the forest, she was now running out of flowers.

"Not much further." Ben glanced at the Jeep's gas gauge. "But we probably need to make one more quick stop for gas before we get there, so start looking for signs of civilization."

Grace squinted and looked deeper into the steep forest lining the road. "Civilization? Yeah, right," she chuckled to herself. "We'll be lucky if we find a place with running water in these mountains."

Ben smiled over at her. The sun, filtered by the trees, made its way through the Jeep's dirty passenger-side windows to form a dotted halo around Grace's entire body. Her ponytail glistened in the mottled sunlight and, without thinking, Ben reached over and gently removed the band holding Grace's hair back. Her long, brown hair fell softly around her shoulders just as she turned to meet Ben's gaze.

"So now you're my Guardian *and* my hair stylist?" She softly smiled.

Ben's eyes were tender and didn't shy away from Grace's gaze. "Sorry. I don't know why I just did that," he spoke with naked honesty and had to restrain himself from touching her again.

"That's okay." Grace looked back out her dirty side window. "It kind of feels better to have my hair down and loose anyway."

Ben placed his hand back on the steering wheel, resuming the ten o'clock and two o'clock positions required by a careful driver, and silently chastised himself. Spending all this time with Grace was making it harder and harder to control his feelings. He needed to concentrate on his job. He needed to focus his energy on being Grace's Guardian.

He needed to get out of that Jeep before he did something really stupid.

"There," Grace pointed out the front window a few minutes later. "Let's pull in there."

A few yards off the side of the winding, narrow road sat an old, dilapidated, one-pump gas station. It looked deserted but an old man sat right by the front door, rocking back and forth in a ladder-back rocker and looking in their direction. He was bald and had lost most of his teeth, but Ben could see his blue eyes were truly blue. Contacts were definitely out of the question in these backwoods.

"We can stop here," said Ben.

The sign above the gas pump said "Cooper's Gas and Groceries" and a neon "Open" sign flickered in the store window.

"At least they have electricity," Grace said, unbuckling her seatbelt. She was ready to escape the Jeep's dirt for a little while.

"Yeah. But do they have gas?" Ben pulled the Jeep off the road and parked it beside the lone gas pump. Before he could turn to ask Grace if she wanted anything from the store, the old man was standing at her window, knocking on the dirty glass with a toothless grin.

The old man's sudden appearance startled Grace. She screamed and jumped over the Jeep's console, contorting herself into Ben's arms.

"Gracie." Ben held her close. "It's okay. He's not one of them." He wrapped his arms tighter around her and gave her a little squeeze. "I promise. No green eyes." He smiled and released his hold on her. Being this close, her sweet smell filled his senses and his heart briefly stopped.

"Sorry. I guess I'm a little jumpy," was all Grace said as she climbed back into her seat.

Ben patted her hand and took a deep breath. His heart started beating again. "Understandable. Why don't we go stretch our legs a little and work off your jitters?" He released her hand and got out of the car.

By now the old man had moved to Ben's side of the Jeep. "Mista, I didn't mean to scare yer lady friend like 'at. I was just goin' to ask ye' if I could pump yer gas." The old man's grin was infectious.

"Oh, she's okay. No problem. Go ahead and fill it up," Ben replied, knowing this was probably going to be the highlight of the old man's day. "Do you have a pay phone I could use?"

"Sure thing," grinned the old man. Being helpful appeared to be his life's work. "Right 'nside th' door thar." The old man pointed to the store and then turned back around to pump Ben's gas.

Ben walked over to Grace's car door and opened it for her. "Come on out now, Gracie. He's harmless." Ben offered his hand for her to use in climbing down from the tall vehicle.

"Thanks," Grace smiled sheepishly, taking his hand for assistance but not letting go of it even after she exited the Jeep.

Ben glanced down at their entwined fingers and subtly, but unintentionally, smiled.

Hand in hand, they silently walked across the small gravel parking lot and into the store. Large windows spanned the entire storefront so, once inside, Ben could still see the old man, the Jeep and the road in both directions. The pay phone was inside, right beside the front door as the old man had said, and Ben picked up the receiver, grateful to hear a dial tone.

"I'm going to call Tom," he said without hesitation. "I think we've worried him enough." Ben didn't want to involve Tom but hearing his brother's voice would help him get his mind back on track and his feelings for Grace in check. He needed Tom to remind him of his place in the world. He needed Tom's voice to remind him he was Grace's Guardian, not the Chosen One.

"Okay," said Grace. "I'm going to go back here to the restroom." She pointed to a door at the back of the store. The sign on the door indicated there was only one bathroom for both men and women.

Ben watched her open the door and he could see there were no windows in the bathroom. With Grace securely locked in the small room, he dialed the operator.

"Hello," Tom's voice finally came through from the other end of the line.

"Collect call from Ben. Do you accept the charges?" the operator's bored voice grated.

"Yes, yes," Tom said excitedly. "Ben? Ben, are you there?"

"Yeah, it's me. Calm down. We're okay. We're okay." At the sound of Tom's voice, Ben took in a deep breath, closed his eyes and then slowly let it out, releasing some of the stress that had built up over the past few days.

"Where are you? What are you doing? Have you lost your mind?" Tom's questions came at Ben fast and furious.

"Tom, listen. We're fine. I know what I'm doing."

"Ben, you need to bring her back. The Council has called me in twice over this and—"

"Called you in? You met with the Council? Face-to-face?" Ben was shocked. He was in more trouble than he had imagined.

"Yeah, thanks to you, I am now on a first-name basis with them all. They're absolutely furious but I think if you brought her back on your own, they may show you a little leniency."

"I'm not bringing her back, Tom." Ben's voice was stern.

"What do you mean you're not bringing her back? You have to bring her back. If you don't bring her back, the Council will—"

"Tom," Ben interrupted. "I'm not bringing her back. I'm her Guardian. I'm keeping her safe. That's my job isn't it? To keep her safe? The Council and their wonderful plan didn't keep her safe in Southern Pines so I'm making my own plans now and taking her somewhere I know she'll be safe."

"Where?"

"The less you know, the better it'll be for you with the Council. I just called to let you know that everything is going to be fine. I'll call you again in a couple of days." Ben paused, thoughtful, then added, "Tom, you know if I bring her back, they'll take her away. I…I can't let that happen yet. I'm…I'm not ready for that yet. But I promise I have everything under control."

Ben hung up before his brother could respond. Tom should understand Ben was just doing his job. That's all this was. A job. Nothing more. He was Grace's Guardian and would keep her safe until he and Dave could figure out what to do next. Until then, he was just doing his job. His call to Tom worked. Ben's mind was back on track now.

But in the middle of Ben's self-convincing, the bathroom door opened. In that moment, everything Ben had tried to accomplish with the impromptu call to Tom was officially lost. The sight of Grace, with her long, brown hair flowing behind her, her endearing blue eyes and a smile that literally made Ben's heart stop, destroyed any hope Ben had of pushing aside his feelings for her. His mind wasn't back on track and the fact he was Grace's Guardian was now irrelevant.

Because at that moment, Ben realized he wasn't keeping her alive because he was her Guardian.

He was keeping her alive because he was head–over–heels, heart–stopping, can't–think–straight in love with her.

Ben swallowed hard, took a deep breath and put his mask back on. Hiding his feelings from Tom was hard, but hiding his feelings from Grace was more challenging than single-handedly fighting off ten Anti-Powers.

"Did you talk to Tom? What did he say?" Grace sidled up to Ben, unaware that her mere presence by his side obliterated his normally logical mind.

"Uh…yeah. I talked to him. He knows we're safe but I…got cut off before he said much," Ben lied. He glanced at the bathroom door and found his escape. A cold-water splash would clear his head. "My turn." He smiled hesitantly and pointed toward the bathroom. He scanned the parking lot one more time. "Stay in the store and let me know if anyone else pulls up for gas. I'll be right back." He gave her hand a squeeze before heading into the bathroom.

Grace stood there, looking around the store. She knew she shouldn't but she couldn't help herself. Ben had called Tom. And no Anti-Powers had suddenly appeared as a result of his phone call. And she just needed to hear her voice.

"Collect call from Grace." Telephone operators must be trained to sound bored.

"Yes," Annie squealed. "Yes. Gracie? Is that you?"

"Annie," Grace sighed. "It's so good to hear your voice. You would not believe everything that's going on."

"Where are you?"

"Cooper's Gas and Groceries. Somewhere in the Appalachian Mountains. Virginia, I think. Maybe West Virginia? Oh, I don't know and it doesn't matter. Look, I just wanted you to know I am all right. Ben isn't losing his mind. He was right. About everything."

"What do you mean he was right about everything? When are you coming home? You know, Julian keeps asking if you're ever coming back to work. I don't know what to tell him."

"Tell him I don't know. Annie, you need to listen to me. Ben was telling the truth. About the Powers, the Council, the Anti-Powers. Everything."

At that moment, the old man reentered the store.

"Whar's yer friend?" he grunted, leaning into Grace by the door.

The hair on the back of her neck bristled and she swallowed hard. "He's in the restroom." Grace placed the receiver back in the phone's cradle, hanging up on Annie in mid-sentence.

"Left ya all alone, did he?" the old man leered.

"No. He's here. Just in the restroom," Grace repeated, wondering where this conversation was going. The old man stood so close to her, she could smell his coffee-tinged breath. Grace decided she no longer liked the smell of coffee.

The old man smiled at her. It wasn't a friendly smile. "Where ya'll going?"

"Uh…the mountains?"

"Don't sound too sure of yerself, Miss Gracie. Ain't ya'll already in the mountains?" The old man moved closer to Grace, if that was at all possible.

"How…How do you know my name?" Grace stammered.

"Ever'body knows yer name, little lady," the old man sneered.

"Ben!" Grace yelled and instinctively backed away from the old man. She felt behind her back, making her way to the bathroom door, her eyes never leaving the old man's toothless grin. Just as she reached the door, it opened and she backed right into Ben's arms.

"Grace? Being clumsy again?" Ben chuckled.

Grace turned around, fear filled her eyes. "Can we get out of here?"

"Sure." Ben looked over at the old man.

"Skeer'd little thing ye got thar," the old man said to Ben as he shuffled behind the store counter.

Grace walked behind Ben as they headed for the door. Her heart pounded and she held onto the back of Ben's tee shirt with both fists.

"How much do we owe you for the gas?" Ben asked the old man as they walked past him.

"Forty should cover it," the old man flashed that toothless grin.

Ben threw two twenties on the counter. "Thanks," he said as Grace moved him quickly to the door.

"Have fun in the mountains," the old man called out the door to them.

Grace let go of Ben's shirt only when they got back to the Jeep. Her hand shook as she grabbed the door handle and pulled herself into the passenger seat.

"What was that all about?" Ben asked once they were both safely in the Jeep and driving away.

"He knew my name. I don't know how, but he knew my name," Grace said, her fear still evident in her shaking voice. "That guy gave me the creeps. How did he know my name?"

"Gracie," Ben said. "Maybe he just heard me call you by name. Who knows? But I told you, I would never leave you alone if I didn't know you were safe."

Grace sighed, "I know. I'm sorry. I guess I'm still a little skittish."

Ben reached over and took Grace's hand. "I promise. Everything's going to be okay."

Grace glanced down at Ben's hand holding hers and let out a deep sigh. "Look." She turned to him. "If I have to go through all this with someone, I'm really glad it's with you."

Ben's heart stopped again before he said, "Me too."

Chapter Fifteen: The Mountains

Tom sat on the couch in his apartment and stared at Ben's recliner. The apartment seemed smaller with Ben gone but the empty recliner loomed ten times larger than usual. After receiving Ben's phone call, Tom's previous worry for his younger brother had been replaced by anger. He could not believe his brother would so blatantly disobey the Council like that. And then to not tell Tom where he was taking Grace was inexcusable. Ben knew better and his reckless disregard for the Council code scared Tom. Ben was officially a fugitive in the Council's eyes and Tom prayed their justice would be painless for Ben when they found him. And if not painless, at least quick.

"I'm taking her somewhere I know she will be safe."

Ben's words tugged at Tom and his inability to decipher their meaning only added to his frustration. When he was younger, Tom's powers and top mental acumen had confirmed his role as Grace's Chosen One for the Council, but today his astute powers did nothing to help him find Ben's safe place. He had no idea where Ben was taking Grace and, for once, his thoughts were ineffective.

Frustrated, he got up from the couch and headed to Ben's room. He had been through this room a thousand times in the past few days, leaving it in more of a mess than he had found it, but he had to do something and searching Ben's room again was all he could think of at the moment.

Tom sat on the bed and looked around. His younger brother had never been a clean freak and Ben's room reflected that aspect of his personality. Clothes were all over the floor. Video games and iPod accessories scattered near Ben's laptop. Papers on top of papers stacked on Ben's desk. And a framed picture of the Three Amigos staring back at Tom from behind one of the stacks of papers.

Tom levitated the cheap wooden frame and it instantly flew across the room and into his open palm. It was a picture from some high school party his brother had attended. Ben was playfully grinning at the camera with his arms casually draped over Annie and Grace who stood on each side of him. Annie was striking her best supermodel pose with her long blonde hair softly falling over her bare shoulders. And then there was Grace. Grace had her sweet smile, crazy ponytail and those blue eyes that ensured her place in this world. Focusing on Grace's eyes, Tom knew that he could eventually love her the way he should. He would be able to fulfill his duties as the Chosen One.

If Ben ever brought her back to him.

Tom levitated the picture back onto the desk and started looking around the room again.

"I'm taking her somewhere I know she will be safe."

The world was large and, as Grace's Guardian, Ben had been trained to never feel safe anywhere, to always be on guard. Ben's safe place now eluded his older brother who was not used to this mental vexation.

Tom moved his search to Ben's nightstand, using his mind's powers to open drawers, pull out the contents and spread the items all over Ben's bed for the millionth time. He shifted each object around on the bed one by one, at times suspending the objects high above the bed so that he could study them more carefully. There was so much junk crammed in the nightstand's two drawers Tom wondered how Ben had gotten it all in there in the first place. A flashlight, a lighter, a couple of issues of *Sports Illustrated,* even a Playboy. But nothing that indicated Ben's safe place for Grace.

Frustrated, he released his mental hold and let all the objects abruptly crash back down onto the bed and, as he did so, a picture fell out of one of the older *Sports Illustrated* magazines. The picture's edges were worn but the faces shining back at Tom were as clear as the day it had been taken. It was an old picture of Tom, Ben, their parents and their father's best friend Dave. Dave stood in the middle, holding up a rainbow trout that, in Dave's large hands, looked smaller than Tom remembered. The good times shared that day were evident in his family's smiles, and nostalgia eased Tom's frustration slightly. Visits to Dave's house had always been more like events than vacations. The kinds of events that only the Powers could experience. Only with Dave were the brothers allowed to openly practice their abilities while they swam in the lake, levitated rocks across the river, and climbed the mountains.

The mountains.

Tom looked closer at the picture and smiled. The answer had been here all along. There was his family and Dave posing so proudly with the trout, the river flowing at their feet, the mountains framing the clear sky behind their heads.

Ben had taken Grace to the mountains. Tom was certain. Not many Powers knew about the Misfits, certainly not any of the Anti-Powers, so the Misfits' Appalachian community would be the perfect place for Ben to hide Grace and keep her safe.

Tom dropped the picture on the bed and ran to the hall closet. Using his powers, he pulled a large cardboard box down off the top shelf and levitated it to the living room coffee table. The box contained all the memories the brothers had left of their parents and Tom had not gone through it since they died. But he knew it was in there. It just had to be.

One by one, he levitated each item out of the box. Family pictures, cards, letters, books, even a couple of old music albums from the seventies. The brothers did not have a record player on which to play the albums, but their father had kept them for posterity so the boys thought they should too. Tom rifled gingerly through the albums, papers, and books. Belonging to his parents and being irreplaceable, Tom gave the items a reverence unmatched by anything else in the brothers' small apartment.

Hidden at the bottom of the box was their father's old *Physical Powers Training Manual.* Tom had seen Ben's manual before and, with his brother and father having similar powers, Tom found nothing new in his perusal of the older manual.

Beneath the manual was his father's Bible. Worn at the edges with pages falling out, this Bible had seen more use than the old training manual. His father had memorized both, but the Bible had been the more influential reference tool. Tom carefully flipped through the pages and finally found what he was looking for.

There, hidden in the New Testament Book of Revelation was an old hand-drawn map. The map to the Misfits' secret community.

Tom's powers practically pushed the phone to his ear. He didn't even need to press the buttons because, under his powers' control, the phone dialed itself. In his first meeting with the Council, they had instructed him to memorize their emergency number, but memorization was not something Tom did. One look at the number and he could instantly recall it forever. He knew the Council had given him special access because of the Ben situation but he had not had to use it until now. Having met face-to-face with the Council and now knowing their secret identities, while nerve-wracking at best, the situation did have its advantages and easy access to the Council members was now one of them.

The Council leader answered on the first ring. "Yes, Tom?" She sounded brusque.

Tom took a deep breath. "I know where they are."

• • •

"Here you are, darling," Mr. Reich said handing his wife a vodka tonic. "With extra lime, just as you like it."

"Thank you," Mrs. Reich purred. "Just put it right here on the side table." She was lounging outside on a chaise, sunglasses on, watching a group of golfers from the country club play past their mansion's expansive back deck. The sun was brilliant that afternoon so she looked somewhat normal in her sunglasses that day.

She took a long sip of her drink. "Mmmm," she sighed.

"Feel better?" Mr. Reich asked, sitting down on the chaise adjacent to Mrs. Reich's.

"Yes. Much," she said, lounging back and closing her eyes with her face full to the sun. Without opening her eyes, she calmly added, "But I still want that girl dead."

"In good time, my sweet Ava. All in good time," Mr. Reich soothed, patting his wife's hand. "The troops are ready. Our scientists have the lab prepared. We just need to pinpoint the girl's exact location."

The Reich mansion sat on the sixth fairway of the Southern Pines Country Club golf course and its location provided a convenient venue for Mr. Reich's twisted entertainment. With the bordering landscape providing cover, one of his favorite pastimes involved using his powers to bend and occasionally break the clubs of the golfers passing by his deck. And today was no exception.

"Watch this, my dear," he said.

Mrs. Reich opened her eyes just as her husband initiated his mental attack on the four unsuspecting golfers. Simultaneously, a club flew out of each golfer's bag and hung mid-air. Like synchronized swimmers, the clubs danced around the golfer's heads, twisting and turning in the air until finally the metal rods shattered in two and fell to the ground. The golfers just stood there in disbelief, their shocked eyes looking back and forth from each other to the golf clubs scattered around them.

"Oh, darling. Again? Really?" Mrs. Reich sighed. "That game is so tiresome."

"So what would you like to do this beautiful afternoon, my love?"

Mrs. Reich looked at the golfers in their white and pastel polo shirts. Her eyes glowed and the edges of her mouth curled up as she suggested, "How about a little blood?"

At his wife's request, Mr. Reich smiled and looked over at the golfers who still stood in the middle of the fairway in disbelief. Immediately, the broken club shafts rose up off the ground and began beating the golfers' heads and backs. Their harsh thumping sounds echoed in the fairway's silence. Soon, blood poured from one golfer's ear, even more from another's nose, and deep crimson polka dots materialized on their light–colored polo shirts.

"Is that enough, darling?" Mr. Reich asked.

"More," Mrs. Reich purred, her voice almost orgasmic at the sight of the golfers' blood.

Mr. Reich looked again at the foursome. The broken, jagged-edged clubs now alternated between beating and jabbing the golfers, tearing at their flesh, and cracking their bones. Two of the bloodied golfers ran for their golf cart, while another golfer lay sprawled out on the ground face down, with a club continuously smashing into his head. The remaining golfer grabbed at the golfer on the ground and tried to pull him toward the cart in between the clubs' erratic swings. Large pools of blood stained the fairway by now and the golfers slipped on them as they tried to escape.

Mrs. Reich held up her hand. "Enough now, dear. We don't want to ruin the grass right in front of us. You know how hard the club works to maintain these fairways."

"You are so right," Mr. Reich agreed. He waved his hand and the clubs instantly fell to the ground. The golfers disappeared in their carts, assumedly racing back to the clubhouse, leaving the broken golf clubs and large red pools of blood dotting the manicured fairway.

Mr. and Mrs. Reich lay on their chaises laughing hysterically at a pitch only they could hear.

"Excuse me, Mother and Father?" Gregory's voice came up behind them.

"Yes, Gregory?" Mr. Reich smiled over at his son who now stood at the edge of the deck.

Gregory glanced over at the pools of blood and grinned. "I'm sorry to interrupt your afternoon but you asked me to let you know the minute she contacted us."

"And?" Mr. Reich raised his eyebrows.

Gregory smiled. "And we now know where Grace is."

Chapter Sixteen: The Trio of Boulders

Cooper's Gas and Groceries was now just a memory and Grace was finally relaxing a little as they made their way deeper into the mountains and away from civilization. Neither she nor Ben had said much since leaving the gas station and Grace assumed Ben was as lost in his thoughts as she was in hers. She did not know why, but images from their high school days kept popping into her head. Football games, exam cram sessions, even the night of their group prom date swirled in Grace's head like a photo album collage. And while those images swirled in her head, her heart was pulling up memories of its own. Like the feeling Grace had when Ben impulsively bought her the silly monkey key chain for no reason at all. Or when he boldly complimented her prom dress in front of everyone at the dinner table. Or when she realized that her lovesick feelings for Ben were not mutual and she had placed him back into her friends bucket.

A bucket he seemed to be slowly but intentionally climbing out of now.

Grace looked over at Ben and softly smiled. His messy black hair made his blue eyes seem bluer, if that was at all possible, and his face revealed the intensity of his concentration on the road. Grace was amazed at how deftly he maneuvered the narrow road's hairpin turns as it wound through the steep Appalachian Mountains, and she assumed that his powers and superhuman reflexes made such quick maneuvers possible.

When they finally reached a portion of the road that was somewhat straighter, Ben slowed the Jeep down slightly. "Here."

He looked over at Grace. "Lean over here and take the wheel for a minute."

Grace reached over and placed one hand on top of the steering wheel. "What are you doing?" she asked without taking her eyes off the road in front of her.

Ben just grinned as he sat up toward the driver's side window and pulled his wallet out of his back jeans pocket. He handed the wallet to Grace before taking hold of the steering wheel again. "Open this for me and pull out that white folded piece of paper. It should be right behind the cash."

Grace did as she was told and pulled out the paper. It was a map, or more specifically, a Xeroxed copy of a hand-drawn map. In the lower left corner were the words "Cooper's Gas and Groceries" and a drawing of a building. Dotted lines crisscrossed the map representing the makeshift roads that weaved in and out of mountainous landmarks, with one dotted line abruptly ending at the upper right corner with the word 'Misfits' circled in bold pen strokes. Then it dawned on Grace. "You mean you know that old man back at the gas station?"

"Not personally. I just know of him. Cooper's been around the Misfits for a long time." Ben smiled over at Grace. "I told you I wouldn't leave you alone unless I know you're safe."

Grace knowingly smiled back at Ben and then began scanning the map, searching for anything she recognized other than the gas station. "Where are we?"

"Here, let me see," said Ben.

"You mean you don't know where we're going?" asked Grace incredulously, holding the map between them so Ben could see it and the road at the same time.

"I know where we're going. I just don't know exactly how to get there," Ben said sheepishly with a grin as he glanced down at the map. "I've been there a thousand times and know we have to turn off the road about fifty miles past Cooper's. But I need the map for after we make that turn."

"Oh, give me this." Grace pulled the map back into her lap. "You drive and I'll navigate." Grace studied the map to get her bearings.

"Okay. Our turn is coming up so you better be ready, Miss Navigator."

"Aye, aye, Captain." Grace saluted and rolled her eyes.

A few minutes later, Ben pulled off the road into the woods and stopped. "Here we are. Where to now?"

Grace concentrated on the map. "First, we need to find a large rock shaped like an Indian arrowhead."

Ben scanned the dense woods and pointed. "There."

Grace followed Ben's point but she saw nothing but trees. "Where?"

"You can't see it, but I do," he replied matter-of-factly as he put the Jeep in four-wheel drive and steered it toward the rock in the very far distance. There was no road now, not even a trail, and the Jeep jostled its passengers relentlessly as it made its way through the woods. The density of the tall trees blocked the sunlight so, in the deep undergrowth of the forest, it looked and felt more like the evening's twilight hours than the mid-afternoon it actually was.

"Okay, your smarty pants eyesight is going to get on my nerves, so why don't I call out the landmarks on the map and you find them? Maybe then I won't feel like just an ordinary human in your presence," joked Grace.

"Gracie, I promise you, there is absolutely nothing ordinary about you," Ben said, shaking his head and smiling. "But that sounds good. What comes after the arrowhead rock?"

Grace scanned the map again after they arrived at their first landmark. "At the arrowhead rock, turn left and go straight until you find a two hundred year old oak tree. I don't think this map is drawn to scale, but this oak tree looks huge. And how are we supposed to know which one is two hundred years old?"

"Got it," Ben said, looking off into the distance. He aimed the Jeep toward the oak tree that stood even deeper in the wood's darkness.

After more than an hour of the pair working together like a well-oiled machine, with Grace calling out landmarks and Ben swiftly maneuvering the Jeep through the thick woods, they were finally reaching the edge of the map.

"Looks like the last landmark is called the Trio of Boulders. They're kind of shaped like Stonehenge but there are only three of them." Grace squinted out the window. "These things look so large on the map even I might be able to find them."

"There they are." Ben headed the Jeep toward a large outcropping of rocks at the base of a steep mountain. Just when the Jeep had almost reached its destination, it came to an abrupt stop in the middle of two small, but sharply sloped, hills.

"What the—" Puzzled, Ben looked out the Jeep's front window. He gunned the engine. The tires spun on the leafy ground beneath them, but the Jeep did not otherwise move.

"Are we stuck?" Grace peered out her window and scanned the mountainous landscape. Nothing but trees, rocks and forest undergrowth surrounded them. The Trio of Boulders was still about thirty yards away directly in front of the Jeep.

"I don't know. Maybe caught up on a root or rock or something. We may have to walk the rest of the way, but let me check it out first." Ben looked intently into Grace's blue eyes. "Lock the doors behind me and do not, no matter what, get out of this car under any circumstances. Do you hear me Grace?"

"Okay." Grace widened her eyes with Ben's sudden seriousness. She glanced out her window again and, for Grace, the woods suddenly seemed darker than they were a few minutes ago.

"Grace, I mean it. Do not get out of this car. Promise me." Ben's intensity increased.

Grace turned back to Ben, her eyes widening even further. "Yes. Got it. I promise."

Ben took her hand and squeezed it with a wink before he exited the Jeep. The minute his door closed behind him, Grace pushed the door lock button and heard a simultaneous thump from each of the Jeep's four doors. Without thinking, she tugged on her seatbelt, testing its usefulness.

Ben walked around to the front of the Jeep. He looked closely at the front tires before peering down to inspect the Jeep's undercarriage.

"Ben?" Grace called. "What is it?"

Ben stood up and looked at Grace crouched in the front seat. "I have no idea. We're not stuck on anything that I can see." He kicked the leaves around the tires, revealing nothing but dirt underneath. Ben then walked to the back of the Jeep and performed the same inspection. Still nothing. He returned to the front of the Jeep. "Hold on," he yelled to Grace. "I'm going to lift it up and try to pull us out of whatever we're stuck in."

"Lift what up? What did you say?" Grace called through the Jeep's dirty windows.

Before Grace knew what was happening, Ben lifted the Jeep over his head, with Grace bracing herself inside. She sat there suspended in the air for a few minutes, trying not to look down. "Ben?" she called out, her eyes focused on the Trio of Boulders up ahead.

Just then, Grace heard an "Ugh" and the Jeep abruptly crashed back down to the forest floor. She looked around but could not see Ben. At first she thought the Jeep had fallen on top of him.

But, unfortunately, she was wrong.

Ben suddenly appeared in front of the Jeep, looking like he was being pulled and pushed in rag doll form. In mid-air, his body was tossed around like a juggler's ball, but Grace could not see who or what was doing the tossing. She just heard soft, but deep, laughter echoing in the trees.

"Stay in the car!" Ben yelled in between tosses. He swung his arms, attempting to strike whatever invisible being was attacking him, but the attacks just kept coming. He was thrown back and forth in front of the Jeep, never hitting the ground, always remaining suspended. His strong powers appeared ineffective against his unseen attacker.

Grace stared into the woods' darkness, trying to see who or what had hold of Ben. She felt helpless watching her Guardian being tossed around right in front of her. She scanned the Jeep for anything that might be used as a weapon. Nothing. She then looked around the dense woods. A stick, a small rock, anything. As she inspected the woods, her eyes stopped on the Trio of Boulders. She thought she saw something move in front of the middle boulder. She stared harder but couldn't see anything else.

At that moment, Ben was tossed hard and pinned against a nearby tree with his entire back pressed to the tree's trunk. His feet dangled up off the ground and his arms were forcefully extended around and behind the trunk, rendering him unable to reach his unseen attacker. His face turned beet red as he gasped for air and it was obvious to Grace that something had hold of Ben's throat, but she still saw nothing but Ben and the trees. Before Grace could blink, Ben's powerful arms pulled loose from their invisible hold and swung around to grab at his own throat. Ben pushed off whatever held him and began pounding the air in front of him. His fist obviously struck something hidden in the air and Ben fell off the tree, his feet firmly planted on the ground before he began striking again.

As Ben struck the air at his feet and whatever hid in it, a body began to appear in the area that was now the target of Ben's intensity. Invisible before, it was the body of a very, very large man crouched in the fetal position. His head was shaved and he was dressed in green camouflage shirt and pants with tall black combat boots, the kind found in army surplus stores. His arms defensively covered his face and head and his deep voice yelled, "Enough! Enough! Stop! Stop!"

At the sound of the man's voice, Ben stopped his punches and looked down at his former assailant who remained in the fetal position on the forest floor. Ben then glanced up at Grace and mouthed, "Stay."

Before Grace could respond, Ben was attacked again, but this time it came from behind. Something grabbed him, tossing him into the air and over his first attacker's head, but before he could land on the ground, something else caught him and threw him back. His first attacker smiled and stood up, rising at least seven feet tall, and now participated in some sick twisted version of the monkey in the middle game using Ben as the ball.

On about the third or fourth toss, Ben finally made his move. Just as he was tossed to his second attacker, Ben thrust his leg out and miraculously kicked the second attacker before it could catch him. With the impact of Ben's kick, the second attacker materialized: a slim, pixie-like woman with wild blonde ringlets framing her face and dressed exactly like her partner. She fell to the ground, clutching her stomach and writhing in obvious pain. Ben then spun around and jumped on the large man in the middle, throwing his thighs around the man's neck and twisting it until he passed out. The large man slumped to the ground and Ben stood silently over him.

Ben didn't move. He just stood there listening, staring at Grace, who by now was almost sitting on top of the Jeep's dashboard in an anxious posture. After a few seconds, Ben finally heard what he was waiting for. A small twig cracked on the ground immediately behind Ben, prompting him to reach behind his head and grab at the third invisible assailant. Ben took hold of the back of the attacker's neck and flung the assailant over his head. The attacker landed on the ground with a thud and instantly became visible. He wore camouflage like his partners and was smaller than the first man, however this attacker did not give up as easily. He jumped up and tackled Ben to the ground.

Ben maneuvered to pin his attacker on the ground and then punched and punched and punched the man until, just as Grace thought he was going to kill the guy, a resounding "Whoa! Stop! Stop!" boomed from the middle boulder. Ben immediately ceased his assault and looked up.

Out of nowhere appeared an older heavyset man dressed in faded blue jeans and a red plaid flannel shirt. His shaggy thinning hair was dirty blonde with gray highlights, and his face looked like he had not shaved in two or three days. He lumbered toward Ben with a huge smile and said, "Sorry I'm late. Petra didn't see all this until just now." He grabbed Ben in a huge bear hug and it was more than a few seconds before the man released his hold.

Ben stepped back from the man and smiled. "Dave. You don't know how glad I am to see you." Ben, barely panting from his fight, turned to Grace who still sat in the Jeep, now with a puzzled look on her face. "It's okay, Gracie. You can come out now," Ben called to her.

Grace's brow furrowed as she looked from Ben, to Dave, to the three attackers who were now standing behind Dave brushing leaves off their clothes. She shook her head at Ben and did not move from the Jeep.

Ben sighed and winked at Dave. He walked over to the Jeep and forcefully yanked Grace's locked door off the Jeep, his strength rendering the door and its lock permanently useless. "Sweetie, I promise you, it's okay to come out now."

Grace unbuckled her seatbelt and silently took Ben's offered hand. She exited the Jeep very slowly, moving with shocked hesitation. She clutched Ben's hand in a double-handed death grip, staying behind but as close to Ben as was physically possible as they walked toward the large man in the red flannel shirt.

"Grace," Ben said, stopping before the large man, "this is Dad's best friend, Dave. Dave, this is the infamous Grace MacKay."

"It is my absolute pleasure to finally meet you, Miss Grace. We are humbly at your service," Dave said with a smile and a sweeping bow.

Grace cocked her head, looking back and forth from Ben to Dave. "Misfit Dave?"

Dave chuckled. "The one and only, my lady."

"Is this your idea of a welcoming committee?" asked Ben, pointing to the trio standing behind Dave.

"My apologies," said Dave. "With the Anti-Powers getting more aggressive and all, we've had to institute a few extra security measures. Here, let me introduce you."

Dave walked over to Ben's attackers who now stood in a military stance, feet apart with their hands clasped behind perfectly straight backs. "These are the Boulder Triplets. They were born with chameleon-like powers and can appear invisible at will. The problem is they become visible if certain parts of their body are hit. Not a very useful power when fighting to protect the humans, so they came here to live with us Misfits after they completed their training. Despite their power's limitation, they're darn good, strong fighters and extremely perceptive guards so they have the prestigious job of protecting our community's entrance."

Dave pointed to Ben's first attacker. "This very, very large man here is Steve."

Steve stuck out his massive hand to Ben and grinned. "Sorry. We had no idea it was you…and her. No hard feelings?"

"No. We're good," said Ben.

Steve turned and bowed to Grace. "Your Highness."

Steve's regal greeting dumbfounded her.

"And this young lady is Carrie," continued Dave, gesturing to the woman.

Carrie was the smallest of the three in stature but had the biggest smile with ruby red lips that curled up almost to her twinkling blue eyes. She looked at Grace and curtsied. "It is such a pleasure to meet you, my lady."

It struck Grace odd to see a woman dressed in camouflage curtsy.

"And last but not least, we have Elton." Dave pointed to the third attacker.

"Hello," Elton said softly. He was considerably shorter than Steve and much wirier but his eyes were loaded with more mischievousness.

"Elton?" Grace repeated, not sure she heard correctly.

"Our parents had a thing for Elton John." Elton sheepishly shrugged his shoulders and smiled. He turned to Ben. "Sorry if I was a little extra rough on you. I got kind of excited. We haven't had any intruders in a while."

"No problem. I appreciate your enthusiasm," said Ben, shaking Elton's hand.

"Miss Grace," Elton continued. "It is truly an honor to finally meet you. I hope we did not scare you too much."

Grace returned his smile. "No. I knew Ben could take you. I really wasn't worried at all," she joked.

"Well," interrupted Dave. "I, too, have the utmost confidence in our Ben's powers, but don't believe today is the day to test them any further. Shall we all go somewhere that's a little less…open?" Dave looked around and up into the trees as he spoke as if they were not alone. He gestured for them to follow him and headed toward the Trio of Boulders.

"Oh. Yeah, right," said Ben, retaking Grace's hand. "Let's go, Gracie." He followed Dave with Grace still staying close to his side.

"Get rid of that Jeep and assume your positions," Dave yelled back over his shoulder to the Boulder Triplets.

Grace looked back to say goodbye to her new friends but they had already disappeared into the trees. When she turned back around, Dave was walking straight into the middle boulder. Grace tugged on Ben's arm and pointed in amazement at Dave who now stood halfway in and halfway out of the large stone.

"It's okay Grace. You can do this." Ben pulled Grace up to the middle boulder and stood behind her. "Ladies, first. Follow Dave and I'll be right behind you."

Dave held out his hand. "Come on, Miss Grace. This is the easy part. Just close your eyes and hang on to me."

Grace took Dave's hand, but before she could look back to Ben, Dave was already pulling her through the large rock and into the mountainside. As instructed, she closed her eyes, and as she passed through the stone, she felt like she was floating in the ocean with waves massaging her entire body. Relaxation overcame her anxiety but, just as soon as the waves had started, they abruptly ended.

"Okay, you can open your eyes now Gracie," Ben whispered behind her ear.

Grace slowly opened her eyes, reluctant to leave the lingering relaxed feeling of the waves, and found herself standing in the middle of the unexpected.

Chapter Seventeen: The Misfit Community

"Welcome to my world," Dave declared with a wide sweep of his hand.

They were inside the mountain, standing on a rocky precipice that jutted out from the steep mountain's inner wall like a woman's well-manicured fingernail. Below them, in a deep wooded valley, stretched a wide dirt road bordered on both sides by log cabins of all shapes and sizes. More cabins dotted up the surrounding mountainside reaching deeper into a dense green forest. The mountainside cabins were almost invisible but for the random trails of smoke escaping from a few chimneys and filtering up through the trees. A clear, rippling creek wound between the cabins and wildflowers decorated the water's edge like an Impressionist oil painting. The air was crisp and the clean smell of early morning dew rushed into Grace's nose, even though it was almost evening.

"Wow," was all she said.

"Like it?" asked Ben who was now standing beside her.

"Who wouldn't? But don't the Anti-Powers—"

"Miss Grace," Dave interrupted her, "don't you worry about those crazies. They don't know anything about this place. Heck, most of the Powers don't even know we're here. We have a pretty special way of staying hidden underneath this fake mountain. Come on down." Dave took a few steps and suddenly jumped off the rocky ledge. "Wahoo!" he screamed as he glided slowly to the edge of the dirt road thirty feet below.

"He can fly?" Grace asked, her eyes squinting at Ben.

"Not really. He's just made this jump so many times he knows exactly how to gage it with the wind and all. You could do it too if you did it enough times," Ben said as if that were a fact. "Come on. Your turn."

Without notice, Ben scooped Grace up into his arms and took a flying leap off the precipice. A few days ago, this jump would have scared the wits out of Grace, but now, having previously experienced Ben's powers, she simply rested securely in his arms, allowing the wind to blow across her face as they glided through the air. Within seconds, they landed with a muffled thud on the dirt road below. Grace looked up at Ben and exhaled, "Thanks."

"No problem." His eyes were soft as he slowly and reluctantly released his hold on her.

"Are you hungry?" asked Dave.

As if on cue, Grace's stomach growled. Ben and Grace looked at each other and hysterical laughter overcame them. It was a good laugh, one they had not had in a very long time and it took a few minutes for each to catch their breath.

"I'm afraid that food hasn't exactly been high on our agenda the past few days," chuckled Ben. "So, yeah, you could say we're hungry."

"Great." Dave had a funny look in his eyes. "Because I can see that Petra has dinner ready now."

Dave started walking down the middle of the road with Grace and Ben following close behind him. They passed cabin after cabin along the road. Most of the buildings appeared to be residences with wide front porches and roughly hewn rocking chairs obviously recycled from the woods' discarded branches. The cabins without front porches resembled storefronts from an old western town. One looked like a blacksmith's shop, one a woodworking shop, but the largest cabin on the road was "Ted's General Store" as indicated by the large, faded blue letters painted on the side of the building. Despite the numerous buildings, however, not a soul could be seen on the road, on the porches, not even in the cabin windows. It was like a ghost town.

"Where is everyone?" asked Ben.

"Ballgame." Dave glanced at his watch. "Should be about over by about now. But there will be another one tomorrow so you haven't missed anything."

Ben looked over at Grace. "Wait until you see a Powers ballgame. I promise you'll finally have some fun tomorrow."

Grace smiled like she knew what Ben was talking about, but, as usual, she did not.

Dave's cabin was toward the end of the road but was built behind the first row of cabins and on the other side of the creek. It sat a little way up the mountainside and appeared to be one of the most hidden cabins in the entire community. It had a wide front porch with six rocking chairs strewn haphazardly all over it and Grace had to fight her impulse to orderly realign them. The cabin's position on the mountainside gave the front porch rockers not only a fantastic view of the creek but also of the entire road and community below. Grace assumed Dave had intentionally chosen this cabin site more for this voyeuristic view than its inherent camouflage qualities.

"Petra!" Dave called through the cabin's screen door. "They're here!"

Upon Dave's loud announcement, out of the cabin walked one of the most beautiful women Grace had ever laid eyes on. She wore blue jeans and a faded Rolling Stones tee shirt, and appeared to be slightly older, around Dave's age, with gray streaks throughout her thick blonde hair and around her temples. The top of her hair was pulled away from her face with a wooden clip, leaving the remaining long strands cascading down her back. But her face. Her face was unlike anything Grace had never seen. Her skin was porcelain, her lips a deep rose, and her eyes the bluest of blues. She wore no make-up and, even with laugh lines dancing around her twinkling eyes, her face had the softness of a very young child.

"Benjamin!" Petra wrapped her slender arms around Ben and gave him a squeeze. "How we have missed you so! Just look at you. So tall and grown up! I'm so happy you're finally here." Her sweet voice made her words sound almost lyrical. "And you must be Grace," she said taking Grace's hand. "It is such an honor to finally meet you and have you in our home. I am so sorry I didn't see you coming sooner or I would have had everything ready. But you know how we Misfits are. Always one step behind."

"Uh…nice to meet you too." Grace looked puzzled and stood a little closer to Ben. She had no idea what Petra was talking about.

"Oh, shoot! Forgive my manners, dear. Here I am going on and on and I know exactly who you are and you have no idea who I am. I'm Dave's wife. At least I am until he finds someone else to put up with him, but we all know *that* is never going to happen," she giggled and winked.

Dave grabbed Petra from behind, his large arms folding around her lean body. "But I don't want anyone else." He grinned and nuzzled the back of her neck.

Petra waved him off. "Oh, pooh. Let's get these young people some supper. I know they're starving. Come on inside, you two."

Grace and Ben followed the happy couple into the cabin, which had an interior that belonged more on the pages of *Architectural Digest* than in the middle of a clandestine forest. To the left was an expansive living room with a stone fireplace that reached halfway across the far wall and several large tufted sofas and chairs that invited afternoon naps. Two floor-to-ceiling windows that were at least fifteen feet tall flanked the fireplace and, looking upward, the high ceiling revealed an upstairs loft area with skylights that captured the dusk's remaining sunlight. To the right of the front door was the kitchen with pine cabinets and a long rustic dining table that stretched between two sturdy benches. The table was filled with more food than was needed for four people and the glistening fine china and crystal place settings looked a little out of place next to the hosts' blue jean attire.

"Please, sit, sit." Petra motioned Ben and Grace over to the table. "Ben, I made your favorite. Hash brown casserole. And Grace, Dave couldn't exactly see what you liked so I made a little bit of everything for you."

Looking at the bountiful table, Grace thought a "little bit of everything" may have been an understatement. Spread over the table were silver dishes filled with chicken, ham, potatoes and more salads and fresh vegetables than Grace had ever seen in her life. "It all looks wonderful. Thank you," she said. "But, um…do you mind if I wash up a little first?"

"Of course! Of course! Right down the hall there and first door on your left," Petra replied.

Grace leaned into Ben and whispered, "Come with me." Her small voice leaked insecurity.

Ben silently obliged and stood guard outside the bathroom door as she requested.

"She's good looking," Dave whispered to Petra as soon as Ben and Grace had left the room. "It's too bad Ben is not the Chosen One. They would have made a good couple."

"Dave," Petra quietly scolded. "No matchmaking. Ben's in enough trouble with the Council as it is."

"Hello! Remember me? Powers guy here!" Ben called out from the hallway. "I can hear you two whispering!"

Dave opened his mouth to reply but before he could utter a word, Grace and Ben reappeared in the kitchen.

"Thank you," Grace said, still drying her hands on her jeans.

"Okay. Now let's eat," said Dave.

The four sat at the long table with Grace sitting closer to Ben than usual. Remembering her own clumsiness, she used extra care when she picked up the stemmed crystal water goblet and slowly moved it to her lips.

Seeing Grace's noted cautiousness, Petra said, "I hope all the crystal and china doesn't make you uncomfortable, dear. We just haven't ever had royalty in our home and I wanted to make a good impression. Besides, I tried to look and did not see you breaking anything on the table so you can relax. You won't hurt anything."

Once again, Grace had no idea what Petra was talking about. She looked over at Ben with the puzzled expression he had now grown accustomed to over the past two days.

As if reading her thoughts, Ben said, "For Dave and Petra to see means something a little different than it does for the rest of us. Petra can see the future—sometimes. She isn't always accurate and doesn't always see everything but she tries."

"That's why we're so good together," Dave said. "She's into the future and I'm into the past. An opposites attract kind of thing."

Ben looked at Grace. "Dave, on the other hand, can see the past—at least some of it," Ben grinned.

"Yeah," continued Dave. "Your father and I used to have a lot of fun with that at training camp. To know who had a crush on whom, who cheated on which test. We had a blast messing with our classmates. Too bad the Council didn't think my powers would be helpful in protecting the humans. Together, your father and I could have stomped the Anti-Powers and you all would not be in the situation you are in today."

At the mention of his father, Ben shifted uncomfortably on the bench. "Dave, about Dad—" Ben started.

Dave held up his hand. "I already know. For once, my powers worked exactly the way they were supposed to and I knew it right after it happened. I'm sorry Ben, real sorry. Your parents were good people. Petra and I lost our best friends that day and they will never be replaced as far as we're concerned."

Tears welled up in Petra's eyes. "I just wish I had seen something coming. Anything. Maybe I could have stopped the Anti-Powers."

Dave put his arm around his wife's shoulders and looked at Ben. "She's beat herself up pretty bad over not seeing their future."

"Petra," Ben soothed. "It's okay. It's not your fault. It's not anybody's fault."

"Except for the Anti-Powers," Dave added. "I'd love to get my hands on one, just one!"

"Ben killed two Anti-Powers," Grace piped in trying to steer the conversation away from the topic of Ben's parents.

"Well," Ben said. "At least one. Maybe two."

"Attaboy! Two down! That's fantastic," Dave proudly beamed. "Now that's the kind of stuff we used to send in to Stan Lee. He could have really used that!"

"Stan Lee? The comic book guy?" Grace was in the dark yet once again.

Dave looked at Ben. "How much have you told her? I can't see."

"Not much," Ben lied. "Just what I thought she needed to know. I told her about the Salem murders and that rogue Council member that started the Anti-Powers. That's pretty much it."

"Hello! I'm right here. Remember?" Grace uncharacteristically interrupted. "No need to refer to me in third person. Now what's this about Stan Lee?"

Dave leaned in and looked hard at Grace seated across the table. "Miss Grace, it appears you need a history lesson." He leaned in even closer to Grace. "Well, if you know about the Salem murders, then you know why the Powers are such a secretive bunch. To tell you, a human, anything is a huge Council code violation, sometimes punishable by death."

Grace's eyes widened as she looked over at Ben, but Ben just stared down into his plate and pushed his food around with his fork.

"But around here," Dave continued, "we don't pay much attention to the Council. Just because we only have one power and just because that power may or may not work the way it should, well…I mean…they seem to think they don't need us to protect the humans so, in turn, we don't need them and their stupid Council code. The Misfits, as they like to call us, well…we live by our own rules."

"Dave? You were telling her about Stan Lee. Remember?" Petra prodded him.

"Oh, yeah. Right. Okay. Anyway, after the Salem murders, the Council decided that all Powers should go into hiding. At first, most were okay with that. They could protect the humans and hide their powers at the same time. No problem. But as things became more modern and weapons deadlier, it became harder and harder for the Powers to protect the humans without openly using their special abilities. So, early in the twentieth century, the Council came up with the idea that, if the humans could view the Powers as their protectors instead of as freaks, then the humans would be more accepting and the Powers would be able to use their abilities out in the open."

Grace was so engrossed by Dave's lesson that, as she leaned closer across the table to hear her host, she unconsciously shifted her hand from her lap to Ben's knee under the table.

Ben smiled to himself but was otherwise afraid to move. He liked Grace's hand just where it was.

"So," Dave said, "in walks Mr. Stan Lee, public relations man extraordinaire. He was genius. Pure genius. The Council secretly hired him to work on the Powers' image with the humans. His idea was to introduce the Powers through comic books to the younger humans. He thought if he could hook the children early, make them understand that the Powers were real and good and all that, then, when they got older, they would accept the Powers as their protectors and the Powers would not have to hide anymore."

"Comic books? That was his great PR strategy?" Grace questioned skeptically.

"Yeah. Sounds simple, I know, but it was a fantastic idea. All the kids loved us. And he had all the great Powers in there. He and his associates filled the Marvel and DC comic books with them. You'd know them as Spiderman, Superman, Batman, Wonder Woman…there are too many to count now."

"Superman was…was real?" Grace was almost laughing now.

"What do you mean 'was'? He's retired and living in Boca Raton now." Dave spoke as if that was a well-known fact.

"He always sends Dave the funniest birthday cards," Petra added.

Grace just sat there shaking her head. Ben had been a comic book junkie when he was younger. Now she realized he was just studying up on his history.

"Who else?" Grace asked excitedly. "Who else is still around?"

"Well," Dave continued. "The guy you'd call Batman is living in Montana. Huge fly fisherman. Even ties his own flies. Loves nothing more than to be out on a river."

"He has the most beautiful cabin up there," inserted Petra. "We actually got some ideas for our cabin from visiting his."

"And Robin?"

"San Francisco, of course." Dave rolled his eyes as if Grace should have known that.

"What about Wonder Woman?"

"She lives in Atlanta," Petra answered. "Owns the cutest little antique store in Buckhead. She needed to live near a major airport since she's always going back and forth between Boca and Montana, if you know what I mean. And since Atlanta was right in between, it was the perfect place for her to retire."

"Between Boca and Montana? You mean—?" Grace grinned.

"Yep," Petra replied. "That woman has been playing those two men against each other for years. She goes back and forth between them with the whim of her mood swings."

Ben laughed. "Grace wouldn't know anything about mood swings."

Grace elbowed Ben playfully. "Anyway…what happened? Why didn't it work? Why are the Powers still in hiding?"

"I honestly don't know," sighed Dave. "The advent of video games, faster technology replacing comic books, who knows? And, of course, having to deal with the Anti-Powers didn't help either. But here we are, still freaks in the human world."

Grace squeezed Ben's knee under the table. "Well, you're not freaks to me," she said to him.

"Thanks." Ben gently patted Grace's hand, which still rested on his knee. Their eyes locked for the briefest of seconds but not without being noticed by both Dave and Petra.

Grace turned back to Dave. "So, the Council really is congress for comic book characters."

Dave let out a deep cackle. "Oh, Miss Grace! I'd never thought of it that way. That is absolutely priceless!"

"But accurate," Petra giggled.

Just then, there was a knock on the cabin's screen door.

"Anybody home?" a voice called out.

"Hey, DJ!" Dave yelled at the voice. "Come on in. We're in the kitchen."

DJ opened the screen door and entered the cabin with sweat pouring from his brow. He had long brown hair pulled back in a ponytail and high, sharply cut cheekbones. He was spaghetti skinny and extremely tall, at least seven feet, and based on his sports attire, must have just finished playing in the Powers ballgame.

"Who won?" asked Dave.

"The Mentals this time." DJ grinned. "But we'll get them tomorrow."

"Dave," Petra prompted. "Where are your manners?"

"Oh, yeah." Dave turned to Grace. "Miss Grace, this is DJ."

Grace slowly stood up and held out her hand. "It's very nice to meet you."

DJ bowed and lightly kissed the top of Grace's extended hand. "Your Highness. Welcome."

Grace's puzzled look was now permanently etched onto her face.

"And you remember Ben?" Petra said.

DJ's smile widened. "Of course. I haven't seen you in a while. You've gotten…bigger. Maybe you could join our team for the game tomorrow.

Ben laughed. "We'll see."

Dave rolled his eyes. "Now, DJ, I don't think it would be fair to have a full-fledged Guardian Power on your team, even if he is a Physical. Odds wouldn't be quite balanced then, would they?"

"No. You're right. Maybe some other time."

"Where's Rebecca?" asked Petra.

"She's right behind me with Vector and a couple of others. I saw your lights on and noticed you weren't at the game so wanted to make sure everything was okay. Obviously I got here first." DJ glanced at Grace. "We had no idea she would be here."

Ben leaned into Grace and said, "DJ's power is speed."

DJ smiled at her. "Well, most of the time it is. It's more like intermittent speed. You know, short bursts that prematurely pop. It's not really the most dependable of powers."

"Oh, sweet DJ," said Petra. "Around here, nobody's power is exactly dependable. If they were, we wouldn't be here."

Grace returned DJ's smile without saying anything. Hearing about someone's power was still foreign to her.

Just then, the cabin door flew wide open and in walked five people excitedly talking and giggling about the ballgame. At the sight of Grace, they stopped cold, looking from Grace to Dave to DJ with questioning eyes.

"Hey everyone!" laughed Dave. "Guess who's here!"

Ben stood, pulling a reluctant Grace up by her arm. He whispered in her ear, "Don't hate me for this," before he faced the newcomers and boldly stated, "Everyone, this is Grace MacKay. Grace, this is…well…everyone."

All eyes focused on Grace who now stood a little closer to Ben, grabbing for his hand until she found it behind her back. It was warm and soft and comforting. Nothing like Gregory's electric grip. Feeling Ben's touch eased her anxiety of being the center of the room's attention, even if only slightly.

A tall, slender woman with short jet–black hair and powder blue eyes so pale they were almost white stepped forward and held out her hand. "Hello, I'm Rebecca, DJ's girlfriend. It's such a pleasure to meet you, my lady." She reverently nodded her head slightly before stepping back.

Dave stood up and turned to Grace. "Rebecca is a shape shifter, a very, very slow shape shifter," he laughed. "Unlike her boyfriend, speed is not one of Rebecca's virtues."

Grace looked back at Rebecca who smiled and shrugged her shoulders. Without saying a word, Rebecca started to transform. Slowly, over the course of more than a few minutes, Rebecca's tall slender body shortened and filled out, her smile widened and her short black hair lengthened to a thick, glistening brown. When the transformation was finally complete, it was as if Grace was staring into a mirror.

"Wow," breathed Grace.

"I'll say!" exclaimed DJ. "You filled out in all the right places, sweetie."

"DJ!" yelled Petra. "Watch your tongue."

DJ glanced over at Grace. "Oh, Your Highness. I am so very sorry. It…it just came out." He sheepishly hung his head.

"No problem. I kind of think those places actually look better on her." Grace softly smiled, still confused over the royal greetings.

Dave tossed his head back and laughed. "Oh, my lady, in this crowd, it's a good thing you have a sense of humor." He glanced at Ben with a knowing smile. "You are definitely a keeper, Miss Grace, definitely a keeper."

Ben was suddenly very uncomfortable under Dave's perceptive eyes. He looked away from his host and quickly changed the subject. "And this older but distinguished gentleman is Vector," Ben said, pointing to the oldest man in the crowd. Vector was balding, slightly stooped, and wore perfectly round wire-rimmed glasses, a sweater vest, and tweed sport coat. His blue eyes twinkled against his dark brown skin and he reminded Grace of her eighth grade science teacher except Vector walked with a cane and smelled of motor oil.

"At your service, my dear," Vector said. He attempted to bow but was already so stooped over, his bow ended up being only a slight head nod.

"Vector is the local mechanic, mad scientist, and all-around Mr. Fix-it around here," Ben continued.

"Vector is a Mental and his powers are mechanical. He can build or fix anything, and I do mean anything," Dave said. "He's the reason our little community stays hidden. His contraption hides us here in the middle of a National Forest and no one, not even the United States Federal Government, knows we are here."

"Oh, it's really nothing." Vector modestly smiled. "But perhaps Miss Grace and Master Ben would like to see my shop while they're here."

"That would be nice, thank you," said Grace without looking at Ben.

"Oh, what are we all doing standing around here?" asked Petra. "Let's move out on the front porch for coffee and dessert." She herded her guests outside before returning to the kitchen to load a tray.

On the porch, there were more people than rocking chairs, and, despite protests of formality and offers of seating from the other guests, Grace sat down on the front stairs next to Ben. As Petra passed around the coffee and apple pie, the remaining three guests introduced themselves to Grace. Ben already knew them all and he and Dave helped fill Grace in on the guests' powers for those who were too shy to reveal them.

In between bites of apple pie, Grace met Lofty, who could fly but only when the sun was shining; Numbers, a first-rate mathematician who worked closely with Vector; and Star, whose entire body could glow upon demand. Star was the only one of the group who seemed to be more interested in Ben than Grace. She kept reminding him of experiences they shared when they were younger, sitting closer and closer to him with each story told. Grace wasn't sure she cared for Star much.

The impromptu gathering turned into a party on the front porch. The group ate and talked and laughed until midnight had closed in on them and the yawns finally outnumbered the laughs.

"Well, folks," said DJ rising from one of the rockers. "It has truly been a pleasure but I need my sleep if I am going to kick some Mental butt tomorrow on the ball field."

"In your dreams," laughed Numbers. He then turned to Grace and bowed. "Sweet dreams, Your Majesty."

One by one, the guests said their regal goodbyes to Grace and headed down the hill toward the main road with Star glowing in the lead. As Star's glow glided through the woods and away from Dave's cabin, she resembled Tinkerbell from Disney's Peter Pan and Grace's pleasant evening was momentarily interrupted with a vision of the twinkling lights from her birthday party. A vision that would have been lovely by anyone else's standards, but now only evoked a sick feeling in Grace's stomach.

She turned to Ben and impulsively said, "You are sleeping with me tonight, right?"

"Uh…uh," Ben stammered with raised eyebrows.

"I'd feel safer with you next to me."

"Of course." Ben only halfway smiled.

They headed back into the cabin where Petra met Grace and took her hand, "Here, sweetie, follow me. I have you set up right back here in our guest room. It has a private bath and I've laid out some towels and clothes for you to use while you are with us." Petra walked as she talked and did not notice Ben following them.

"Where are you going, son?" Dave followed them down the hall.

Ben flipped his head around and stopped in the guest room doorway. "I'm staying with Grace…protecting her. I'm her Guardian, remember?"

Dave smiled at Ben. "Oh, I remember. I'm just making sure you do," he said matter-of-factly before turning around and heading up the stairs to his room.

Petra scooted past Ben to follow Dave. "You just let us know if you all need anything. We'll see you in the morning." She waved back before leaving the pair alone.

Ben stood in the doorway and stared into the room. Grace had already gone into the bathroom to change into Petra's old pajamas and he was glad she was not there to see his face.

Because the guest room no longer housed the twin beds Ben remembered from his youth.

Now the guest room was filled with one very large, overstuffed, king-size bed.

Grace emerged from the bathroom and got into the bed without looking at Ben. She pulled the covers up to her chin, rolled over away from him and mumbled, "Aren't you sleeping tonight?"

Ben swallowed hard before he hoarsely said, "I'm going to try."

And like in the Stardust Motel the night before, Ben, still in his jeans, tee shirt and tennis shoes, lay down on top of the bedcovers.

This time he was able to strategically leave plenty of space between himself and Grace on the king-size bed. He folded his hands over his chest and stared up at the ceiling. He could try, but sleep was not going to come easily tonight.

Without turning over, Grace reached behind her back and pulled Ben's arm up and over her body, wrapping his body around her and nuzzling his hand under her cheek like a security blanket. Ben's breathing deepened as he slowly turned his body toward Grace with a move that now totally eliminated any space between them on the bed.

"Ben," Grace whispered without opening her eyes. "Thank you. You feel good next to me."

"You feel good too, Gracie," Ben sighed, allowing the position of his arm around her body to become less of a protective hold and more of an embrace.

Chapter Eighteen: Forbidden Feelings

Grace woke to the warm smell of bacon. Sunlight streamed through the room's only window and Grace turned over to find the other half of the bed empty. The bedcovers weren't even wrinkled.

"Ben!" Grace bolted straight up.

"Yeah," his voice filtered in from the other room. Within seconds he appeared in the guestroom's doorway, wiping his hands on a dishtowel. "I'm here, sleepy head. What do you need?"

"Nothing. I just didn't know where you were and wanted to make sure you were still here."

Ben shook his head and crossed the room to sit on the edge of the bed next to Grace. "Of course, I'm still here, silly. Where else would I be?"

"I…I don't know. I just didn't like waking up without you." Grace looked down, pretending to study the wooden slats of the floor beside the bed.

Ben's hand gently tilted her chin up to face him, their eyes now inches apart. "Grace MacKay," he said intently. "I promise I am not going anywhere without you. Okay?"

"Okay," Grace exhaled.

"So get up and get dressed." Ben was now grinning. "Dave and I have cooked a huge breakfast and we need you to eat it. Now."

At that moment Petra's head peeked around the doorway. "Good, you're up," she said in her singsong voice. "Please let me know if you need anything, Your Highness."

"Uh…no…I'm good." Grace half-smiled at her hostess.

"Well, okay then. Breakfast is ready when you are," Petra called back to Grace as she returned to the kitchen.

Grace turned to Ben. "Why do they do that?"

"Do what?"

"Say 'Your Highness' and 'my lady' and all that stuff to me. It's weird."

"You've been attacked by Anti-Powers, met invisible triplets, and seen your best friend throw a car, and you think my friends referring to you as royalty is weird?" Ben chuckled.

"Well, yeah, kind of." Grace grinned.

"Okay," Ben paused. "Well, in their world…my world, the Family, your family, has always been thought of as royalty, granted it's been a secret royalty, but a kind of royalty just the same. We don't have kings or queens or any of that stuff since we're governed by the Council, but without the Family, none of us would exist, none of us would be…special. So to us, your family is our own unique brand of royalty that's been passed down through generations of Powers. I don't know why. That's just the way it's always been."

"Yeah, but that doesn't really help when my whole goal in life is to avoid being the center of attention, now does it?" Grace said.

"Grace," Ben's voice took on a serious tone. "You are the last of your family line. You're all the royalty we have left. It's kind of a big deal for the Misfits to have you here. It's truly an honor for them and it makes them feel good to be helping you. I know you hate it but let them be respectful and treat you like royalty for now—at least until I can figure this whole Anti-Powers situation out. Okay?" Ben's blue eyes intentionally tore through Grace.

"Okay," she nodded.

"Thanks. Now get up. After breakfast I'm going to show you the town. Literally." Ben patted Grace's hand and stood up. "And I can't wait for you to watch the ballgame. It's quite a…spectacle."

Ben left Grace smiling even though she still felt uncomfortable as a royal guest in the Misfit community. Shaking off her shyness, she quickly changed into the jeans and tee shirt Petra had laid out the night before. Seeing The Who's Roger Daltry screaming across her chest in the bathroom mirror, Grace assumed Dave and Petra must have been concert junkies in their younger days. Without thinking, Grace began to pull her hair back into her usual tight ponytail but, looking at herself in the mirror, she stopped. She released her hair and it fell full along her shoulders and down her back.

"There. That's better," she said to herself before throwing the rubber band in the trash and heading to the kitchen.

The breakfast table looked more plentiful than the night before, if that was at all possible, and once again, Petra had brought out her fine china.

"Did you sleep well, Your Majesty?" Dave asked, placing a heaping bowl of scrambled eggs directly in front of Grace's plate.

Grace glanced over at Ben knowingly, the regal greeting ringing in her ears, before she smiled up at Dave and said, "Yes, thank you."

"Good, good. Glad nothing…interrupted your dreams," Dave said, nudging Ben behind his back.

"You're real funny, Dave," Ben whispered in his host's ear as he pushed Dave aside and sat down next to Grace.

Like the night before, the foursome practically licked their plates clean and, watching Petra's slender arms reach for her twelfth slice of bacon, Grace wondered if the Misfits ever gained any weight. If living here meant she could eat that much processed meat and still keep her weight down, Grace was moving in to stay.

After the hearty breakfast, and after Grace had washed the dishes despite Petra's shrieking protests against royalty doing any type of labor in her home, Ben led Grace back down the mountainside to the dirt road running through the center of the

Misfit community. Unlike the day before, the community was bustling with people and, as expected, everyone already knew about Grace because each person they came across either bowed or curtsied in a grand fashion.

"I'm sorry," Ben whispered in her ear after they had encountered the umpteenth bow. "I know that makes you uncomfortable but thanks for being such a good sport about it."

"If that's what makes them happy, then I'll live with it," Grace whispered back. "But if you ever start doing that, as royalty I will have no choice but to have you killed by the palace guards."

"Got it," laughed Ben.

They passed by Ted's General Store and found Numbers hanging around the old wooden steps leading up to the front door. "Your Highness," he said with a bow. "Welcome to my humble establishment."

"You? You're Ted?" asked Grace pointing to the sign on the side of the building.

"Yes, Madam," Numbers chortled. "My real name's Ted. Numbers is only a nickname Vector gave me a long time ago and it just kind of stuck."

"Is he in his shop?" asked Ben, peering around the side of the building.

"Yes, sir. Go on back. He was hoping you'd stop by."

Ben took Grace's hand and led her to a building behind the General Store. It too, was a log cabin, but it had various satellite dishes in all shapes and sizes covering its green tin roof. The large modern steel front door, measuring at least five feet wide, resembled the entrance to a bank vault and looked very out of place sitting in the middle of the cabin's log walls. Beside the front door was a small red button which, when Ben pushed it, sang Aretha Franklin's "Respect" both inside the shop and out on the front porch.

"Cool doorbell," Grace grinned.

"Yeah. Vector had a thing for Aretha back in the sixties. Rumor is that she still visits him here from time to time."

Grace raised her eyebrows. "You mean she's a—?"

"With that voice? What do you think? I told you Grace, Powers are everywhere."

Inside the shop, amid more than a few grunts, Vector unlocked the large door and attempted to pull it open. Hearing the old man struggle, Ben used his superhuman strength to push the door open the rest of the way.

"Thank you, thank you, young man. I really need to work on that thing but I never do seem to find the time." Vector was stooped over his cane but, upon seeing Grace, attempted to straighten himself, notwithstanding the physical impossibility of his effort. "Welcome to my shop, Your Majesty." Vector swept his arm out in a broad stroke as if he were showcasing a game show prize.

The shop was larger than it looked from the outside. Despite the numerous computers, monitors, and metal gadgets that filled the room and made it look like a high school science lab, it still had a few homey touches. In the far right corner of the room was a small stone fireplace anchored by an old red leather club chair. The chair held a square needlepoint pillow depicting a pheasant and beside the chair was a small table stacked high with books and papers. An ashtray sat on the table to the left of the books and a pipe leaned on its rim with a thin line of smoke disappearing up into the air.

"I hope we aren't interrupting," Ben said, eyeing the still-lit pipe.

"No, no, of course not," Vector shook his head. "Just studying some charts I pulled from last night. There's something strange going on right outside the fourth quadrant but I'm sure it's nothing."

"What do you mean 'strange'?" asked Ben.

Grace immediately tuned into Ben's altered tone.

"Oh, I promise, it's probably nothing more than my paranoia," Vector said shuffling over to the nearest computer screen. He punched on the keyboard, his crinkled fingers moving faster than expected for such a stooped old man. "See, here," he pointed to the screen.

A large blue blob filled the computer screen and blurred red images outlined in yellow moved sporadically throughout the blob.

"The red indicates heat," Vector said. "I just haven't seen this much heat in one area before. It's been accumulating all night."

"Could it be a herd of deer or something?" Ben asked.

"Maybe. But I don't think so." Vector pointed to one of the red images on the screen. "See how that thing is moving. Deer don't move like that." He smiled over at Grace. "But, as I said, I'm sure it's nothing."

"Do you want me to go check it out?"

"No, son, but thank you. I'll send one of the Triplets to look into it. We'll get their report soon enough."

Ben feigned a smile at Grace. "I'm sure it's nothing. Like Vector said."

Grace's eyes smiled back but her hand nervously reached out to clutch Ben's hand behind his back.

"Would you like to see my masterpiece?" Vector asked Grace proudly.

"Sure," she said hesitantly, her eyes still on Ben.

Vector shuffled over to the largest computer in the room. It hummed warmly and looked as old as a Smithsonian relic. "This," he beamed, "is what keeps us hidden."

"How?" Grace asked skeptically.

"Let's just say it makes mountains," Vector chuckled.

Ben shook his head. "What Vector means to say is it pretends to make mountains. Somehow, only Vector knows how, this invention has hidden the entire Misfit community under a fifteen-mile, translucent covering that, from the outside, looks and feels like one of the many mountaintops filling the Appalachian range. Humans drive and hike all over this covering never knowing there's a whole community under here. The Misfits live inside a mountain that is not really there."

"The hardest part was making it translucent," Vector beamed. "But we got it, didn't we young Benjamin?"

Ben nodded. "Vector is pretty proud of that part. Air, sunlight, even rain, filters through the covering as if it were not even there. Makes living here a whole lot easier."

"Yep," said Vector. "Sure does. We have everything we need right here. And with the Boulder Triplets guarding the only entrance and someone constantly watching these computer screens, no one gets in or out without me knowing."

"I told you we'd be safe here." Ben squeezed Grace's hand and glanced at his watch. "Well, Vector, we better get going. We have another stop to make before we head out to the ball game. Are you going?"

"No, son, I went to the game last night. I need to stay here and keep an eye on my computers so my assistant, Marshall, can make the game today. If you decide to play, the Mentals are going to need all the help they can get, and Marshall is pretty good with a ball. But you all have fun without me and tell Dave I'll see him later," Vector chuckled, waving Ben and Grace out the door.

"Where are we going?" Grace asked once they were outside.

"You'll see." Ben bent over. "Now climb on."

Now accustomed to following Ben's instructions without question, Grace hopped on Ben's back and clutched his chest. She had not noticed the other day, but Ben's chest felt firm, muscular, not at all like she thought it would.

Ben ran his invisible run and instantly they were standing in another part of the forest. Grace looked back but the Misfit community had disappeared.

"Where are we? Are we still under the mountain?" Grace asked as she eased off Ben's back.

"Yeah. Don't worry. We're still hidden if that's what you mean. Come on." Ben pulled Grace through the trees and up a small hill. They were nearing a clearing when Ben said, "Now close your eyes and no peeking."

Ben placed his hand over Grace's closed eyes and led her into the clearing. She could feel the sun's warmth on her face and the smell of lilacs filled her lungs.

"Okay. Now open them," he said, his fingers lightly brushing her cheek as he took his hand away.

Grace blinked and before her stood the most brilliant display of lilacs she had ever seen. She was standing right in the middle of the clearing and everywhere she looked, large clusters of lavender and white flowers, in every shade imaginable, screamed at her. The lilacs encircled the clearing like a halo and had grown so thick and tall, the forest behind them was almost invisible.

"Ben!" she exclaimed. "This is gorgeous!"

"I thought you'd like it," he beamed. "Aren't lilacs your favorite?"

"Yes," she breathed. Grace stood there turning in a circle, taking in each flower, each color, and each smell that surrounded her.

"These are magnificent. And they're everywhere! I can't believe a place like this exists."

"Yeah," said Ben wistfully, looking around the clearing.

"Why…how did they get here? Are they wild?"

"No. Well, they may be considered wild now, but they didn't start that way. Mom planted them," Ben quietly answered.

"Your mother? Why was she here? I thought she didn't have any powers? I thought she was from my family?"

"She was and, no, she didn't have any powers like you think. But Dad got special permission from the Council to tell her about the Powers so she got to come with us when we visited Dave.

While we were off messing with our Powers, Mom would come up here and doodle and plant and do whatever it is gardeners do."

"Special permission? So your mom knew about me…about my family?"

"Yes. Not to sound sexist, but Dad argued to the Council that he and his two sons would not know what to do with you, a girl. So the Council let Dad tell Mom so, you know, she could help with you."

"You make me sound like a project."

"Well, for my family, you were…are…kind of."

"Thanks." Grace rolled her eyes.

Ben playfully elbowed her. "Gracie, my parents loved you like a daughter and you know it."

"I know. But why lilacs? Why did your mom plant all these lilacs?"

Ben's eyes softened then. "Because they were her favorites… and yours." He shuffled his feet and stared down at the thick grass blanketing the ground below. He felt Grace move closer and his heart stopped. It was on the tip of his tongue, but he just could not bring himself to say the words.

But he didn't have to.

Ben looked up just as Grace's arms were reaching around his neck. Her closeness was dangerous now, he knew it, but he didn't stop her. She pressed her body against his and he felt her breath on his neck when she said, "Thank you. They're beautiful."

"You're welcome," he whispered in her ear.

They stood there in silence for a long time, breathing in their embrace, their arms wrapped tightly around each other for no reason at all. Finally, without forewarning or permission, Grace's head turned. Her lips lightly brushed against his cheek before they softly started to make their way down Ben's face toward his waiting lips. Her arms wrapped tighter around him the closer her lips got to his and Ben knew he was about to experience the first kiss he had waited so long to savor.

The first kiss he was forbidden to experience.

The first kiss that belonged to his brother, Tom.

The first kiss he needed to end before it even began.

"No." Ben softly shook off Grace's lips and pulled her arms away from his neck. "Gracie, I can't," he murmured.

"Oh," Grace whispered. She turned her back to Ben and hid her face in her hands.

It was déjà vu for Ben as he watched Grace's tears hit the grass below. His second rejection of her felt worse than the first and Ben did not want to relive this high school scene again.

Grace swallowed hard and shook her head. "I'm sorry...I shouldn't have. These last few days...I just thought...I mean... well...maybe your feelings for me had...had changed." She took deep breaths as she spoke, as if she was trying to hold it all in.

Ben gently placed his hands on her shoulders and turned her around to face him. "My feelings haven't changed." He tried to look into her eyes but she kept her head down.

"It's okay. Don't worry about it," she shook her head and sighed. She stared intently at the ground below, as if trying to suck the tears back into her eyes. "We...we can forget this ever happened."

"No, Gracie, it's not that. You...you don't understand!" Ben shook his head and stepped away from her, now trying to get as much distance between them as possible. "My feelings have never changed. I...I love you. I've always loved you. But I'm your Guardian. I'm not the Chosen One. I'm not supposed to love you!" His words came out like bullets from a machine gun.

Grace looked up at him, her eyes wide with tears pouring down her face. "You...you love me?"

Ben's eyes locked onto hers. "Yes."

"You love me," Grace exhaled as the words slowly sunk in.

"Yes, sweetie, but there is nothing I can do about it so forget I ever said anything." Ben's chest felt tight. It hurt.

"I don't understand. What do you mean there is nothing you can do about it?" Grace spoke slowly as if she were speaking a new language for the first time. "Why? Why can't you love me?"

"I told you. I'm not the Chosen One." Ben's chest tightened even more as if all the air had been sucked out of the clearing. He could not even smell the lilacs now.

"What are you talking about? What's a Chosen One?" It was obvious that Grace's mood was swinging in the wrong direction again and that she didn't care. She seemed tired of not understanding.

Ben tried to take a deep breath but he couldn't find any air. "It's a *who.*"

"What?"

"The Chosen One. He's a *who* not a *what.* The Chosen One is who the Council has picked to marry you…to have children with so you can continue the Powers. It's who you're supposed to be with and it's *not* me."

Grace paled and clutched her stomach with both arms. "Marry? Who…who is it?"

Ben looked away, trying to catch his breath. All the air was finally gone and his chest was paralyzed with pain. Where did all the air go?

"Ben? I said who is it?" Grace's voice escalated but her arms remained clenched around her waist.

"Tom!" Ben spurted out with what felt like his last breath, his eyes flipping back and boring into Grace in that same instance. "Your Chosen One is Tom!" he yelled.

Grace slumped, almost doubling over. She looked around the clearing but her eyes did not focus. For a moment, Ben thought she was going to pass out, but then her glassy eyes bored into him.

"But what if I…? I mean, Tom's nice and all…but I…I don't want Tom. I want *you*! I love *you*!"

Ben shook his head. "It doesn't matter what you want. It doesn't matter what I want. And love has nothing to do with any of this. You're the last of your family…of *the* Family. If you and Tom don't…get together, then that's it. No more Powers, no more Council, no more anything."

Grace bent over more, still clutching her stomach. Her breaths were rapid and erratic. "All a lie," she panted. "Whole life a lie." Her breath was shallow now. "A stupid waste of a lie. Just part of some stupid secret arranged marriage for some stupid secret world I don't care anything about." She straightened up and started to stumble around the clearing. "Take me back. I want to go back home. I need to get out of here!" Grace frantically looked around for a way out of the clearing but all she could see were the blasted lilacs blurring in a circle.

Ben was still shaking his head. "Grace, you know I can't do that. The Anti-Powers, they'll—"

"Okay! Okay! Then just take me to Dave's. And then…and then you just leave me alone!"

In an instant, Ben and Grace were standing on Dave's front porch. Grace burst through the cabin's screen door, purposefully smashing it back into Ben's face. She marched straight back to the guest room and slammed the bedroom door without a word to her hosts who were seated on one of the overstuffed couches in the living room.

"You told her about Tom," said Dave. It was a statement, not a question.

"I had to." Ben stood at the fireplace with his back to his hosts, looking out the window.

"You did the right thing," Petra nodded her head.

"I know," Ben sighed. He continued to stare out the window. Dark clouds hovered outside as if tied to Grace's mood. "Looks like rain."

"Yeah, Petra saw it earlier. We've already rescheduled the ballgame to tomorrow."

"Good," Ben sighed. "Maybe she won't be mad at me by then."

Dave shook his head. "I wouldn't count on that, son."

Chapter Nineteen: The Ball Game

Cooper watched a rarely seen Mercedes pull up to the gas pump and instantly knew its occupants were not locals. The driver and passenger exited the silver car but neither went over to the pump for gas. Instead, they both crossed the gravel parking lot and headed directly toward the store. They walked in synchronized strides that reminded Cooper of a German soldier's goosestep, not so much in the way they marched, but more so in the smooth evenness of their step. The older, more brutish driver held the store's front door open for the passenger who was leaner but no less muscular in form.

"Coop, my man!" The passenger's fake smile reminded Cooper of a used car salesman who had not yet made this month's sales quota.

"Yeah? Can I hep ya?" Cooper's old memory failed him every now and then so he had learned to feign recognition with his customers until it was sufficiently jogged by subsequent conversation.

"Well, sir, we certainly hope so," the brutish driver grinned.

There was something about the driver's emerald eyes that made Cooper uneasy. He stood behind the checkout counter and instinctively placed his hand on the cash register.

"We're not here to rob you, old man," the driver laughed.

"Well, it don't look like yer here fer gas," Cooper half-grinned, pointing to the gas pump outside.

"No. No, you're right about that. You see, we need some directions," the passenger said as he leaned over the counter.

Cooper's uneasiness had moved into the outright uncomfortable range and his hands started shaking behind his back. "Whar… whar ya' goin'?"

The passenger grinned and stared deep into Cooper's eyes. "To the Misfit community," he said matter-of-factly.

Cooper's heart pounded and his eyes instinctively darted to the front door.

"Andrew, he thinks he can make a run for it. Isn't that funny?" the passenger laughed.

Andrew moved to stand in the middle of the doorway. He crossed his arms over his chest, his broad shoulders touching each side of the doorframe. "Yeah. Funny."

"Now, Cooper," the passenger continued, his eyes boring into the old man, "I know you know what I'm talking about and, as long as you cooperate, we'll all get along just fine. So, why don't you give me those directions? Now."

As those green eyes bored into him, Cooper began to feel strangely relaxed. His slumping back leaned against the wall behind him and his head wobbled on his neck like a golf ball balancing on a toothpick. "Yer an Anti-Power," he mumbled. "What're ya…what're ya doing to me?"

"Gregory, your power is too much for that old man," Andrew yelled to the passenger. "You're going to make him pass out! Get those directions first!"

"Oh calm down, he's fine," Gregory yelled back over his shoulder, his eyes never leaving Cooper's.

Even in his relaxed state, Cooper tried very hard not to think of the directional landmarks to the Misfit community. He did not know if either of these boys could read minds, but he did not want to take any chances.

"Old man, I'm waiting," Gregory's voice deepened. "And I don't have time to wait." Without taking his eyes off Cooper, Gregory's right arm extended straight out to the side and then swung around to stop right in front of Cooper's face. In the instant of that movement, a glass display case sitting on the corner of the counter shattered and a large, bone-handled hunting knife flew out of the rack. The levitating knife followed the motion of Gregory's arm until it stopped right at the base of Cooper's throat. The knife edged a little too close and nicked the old man's protruding Adam's apple. Blood slowly seeped from the wound and dripped down Cooper's scrawny neck. "Well?" Gregory raised his eyebrows.

"I…I don't know what yer talking 'bout," Cooper stammered. Beads of sweat started to form on his upper lip and forehead.

"Andrew," Gregory calmly called to his brother, his eyes still intent on Cooper's.

Andrew left the doorway and walked behind the counter. He grabbed Cooper's thin arms from behind his back and pulled them around to the counter, slapping the old man's palms down flat on the smooth surface in front of him.

"Maybe this will jog your memory," Gregory smiled. He raised his hand up and sliced it through the air directly in front of Cooper's face. With that movement, the levitating knife suddenly pushed off Cooper's throat and slammed down across his right hand, swiftly and simultaneously chopping off four fingers.

"Aaww!" Cooper screamed, bile rising into his throat from the pain.

This process slowly continued for the next few hours and, for the first time in his long, quiet life, Cooper gave directions to the Misfit Community, one landmark at a time. One landmark for each body part lost until the old man had no more body parts to lose.

• • •

Grace slept for fifteen hours that night and still did not want to get out of bed the next day. She was embarrassed to have silently stormed through the house in front of her hosts the night before but her embarrassment was outweighed by the anger she still felt toward Ben. All the secrets he had kept from her, all the lies he had told her, and he had still let her try to kiss him in the middle of that stupid clearing. That stupid, lilac-filled clearing where he let her lips touch him, where he let her arms wrap around him, where he let her love him.

Again.

Grace pulled the covers over her head and decided she was never going to leave that bed.

"Knock, knock." Petra's singsong voice sailed through the air as she cracked the door and peeked her head through. "Your Majesty? Are you up?"

Grace hesitated, as if her silence would make her invisible. But then she remembered Petra's sporadic visions of the future and Dave's occasional views of the past and realized that she could not make herself invisible. Not here. Not anywhere. Ever again.

"Yes, Petra, I'm up," Grace said, slowly sitting up in the bed.

"Did you sleep well?" Petra asked as she reached over the bed to open the only window's curtains.

"Where's Ben?" asked Grace, ignoring Petra's stupid question. Of course, she didn't sleep well.

"He and Dave have already headed to the ball field. You've slept almost until game time!"

"Couldn't I just skip the game? No offense but I'm not really in the mood for…for all that Powers stuff today."

Petra stood a little straighter at the end of the bed. "Miss Grace, I understand if you feel a little overwhelmed right now. Ben's mother felt the same way the first time she visited us. But, honestly dear, Ben instructed me to bring you to the ball game and…well…he is your Guardian and all…and…well…I kind of have to do what he says right now. Even if you are who you are."

Petra tried to smile when she spoke as if that would make the words easier for Grace to swallow.

"You know I'm getting a little tired of all these rules," Grace sighed, more to herself than to Petra, as she got out of bed.

Petra was already heading out the door when she stopped and turned around. Her eyes were stern when she said, "Yes, dear. But all these rules are keeping you alive." Petra then softly closed the door behind her and left Grace alone with her thoughts.

Grace's face developed a permanent scowl as she got dressed and she could not find any incentive for it to go away that day. Not in breakfast, not in Petra's lyrical voice, not even in the scenic walk she and Petra took to the ball field after breakfast.

"Sun's out." Petra interrupted Grace's foul mood. "Lofty will be playing his best today. Should be a fun game to watch."

"Lofty? Oh, yeah. That flying guy," Grace mumbled. Yesterday's rain had erased the dust from the road so Grace cleanly shuffled her feet a little when she walked. She was in no hurry to see the game. Or Ben.

"You know he can't help what he is, Your Highness."

"What?" Grace wished Petra's visions were working. Her hostess could have seen that she was in no mood to talk right now.

"Ben. He did not choose to be your Guardian any more than Tom chose to be the Chosen One."

"He's my best friend. He should have told me about Tom."

"Yes, he's your best friend and he would have told you if he could. But he has to live by the Council's code, remember? If telling a human about the Powers could be punishable by death, can you imagine what's going to happen now that he's told you about Tom? About who you *really* are?" Petra paused and gathered her thoughts before she calmly continued. "Please don't think me disrespectful, Your Highness, but you don't seem to appreciate how much trouble he's in with the Council for telling you everything he has. Between the Council and the Anti-Powers, that poor guy really is getting it from all sides."

Grace had no response. Her fingers started tingling again so she just shoved her hands in her pockets.

But now, luckily, Petra had seen just enough into the future to know that she should not interrupt Grace's thoughts for the remainder of their walk.

The ball field turned out to be a perfectly maintained, half-size football field. It was located in a large clearing that sat about a mile from the main road at the end of a long, winding dirt path. Trees surrounded the clearing and sitting at one end of the field were two sets of makeshift bleachers, again made from the forest's discarded branches. The bleachers were crowded with elderly Misfits, unable or unwilling to play in today's big game, so Ben's dark wavy hair stood out from the top row like a spot on an albino Dalmatian. He sat next to Vector, who waved furiously at Grace and Petra.

"Miss Grace! Petra!" the old man called. "Over here." He motioned for them with a wave of his feeble arm.

With Vector's yell, every white-haired Misfit on the bleachers turned to look at Grace and, with all eyes on her, she had no choice but to duck her head and join Vector where he sat. Right next to Ben.

"Hello, Your Highness! Welcome to your first Powers game," Vector excitedly said, struggling to scoot over so Grace could sit next to Ben.

Instead, Grace purposefully crossed over in front of Ben to sit on the other side of Vector. Petra followed and took her seat on the other side of Grace.

"I thought you weren't coming to the game?" Petra leaned over to ask Vector.

"I wasn't. I was going to work Marshall's shift so he could play for the Mentals but he hasn't returned from meeting the Triplets yet. It's too nice of a day to be inside and, since Numbers is doing inventory, he offered to watch the computers for me so I could still come to the game."

Ben's ears perked up. "Did Marshall get the report on that stuff going on outside the fourth quadrant?"

"I assume that's what he's doing now. You know, he's kind of sweet on that Triplet Carrie so he is probably out there trying to flirt with her as we speak. With her blonde ringlets and rosy complexion, he may even forget to come back and bring me the report altogether!" laughed Vector.

Ben shot a glance at Grace who seemed oblivious to the conversation.

"There's Dave," Petra said to Grace, pointing to the large man standing in the end zone. "Dave's a natural referee with his powers. Kind of like our own special brand of instant replay when they're working right." Petra proudly beamed.

Grace just nodded at Petra. She really was not in the mood for this.

"Play ball!" Dave shouted and the crowd clapped the teams onto the field. All but two of the players spread out and faced each other in two parallel lines that stretched from one end zone to the other.

"The Mentals are batting first," Vector proudly waved to the team on the left as if Grace knew what was going on. "That's my team."

Grace followed Vector's point and watched the first player saunter up to the goal post. He was swinging a large bat but held it more like a tennis racquet than a baseball bat. "Wait. Is this football or baseball or tennis?" she asked no one in particular.

"It's a combination of all those sports with a little basketball and soccer thrown in as well," Petra said. "With Powers, none of those sports are really challenging by themselves, so a while back the Powers kind of combined them all into one."

Grace still looked confused. Sports had never been her strong suit so everything about this game was over her head.

"It's easy," Petra continued. "All you need to remember is that the object of the game is to move the ball up and down the field five times before getting it into the goal on the far side of the field over there." Petra pointed to a basketball goal that stood forty feet high in the opposite end zone. "There are outs just like in baseball, but you can only get them if someone on the opposite team catches the ball right after the batter bats. After that, you can pretty much do what you want with the ball and the rest of the game is more like soccer or football. The players just try to move the ball up and down the field the fastest way they possibly can. The players can use any powers they have as long as no one gets injured. If a player gets injured, the other team automatically gets two points. We don't want anyone getting too zealous with their powers and forget we're all friends here."

The Physicals team pitcher stood in the opposite end zone under the basketball goal and was tossing a ball that looked to be a little larger than a baseball in size but was neon orange in color. Had it not been so brightly colored, Grace doubted she could have seen it so far away. At the sound of Dave's whistle, the pitcher wound up and threw the ball so fast, Grace didn't even see it. "Where'd the ball go?" she asked no one in particular.

"There," Petra pointed to the ball that had stopped in mid-air and now hung suspended over the middle of the closest end zone and directly in front of the batter who was grinning at the pitcher with a sportsman's taunt. The batter swung his bat at the levitating ball, causing it to fly out to the field beyond.

Seeing the speed with which the Physicals players were gunning for the ball, Grace stated to no one in particular, "He's out."

"Not so fast, Your Highness," Vector grinned.

Just before the ball landed in the opposing team's hands, it weaved, mid-air, and started flying in another direction. Grace's eyes flew open at yet another violation of the laws of physics before she glanced down at the batter who had dropped the bat and was now charging down the field and apparently yelling at the ball.

"Is he doing that?" Grace asked, pointing to the ball jerking from one player to the next, never landing in anyone's hands.

"Yes," laughed Petra. "Hilarious, isn't it?"

"Yes," chuckled Grace. She had to admit the game was more enjoyable than she had expected.

The batter continued to yell at the ball while the Physicals team raced from side to side trying to catch the ball that weaved back and forth in mid-air. Even Lofty, who quickly flew from one side of the field to the other in the bright sunshine, could not catch up to the zigzagging ball. After the ball had flown over the field five times, it raced back to the opposite end zone and swooshed through the basket perched high atop the goal. As soon as the scoreboard reflected the Mentals point, the batter waved his hand and the ball dropped instantly to the ground at the base of the basketball goal. The crowd cheered and Grace assumed most of the gray-haired fans in the bleachers were Mentals fans.

Vector leaned over to Ben. "We may beat you Physicals again today, my boy," he chuckled.

Ben laughed, "Not if I can help it." He stood up and yelled to Dave, "Hey Ref! Can I get in on this?"

Dave smiled and looked over at the coach for the Mentals. The coach cocked his head for a moment and then waved Ben in, grinning, "Bring it on, Benjamin!"

The team members sitting on the Physicals bench cheered when Ben jogged out onto the field. The other Physicals fielders clapped and waved Ben out almost to the edge of the field before he stopped and turned around. He bent down into a catching stance, even though he had no mitt.

Even at that distance, Grace thought she could still see the blue in his eyes.

"This ought to be good," Petra said, nodding toward the field.

The next batter stepped up and again stopped the ball mid-air before taking a hard swing. The ball flew into the air, but this time, Ben was faster. Before the batter could maneuver the ball between the fielders, Ben jumped twenty feet into the air and caught the ball in his bare hands. He landed in the field, his two feet firmly planted, and held the ball up high over his head with one hand. The crowd let out a collective disgruntled sigh as Dave yelled, "Out!"

And so it went with the next two batters until the inning was over and the Physicals came to bat. Ben was the fourth batter for the Physicals team and, although he tried to hold back, he hit the ball so hard it disappeared into the trees beyond the clearing.

"That's an automatic score. I certainly hope we have enough balls to finish the game," Dave smarted to Ben when he ran into the end zone.

Ben laughed as he headed back to the Physicals bench. On his way, he glanced up at Grace who actually returned his smile for the first time today. She appeared to be enjoying herself and Ben hoped the game was erasing the edge she had developed yesterday.

"He's a cute one, that Ben. Isn't he?" Petra asked Grace when she saw their quick exchange of smiles.

"Yeah," Grace whispered sheepishly.

Still looking straight ahead at the field, Petra continued, "You know Grace, I can't see everything in the future, but what I can see is not always set in stone. Sometimes things change. Sometimes for the better."

Grace did not reply but kept her eyes on the Physicals team bench. And Ben.

The game progressed with each team taking turns being in the lead. Finally, with Ben's help, the Physicals team won, much to the dismay of the elder fans in the bleachers.

"Better luck next time, Vector," Dave shook the old man's hand after helping him exit the bleachers at the end of the game. "It was about time the Physicals had a fighting chance against us Mentals."

Vector laughed, "Yes, I guess you're right about that. And I did enjoy seeing young Benjamin in action. Reminded me of his father." Vector turned to Grace and bowed as much as his stooped back would let him. "It was a pleasure experiencing your first game with you, my lady, and I look forward to seeing you tonight." Without waiting for a response, Vector hobbled out of the clearing toward his shop.

Grace turned to Petra. "What's going on tonight?"

"Oh, just a little get together at our community center. Nothing special. We have them at the end of each week," Petra smiled. Seeing Grace glance down at her blue jeans, she added, "Don't worry, Your Majesty. We'll find something for you to wear. Come on. Let's go home and freshen up." Petra pulled Grace toward the path, leaving Dave at the bottom of the bleachers and Ben on the sidelines.

As soon as Petra and Grace were out of sight, Ben darted over to Dave. "Can you see if she's still mad?" he asked.

"It's not real clear, but the way she was smiling and all, she might have cooled down a little," Dave said without looking at Ben.

"I sure hope so," Ben sighed as he headed down the dirt path. He walked slower than usual and Dave had to work at curtailing his own long stride to maintain his pace alongside Ben.

Neither said much at first but Dave's thoughts finally got the best of him.

"I know you love her, son," Dave said, still staring at the path in front of him.

Ben let out a deep breath. "I know you know. You weren't exactly subtle the other night."

"So what are you going to do about it?"

"Not much I can do. I'm just her Guardian. Tom's the Chosen One, remember?"

"Does your brother know how you feel?"

"He might have suspected it a while back, but probably not now," Ben said hopefully. "I mean…I've told him over and over again…I know my job. I'm her Guardian."

"How does Tom feel about Grace?"

"I don't know. We never really discussed it."

"Huh," Dave grunted.

"What do you mean 'huh'?"

"Nothing. Just can't believe you all never discussed it."

Dave noticed that Ben's pace quickened slightly just then. Nothing was said for the next few strides as Dave now reworked the speed of his steps to keep up with Ben.

"Did I ever tell you how Petra and I met?" Dave asked once his steps were back in pace with Ben's.

"No."

"Do you remember Studio 54 in New York?"

"It was kind of before my time, old man. Way before my time. But I know what you're talking about." Ben sounded like he was quickly losing interest in Dave's conversation.

"Man, that was *the* place to be when I was younger. Your father and I practically lived there. We were so socially naïve back then, we actually thought we could dance," Dave chuckled. "If you were a Power secretly looking for other Powers, that's where you'd go. It was an absolute blast."

"Good to know." Ben rolled his eyes.

"Yep. It truly was a blast," Dave continued to reminisce, ignoring Ben's tone. "And then one night we walked in and there she was. You couldn't miss her. Petra was all decked out in this tight, silver metallic jumpsuit from head to toe. She was so shiny she reflected every light in the room. I don't know what sparkled more, the huge Studio 54 disco ball or Petra. She was perfectly beautiful. And the minute your dad and I walked in, do you know what she did? She came right up to me and said she'd been waiting for me. Over everyone else in the room, that gorgeous stranger was waiting for *me*! I couldn't believe it," Dave laughed, shaking his head.

"Why are you telling me this?" Ben asked.

Dave continued to ignore Ben. "You see Petra had seen the future. She knew she was supposed to be with me. But instead of waiting for it to happen, she made it happen. Kind of sped up the process, so to speak. She didn't wait for the future to come to her. She met up with her future on her own schedule."

"So?"

"So, it just goes to show that the future is not always concrete, son. Sometimes you have to make your own."

Without another word, Ben instantly disappeared. He sped down the path and away from Dave, leaving nothing but a little dust to evidence he had been there.

Dave smiled to himself. "Yep, sometimes you have to make your own."

Chapter Twenty: The Dance

The butterfly's large frozen wings spread wide across the cabin's front porch railing, splayed out as if encased in an entomologist's shadow box. Despite the insect's evident lack of life, Grace was envious of its stillness, its vibrant colors now forever motionless perched atop the wooden rail. Death had not touched the beauty of the butterfly's wings, only its mashed and crooked body revealed its now-determined fate. Grace stared at the wings, hypnotized by their quiet waves of delicate color. Without thinking, but with an unrecognized need, she reached out to caress one of the large wings, to feel its fragile softness. Her tingling fingers had barely touched the velvety wing when it suddenly began to move. Grace quickly pulled her hand back, afraid that her closeness would ruin the moment. She held her breath as she watched the wing slowly move up and down, up and down. The other wing joined in the dance and, within seconds, the previously lifeless butterfly was standing, stretching and pumping its wings to the rhythmic beat of Grace's heart, its crooked body now straight and lean and ready for takeoff. The butterfly's wings worked furiously now, it's vivid colors now indistinguishable with the wings' speed and, before Grace knew what was happening, the butterfly floated off the railing and flitted into the dense forest surrounding Dave's cabin. Grace watched the resurrected butterfly disappear into the trees' green leaves and assumed that, perhaps, death worked differently in the Misfit community.

She thought of the butterfly's brilliant colors as she looked down at the simple black dress Petra had chosen for her for the evening's festivities. It was short, fun, and nothing like what she would normally wear. She tugged at the top of the dress, trying to close up the deep V-neck bodice that barely covered her full beasts. It was the kind of dress Ben would have teased her about if he had seen her in it, but given that she had not seen Ben since the ball game that afternoon, and that Dave and Petra were just as clueless regarding his whereabouts, Grace had been unable to get his opinion of her attire before she left Dave's cabin for the evening.

"You look beautiful, Your Highness," Petra said, exiting the cabin's screen door. She wrapped her arm around Grace's waist and the two ladies stood together on the front porch waiting for Dave who, as usual, was running late, unable to find his belt for the party. Twilight was pushing aside the day and the forest surrounding the cabin would soon be darkening. Petra left Grace's side and lit a lantern to guide them through the woods.

"Thanks," Grace smiled. "But are you sure this dress isn't a little too tight?" She looked down at the little black dress that was discreet by normal standards. However, in Grace's self-conscious mind, all she could see were the tops of her breasts trying to hide below the low-cut neckline.

Petra patted Grace's hand. "Your Majesty, that dress was practically made for you. I've already seen that you will be the most beautiful girl there tonight."

Dave burst out the cabin door, still putting his belt on. "Come on, ladies. If we don't go now, we'll miss dinner and I'm starving." He grabbed the lantern out of Petra's hand and then pulled her down the cabin steps in a rush.

Grace followed the couple down the almost dark path through the woods but before they reached the main road, they turned onto a new path that veered to the right and up another hill. At the top of the small hill sat the largest cabin in the Misfit community. It had a wraparound porch and steep roofline, and the sign stretching across the front entrance indicated it was the community center. Strings of white lights outlined the roof, porch banisters and stairs, and the smell of barbeque filling the outside air combined with the tiny, twinkling lights to make it feel like Christmas in July. People overflowed from the porch and stairs and Dave had to fight his way through the crowd to get to the building's entrance.

"I thought you said this was just a little get together," Grace whispered in Petra's ear as they climbed the front steps. Everyone they passed stared at Grace as if she were a rarely seen masterpiece painting from some traveling art exhibit.

"Well, that's what this was supposed to be, a little barbeque after the game, but I guess Your Majesty's presence has brought out the gawkers too," Petra whispered back, holding onto Grace's hand a little tighter as they reached the top step.

The trio entered the community center whose interior looked like King Arthur's banquet hall had mated with a seventies discotheque. The expansive room was beautifully decorated with ancient tapestries and oil paintings covering the log walls. Large rustic, round, wooden tables with heavy matching chairs scattered the room's edges, but it was the center of the room that caught Grace's immediate attention. The tables bordered an open dance floor in the middle of the room and the largest disco ball she had ever seen twirled from the wood-beamed cathedral ceiling above, catching and reflecting the glittering lights of the candles on the tables below. The smell of vanilla filled the room and, despite the hall's enormous size, an air of comfortableness fell over Grace, as she stood in between Dave and Petra in the massive doorway.

"Pretty cool room, isn't it?" Dave leaned over and nudged Grace. "But try not to spill anything on the tapestries or touch the paintings. Originals are hard to replace, you know," he whispered matter-of-factly in her ear.

The painting hanging nearest to Grace beside the door looked familiar to her and she tried to recall what little she remembered from her high school art history class. "Wait…is that what I think it is?" she asked, squinting her eyes to take a closer look at the picture.

"Yes," Petra replied. "Vermeer's *Milkmaid*. The original. The Rijksmuseum in Amsterdam thinks it has the original, but it's just a really, really, really good copy."

"Was he a Power?"

"How else do you think we would have the original?" Dave laughed. "Of course he was a Power. He was one of the lucky ones who got to practice his powers out in the open. Before all that Salem murder mess. But forget those stupid old paintings." Dave pulled Grace away from the doorway, toward the center of the room and pointed to the ceiling. "Check out the disco ball. Isn't that a beaut?"

Grace had to admit the ball was better than any disco ball she had seen, but she was now really more interested in the various paintings hung haphazardly and unprotected around the room.

"Came from Studio 54 where Petra and I met," Dave continued, still looking up at the large spinning ball.

"Oh, Dave," Petra said. "Can't you see Grace is not as enamored with that blasted ball as you are? Go get yourself some food and leave Her Majesty in peace for a moment."

Dave pulled Petra to him and kissed her cheek. "Sorry. I just get so excited thinking about you in all that silver," he laughed before heading back out the door.

Looking around the room, Grace spotted a few of the Misfits she had met the other night. But no Ben.

"Ben's not here yet. But I saw that he will be very soon," Petra smiled knowingly. "Come on. I see Rebecca over there."

Petra took Grace's hand and guided her to one of the large round tables near the dance floor. The table was full of women but

Rebecca was the only face familiar to Grace. The shape shifter was just as beautiful as Grace had remembered and she actually stood and curtsied when Grace approached.

"Welcome, Your Majesty," Rebecca said. "Would you like to join us?"

Grace sat down next to Rebecca and was quickly introduced around the table. On the other side of Rebecca was her younger sister, Sarah, who was empowered with the ability to imitate other people's voices. She, too, had short spiky hair but she had dyed hers brilliant neon blue, as if she was trying to become more parrot-like in her appearance in order to match her power. Directly across from Grace and beside Sarah sat a short, fat older woman named Birch who, despite her looks, could stretch, twist, and turn her arms, legs, and torso to inhuman lengths.

"Such a great pleasure to meet you, Your Highness," Birch smiled as she reached her elastic arm out and over the table's four foot diameter to shake Grace's hand.

"You too," Grace smiled. She hesitantly took Birch's hand, which, despite the rubbery look of her extended arm, revealed quite a firm handshake.

"So what do you think of our little community?" Sarah asked.

"It's lovely," Grace replied.

"Oh, tell us the truth, honey," Birch laughed. "I know you are freaking out over all our little eccentricities, as I like to call them. Shoot, we're a bunch of weirdoes even in the Powers world!"

"Birch has lived here longer than almost anyone else here," Petra leaned over to Grace. "She was one of the founders of the Misfit community."

"Oh, Petra," Birch smirked and rolled her eyes. She looked over at Grace. "What she's really saying is that I'm as old as the hills. Or in our case, our mountain itself. But I still get a kick out of meeting first-time visitors here and seeing their reactions. So, tell us. What do you really think about this place, Your Highness?"

Grace thought for a moment. "Honestly, it is a little overwhelming. I mean, just last week, I was some silly waitress trying to figure out what to do with my life—"

"And now," Birch interrupted, "now you are smack dab in the middle of some stupid battle for control between the Powers and Anti-Powers. But don't you worry, honey. You're safe here with us. The Council may not see us fit to be Guardians in the outside world but surely with all of us here we can protect one little human. Statistically, the odds are in our favor."

"Great." Grace half-smiled. Fantastic. Now she was a statistic.

"Rebecca, is DJ coming?" Petra asked, steering the subject away from Grace's pending doom.

"Already here." Rebecca pointed to the far back right corner of the room.

There, behind an elaborate sound system, DJ was preparing to live up to his name. As if he heard the ladies talking, the tall, slender man with a ponytail looked up and winked at Rebecca just as the lights softened and an old Bee Gees ballad flowed from his surround sound. The disco ball twirled slower to the ballad's beat and the room was instantly transformed into an imitation Studio 54.

"That's their song," Sarah turned to Grace and pointed to Rebecca. "DJ always plays it first. That's how we know when the party is *really* getting started."

Rebecca's blush was so deep that, even in the room's soft light, she could not hide her flushed cheeks.

"Oh, to be young and in love," Birch sighed to Rebecca. "I remember those days."

"Yeah, me too," Sarah spitted sarcastically.

"What are you talking about? You're still young!" Birch laughed.

"She's just not in love." Petra then looked over at Grace. "At least not now. Sarah and her boyfriend just broke up so she is a little jaded right now."

"She caught her boyfriend Elton cheating on her with Star," Rebecca said, placing her arm around her sister's shoulders and giving her a squeeze. "But there are other fish in the sea, sis. We'll find you someone else!"

"Well you better hurry and find that someone before I lose my mind and try to kill Star. She is such a slut!" Sarah half-joked through gritted teeth.

"Star kind of…gets around," Petra informed Grace.

"And speak of the devil," said Birch, pointing to the far left corner directly opposite DJ's sound system.

Grace turned around but all she could see in that dark corner was a soft yellow glow. She squinted a little and in the middle of the glow she could now see a young woman's back with long blonde hair cascading down like silk. If she had not known better, Grace thought she could have been looking at Annie.

"Star always gets who she wants," Sarah scoffed. "If she sets her eye on someone, consider them off the market."

Yep, thought Grace. *Sounds exactly like Annie.*

"Who's she talking to?" Petra asked, straining to see through the glow.

"Whoever it is, she has them absolutely cornered," Birch said, stretching her elastic neck in an attempt to see around the glow.

"I feel sorry for whoever it is," Rebecca shook her head and laughed. "They don't stand a chance now."

The five women spent the next few minutes trying to unsuccessfully determine Star's victim for the evening without being too obvious. Grace really didn't care about Star or her sexual conquests but it seemed important to her table partners, so she feigned interest until Star shifted her stance slightly to the left. At that point, Grace murmured, "Oh" and quickly turned around to face the table again.

Because in the instant that Star shifted, Grace's heart sank.

Standing in the corner, shrouded by Star's glow, was Ben. He was laughing and animated and talking to Star as if she was the center of the universe. Grace had seen him like this before. Ben was in flirt mode.

The other ladies at the table were silent until Petra spoke up, "Now, Your Highness, I'm sure it's nothing. You know Ben. He's probably just being polite."

"Of course, dear. He's just being a gentleman," Birch chimed in.

"Besides, he's your Guardian. He can't do anything with her while he's on duty," Sarah said.

Grace's eyes widened at Sarah's bold, blunt statement and then darted to Petra.

"It's near the front door, to the left," Petra replied to Grace's unspoken question.

"How did you—" Grace started before she realized that Petra had foreseen her in the bathroom. Grace stood up without another word and tried to discreetly make her way to the ladies room before her waterworks started again.

"I'm confused," Rebecca said. "I thought Tom was the Chosen One. Am I missing something?"

"Oh good gosh, sister!" Sarah knowingly smiled. "Love truly has made you blind. Tom may be the Chosen One, but he's not the one that Grace would have chosen!"

While Sarah and Birch tried to get Rebecca up to speed, Petra searched the room for Dave. She found him at the front near the food table, of course.

"Did you see?" she asked him.

"I saw," he replied still going through the food line. "Did you see anything?"

"No. I tried but their future is still too hazy." Petra paused expectantly. "Well? What are you going to do about it?"

"About what?"

Petra punched Dave's arm and almost caused him to drop his full plate of food. "About Star and Ben, you idiot!"

"Oww! Watch it! What do you want me to do?" Dave replied, rubbing his arm. His wife still had a mean punch in her when she wanted to.

"Go talk to Ben and fix it now. That boy has enough on him as Grace's Guardian without Star trying to get into his head."

"Or his pants," laughed Dave.

"Not funny. Go fix it now!" Petra fumed before she turned and stormed back to her table.

"Oh for Pete's sake," Dave said to himself, shaking his head and scanning the room for Ben. He spotted Star's unmistakable glow in the dark corner and assumed the dark wavy hair towering over the glow belonged to Ben. He headed to the corner, placing his plate on a nearby table.

"Good evening, Star," he said as he approached her from behind. "Do you mind if I borrow Ben for a moment?"

Star turned and smiled seductively at Dave, "Of course, dear Dave. It's time I freshen up a little anyway." She smiled at Ben and touched his hand before walking straight through the middle of the dance floor, her glow becoming true to her name as it reflected off the large disco ball and caused a million dancing lights to suddenly bounce around the room. She was her own one-woman galaxy and an obvious professional when it came to capturing attention.

"What are you doing?" Dave confronted Ben as soon as Star was out of earshot.

"What do you mean?"

"I mean, what are you doing flirting with Star? You are supposed to be Grace's Guardian. You're on duty, young man."

Ben stood straighter, his eyes scanning the room. "Why? Is Grace okay? Did something happen?"

"No, you idiot! Grace is fine. She's hanging out with Petra and Rebecca and a bunch of ladies back there. But you didn't answer my question. Why all the flirting?"

"I'm not flirting." Ben laughed incredulously.

"You're not?"

"No. Of course not. Star and I are just talking about old times. We used to play together as kids. Remember?"

Dave rolled his eyes at Ben's naiveté. "Get over here," he said, yanking Ben's arm toward the table where Dave's plate of food was waiting. "Sit down."

Ben did as he was directed.

Dave sat down opposite him and leaned in, his face inches away from Ben's. "Son, I had hoped that by leaving you alone all day you would have had this figured out by now."

"Had what figured out?" Ben felt like he was being scolded but had no clue what he did wrong.

"The whole Grace thing, that's what."

"I have no idea what you're talking about." Ben pretended to study the closest wall tapestry he could find.

"Now, I know you're smarter than that. And I know you know I'm smarter than that. So stop pretending to be stupid and let's get to the point. What did you decide to do about Grace?"

"There is nothing to decide, Dave, remember? I'm her Guardian, end of story."

"So." Dave raised his eyebrows.

"So?" Ben shook his head.

"So, I can't believe you're this dense! I saw the past. I know you love her and she loves you. Petra has tried, but your future is not as easily seen. But despite all that, we still have the present. You two are here, in the safest place in the world for Grace, where you don't have to be on guard one hundred percent of the time, where you all can take the time you want to be yourselves, to love each other."

"But Tom—"

"Forget Tom. He's not here right now. You are! Take this time to be with her because it will probably be the only time you ever get. Who knows what will happen when you leave this place? But the least you can do is leave this place with no regrets!"

Ben sat frozen. As scary as it seemed, Dave actually made sense right now. He looked at Dave and whispered, "You're right. What am I doing? I've already broken every Council law out there. What's one more? I may never get another chance like this." Ben was now musing more to himself than Dave.

"So fix it. Now," Dave sternly said, repeating Petra's earlier instructions.

Ben left Dave shoveling the now-cold food into his mouth and headed to talk to DJ just as Grace exited the bathroom.

She had taken enough time to compose herself so that her reddened eyes had turned back to their original blue. They were not sparkling yet but at least they no longer revealed the sadness that had engulfed her earlier.

"Better?" Petra asked as Grace sat down beside her.

"I will be." Grace half-smiled.

"Rebecca, why don't you get DJ to play something fast?" Birch asked. "You know, maybe one of those old disco songs that gets everybody on the dance floor?"

Rebecca, now tuned into Grace's emotional state, smiled at her sympathetically and said, "Sure."

But just as Rebecca started to stand, a familiar beat floated from the sound system, causing Grace to suddenly grab Rebecca's arm and yank her back down into her seat.

"What?" the shape shifter gasped at Grace.

"Shhh!" Grace replied, her hand still clutching Rebecca's arm.

The entire table froze at Grace's command.

The familiar beat grew louder and soon Grace heard Peter Gabriel's voice join in with the rhythm. The singer belted out the chorus of "In Your Eyes" just as Grace slowly turned. There, walking through the middle of the dance floor, staring directly and purposefully at her, was Ben.

"You know, you never did get your birthday dance." He held out his hand and smiled.

Grace's heart pounded as she placed her hand in his and followed him. He guided her to the middle of the dance floor and tenderly wrapped his arms around her, pulling her body tightly against him. Oblivious to the entire room watching her, Grace simply and silently stared up into Ben's eyes and allowed her body to be enveloped by his. She drowned in his blueness and for the longest time she was lost in his eyes.

"I love you," was all he finally said.

"But what about Tom?" she murmured, her eyes never leaving Ben's.

"I don't care. Right now, I don't care about anything but being here with you," Ben whispered. He leaned his head down until their foreheads touched and Grace could feel his sweet breath on her cheek. "Just be with me right now." His voice was soft. "It'll be just us. Just us for right now."

Grace nodded as Ben softly pulled her closer and deeper into his strong embrace. Her head rested against his chest and she could feel his heart beating with the rhythm of Peter Gabriel's drums. His arms surrounded her with a sweet and gentle peacefulness she had never known and Grace knew that everything she ever wanted was in that moment. Everything she ever wanted was in Ben's arms. In his eyes. In his warmth. In his tenderness. And when she closed her eyes, she couldn't see everyone in the room staring at her. Instead, all she saw were the twinkling lights of the disco ball. Even with her eyes closed.

Chapter Twenty-One: Expectations

He sat in his tent, head in his hands, choosing his words carefully. His team was assembled outside, waiting. Waiting to receive the day's instructions. Waiting to be inspired.

Waiting for him to prove himself. To them. To his brother. To his father.

This was it. All or nothing.

Andrew poked his head through the tent's front flap. "They're ready for you, brother."

Gregory looked up, still lost in his thoughts. "Why do you think Father stayed home? Why do you think he wanted us to do this alone?" he asked. The question seemed posed to himself as much as it was to Andrew.

Andrew immediately closed the tent flap behind him and whispered, "Shhh! What are you talking about?" He thought he heard a slight note of self-doubt in Gregory's tone but that was impossible given his younger brother's ego.

"Why do you think Father sent us on this mission without him? This is the most important thing the Anti-Powers have tried to accomplish in decades and he didn't want to be a part of it? Don't you think that's a little strange?"

Andrew shook his head. "But he *is* a part of it. He's back at the lab getting it ready and will come meet us at the cabin once we have the girl. Stop being so melodramatic and get out here. The troops are getting restless." Andrew left the tent in a huff. He didn't have time to deal with his brother's weirdness right now.

Ben's glaring blue eyes were burning a hole through Andrew's brain and the troops were not the only ones getting restless.

Gregory stood and took a deep breath, shaking off any lingering misgivings. He did know what he was doing. His father wouldn't have sent him on this mission if he didn't think he could complete it. All he had to do was capture one little human and take her to the cabin. Simple.

He exited the tent, broad shoulders squared and head held high. He smiled at Andrew and walked slowly to stand with his brother before twenty or so men and women who were assembled in a wooded clearing only a half mile away from the Misfit community entrance. Dressed in soldiers' camouflage, the team was anxious for battle. Gregory could tell by the look in their dark emerald eyes.

"Fellow Anti-Powers!" Gregory's voice boomed from his taut, muscular chest. "Our time has finally arrived. We have trained for this day. We have studied our opponents. We have memorized their maps. We know everything we need to know to conquer these supporters of peace. The Misfits are no match for our great powers. This, I am certain. We will capture the girl and we will complete our mission. Our success today will secure the Anti-Powers' rightful place in the future and we will no longer have to hide the immense powers we possess!"

"Anti-Powers! Anti-Powers!" the soldiers shouted in unison, thrusting their fists high into the air. Their adrenaline had been building for days and each was anxious to use their powers in combat.

"I could get used to this," Andrew whispered in Gregory's ear.

"All in good time, big bro. All in good time," Gregory smiled as he too thrust his fist in the air, egotistically joining in the soldiers' chant.

Out of the woods to their left, a solider appeared and approached Andrew with his head bowed. "Excuse me, prince?"

"Yes?" Andrew did not like being interrupted in the middle of their pep rally.

"My partner and I just returned from our scouting mission as Prince Gregory had instructed and we found something you should see." The scout kept his head bowed as if he knew he was bothering Andrew.

"Well? What is it?" Andrew's voice boomed at the scout. By now, the other soldiers had ceased their chants and, along with Gregory, directed their attention to the scout with the bowed head.

At Andrew's command, the scout waved to his partner behind him. The partner emerged from the woods leading a young man with wire-rimmed glasses and a young woman with tight, blonde ringlets and ruby red lips. Their eyes were midnight blue and full of fear.

"Well, well, well. What do we have here?" Gregory grinned as he crossed over to the couple.

"Misfits," the first scout stated proudly, sounding certain that his find would please the princes. "They were in a somewhat compromising position in a clearing about a half mile away. All lovey–dovey and sweet on each other. They didn't know we were there until we were standing right over them."

Andrew eyed the couple and marched in a circle around them, inspecting them with his trained eye. "What's their power?"

"The guy is some sort of Mental. He hasn't put up much of a fight," the second scout replied. "But the girl here, well, she's a wild one. She can turn invisible, but if you hit her here," the scout punched Carrie in the stomach, hard, "she becomes visible again."

Carrie doubled over in pain, her face crimson red, but her blue eyes never left Gregory's face. "My brothers will find you. All of you," she gritted through her teeth.

"Well, you see, you are wrong on that Miss Lovebird," Gregory hissed. "Because we already found them first."

• • •

Grace leaned back in the grass and took a deep breath. "I love that smell." She looked at the lilacs surrounding her, memorizing the placement of each flower's petal, each leaf, and each branch. The clearing created by Ben's mother was now her most favorite place in the entire world.

"And I love *you*," Ben leaned over her and smiled. His hand reached down and caressed her temple.

Correction. The clearing created by Ben's mother *with Ben lying beside her* was her most favorite place in the entire world.

"Why do you think she did this?" Grace asked without moving from beneath Ben's soft caress. She loved his warm touch and the gentle way he held her in his arms.

"I don't know. You were like part of her family. Like her daughter. I'm sure she missed you when we were all here so maybe this was her way of feeling close to you. Did she really have to have a reason other than she loved you?"

"No. I guess not," Grace softly smiled. She reached up to touch Ben's face, her fingers caressing his forehead before gently entwining in his dark, wavy hair. She wanted to pull his face down to hers, to quickly stretch her lips up to meet his before she could even close her eyes. The thought of having their first kiss, of the slowness of his lips moving with hers as their mouths embraced, left her body feeling like gelatin and her heart racing with anticipation. But this time she could not bring herself to make the first move. Her last attempt at their first kiss in the middle of these lilacs did not turn out as planned and Grace was afraid that any overt gestures on her part might ruin what was turning out to be a perfect day. So Grace had decided there would be no first kiss until Ben's need outweighed hers.

"You know, at some point we have to return to reality." Ben smiled down at her.

"I know," Grace sighed.

"Vector and Birch are pressuring me to deal with the Anti-Powers and get you back to the Council."

"I know."

"But I'm not ready to give you up yet." Ben's voice was almost a whisper now.

"I know. And I'm not ready to be given up either."

Ben leaned back on the grass beside her and stared up at the sky. He pulled her hand to his lips and softly kissed it. "Look, Gracie," he sighed. "I've thought about it and I don't think I'm too worried about the Anti-Powers now, but the Council…well, that's another story. I don't know what they'll do when we get back but I'm pretty sure I'm in a lot of trouble. And I'm most definitely sure you're still supposed to be with Tom."

Grace did not respond but turned her head to join Ben's gaze up to the sky. A breeze pushed the lilacs around her peripheral vision and their smell swirled around her head.

"So." Ben continued to stare up at the sky. "I've been thinking, whatever the Council decides to do, I'm just going to hang on to us. Like I said the other night…just us. Even if the Council won't let us be together, they still can't take away what we have right now, the way we feel. We have each other, together or apart. We have us and, I promise you, no one will ever love you like I do. No matter what happens, remember that, okay?"

A single tear escaped Grace's eye and she realized she had not breathed since Ben started his declaration. She slowly exhaled, afraid if she spoke more would join that single tear.

Ben turned on his side and leaned into her, his lips now inches away from hers. He wiped away her tear and smiled, "But do you know the one thing that would make us complete?"

Grace shook her head, forcing a smile.

"Our official first kiss." Ben smiled in return.

Grace's smile was no longer forced.

"You know, there's a lot of pressure on a first kiss." Ben's smile widened.

"Uh-huh," Grace nodded.

"So we really need to get this right, don't we?"

"Yeah."

"Cause, whatever happens, the memory of this kiss will need to keep us going even when we're apart."

"You've thought a lot about this, haven't you?" Grace could not stop smiling now.

"I've thought about this kiss for a very, very, very long time. So," Ben took a deep breath, "I believe there is no better place for such a momentous kiss than this clearing."

"And no better time than the present," Grace urged.

With Grace's implicit permission, Ben's arms wrapped around her and cradled her as if she were a fragile Faberge egg. He held her close as he brushed her flyaway hair away from her face before leaning down and tenderly kissing her cheek. Grace was almost embarrassed by the roar of her heart's rhythm but then she felt Ben's heart beating through his chest with a synchronization that was just as loud as hers. The anticipation, the joy, the thrill of their first kiss that had been years in the making mixed with the lilacs' smell to make Grace feel almost dizzy. She relaxed into Ben's arms as his soft lips moved closer to hers. Her eyes were mesmerized by the pureness she found in Ben's face, in the serene blueness of his eyes and, feeling his breath on her waiting lips, she knew she was about to experience true happiness for the first time in a very, very long time.

"Ahem…Excuse me," a voice broke into Grace's dreamlike state and she froze at the realization that they were no longer alone.

Ben released his hold on Grace and sat upright, glaring at the intruder. "What?"

DJ did not even dare look up but, instead, concentrated on the grass surrounding his feet. "I apologize for interrupting but Dave sent me to find you. He needs you to come to the community center." After a few moments of uncomfortable, silent stillness, DJ finally looked up to meet Ben's glaring eyes. "Now," the Misfit with the sometimes super speed grimly asserted without any hint of the embarrassment he showed a few seconds ago.

"This better not be some stupid trick to keep us apart," Ben whispered to Grace as he helped her to her feet. Their eyes locked for the briefest of seconds and each knew their first kiss was going to have to wait a little while longer. Ben turned to DJ, "Do you know what Dave wants?"

DJ looked guiltily at Grace before leaning into Ben and whispering, "It's the Anti-Powers. They're here."

Chapter Twenty-Two: The Gift

Grace only felt a whoosh of lilac wind as Ben hoisted her onto his back with one hand before sprinting out of the clearing with DJ close behind. She closed her eyes and intended to lean her head into Ben's shoulder but they arrived at the community center before she knew what was happening. With Grace still on his back, Ben took the front stairs three at a time and burst through the double-door entrance. Only when DJ locked the doors behind them did Ben gently release his hold on Grace. She stood between Ben and DJ, who positioned themselves like sentries at her shoulders. Ben immediately knew something was wrong as he surveyed the massive hall as if seeing it for the first time.

Gone was the elegant ambiance of the other night and in its place hung a dull, thick air. Even the disco ball seemed to have lost its glitter and the only light in the room focused on the center of the dance floor. There, huddled solemnly around a large cardboard box, were the few Misfits Grace could call friends. Petra hung on Dave's arm, staring down at the box and wiping away tears that would just not quit. Rebecca hovered over her sister Sarah, who knelt beside the box with violent sobs. Even Star, red-eyed and as dull as the air, tried to comfort Sarah with no results.

"What happened?" Ben asked, taking a step closer to Grace.

With bloodshot eyes, Numbers looked at Dave and said, "You tell him."

Dave stood next to Numbers with arms crossed and a face so grim it unnerved Ben. He didn't look at Ben, but instead focused on Grace when he said, "We have a situation."

"What kind of situation?" Ben pressed.

Dave kept his eyes on Grace as he pointed to the box. "Star found this just inside the Trio of Boulders entrance."

Grace and Ben both started to walk toward the box when Dave yelled, "No, Grace! Don't come any further! Just Ben. Grace, you stay with DJ."

DJ reached for Grace's arm and pulled her back to his side with a gentle force. She stood without moving, without breathing, as Ben continued across the dance floor to Dave. Dave opened the top of the box for Ben, and at that instant, Sarah's sobs turned into screams as she threw herself face down onto the hardwood floor. Rebecca and Star quickly carried her to a side table where Sarah could continue her laments without the concrete visual of the box's contents.

"Look in the box, but keep your emotions in check in front of Grace," Dave whispered his instructions to Ben.

Ben slowly peered down into the box and instantly felt sick to his stomach. There, posed as two lovers kissing, were the decapitated heads of Carrie and Marshall, Vector's assistant. With their closed eyes and postured lips, they almost looked asleep but for the dried blood encircling the jagged edges of their throats. Without turning around, Ben sternly called back, "Gracie, stay where you are!"

Grace felt every eye in the room on her, but despite her normally paralyzing self-consciousness and Ben's clear instruction, she wrenched her arm out of DJ's grasp and ran toward the box.

"Grace!" yelled Ben. "I said no!" Just as she reached the box, he caught her waist from behind and wrapped his arms tightly but gently around her, pulling her back. "You don't need to see that."

"What is it?" Grace strained to see inside the box. She seemed afraid and curious all at the same time.

"The Anti-Powers," Ben replied with trusting honesty. "They… they killed Carrie and Marshall, Vector's assistant."

Grace's head swirled. "Are they in there?" she mumbled, pointing to the box.

"You don't need to see that," Ben repeated.

"What's in the box?" Grace's voice was not quite a whisper now.

Ben sighed. "Their heads." He held Grace tighter as her whole body began to shake and her sobs filled the hall's silence.

"Don't…let go…of me," Grace cried between breaths.

"I won't, sweetie, I won't." Ben picked up Grace's trembling body and carried her to the table where Sarah was finally getting herself under control.

Still in Ben's arms, Grace looked at Sarah and said between sobs, "I'm sorry. I'm so very sorry. This is all my fault."

"Carrie was my best friend." Sarah looked up at Grace with accusing eyes tinted more with tearful red than sparkling blue.

"I'm sorry," Grace repeated to Sarah in a whisper. She looked at Ben, "I really am sorry."

"I know. I know," Ben said, holding her closer. "It'll be okay."

Petra walked over and gently pulled Grace out of Ben's arms. "Dave needs you," she whispered to Ben. "Don't worry. I've got her." Petra helped Grace to a chair right beside Sarah. "I know you two will stay friends," she said to the two sobbing girls. "I've seen it."

Grace could not see Sarah through her tears but she felt a warm hand on her knee and knew Petra was right.

Ben squeezed Grace's shoulder. "I'll be right over here." He strode over to the box where Dave, Numbers, and DJ were still standing watch over their friends' severed heads.

"What do you think we should do?" Dave asked Ben.

Ben looked at the three men and their eyes told him he was no longer his father's son. Now, standing before them, their eyes confirmed Ben was a Power, a full Power, trained by the Council to protect Grace from the Anti-Powers. These grown men were looking to him, depending on him to guide them, so he took a deep breath and instinctively moved into Guardian mode to begin his interrogation. "Have you been able to see what happened?" he asked Dave.

"No," Dave sighed. "This has all happened so fast…I mean…no one's ever been murdered here before. I…I tried to see but everything…everything's so messed up now."

"Okay." Ben took a deep breath and switched gears. "Okay, where's Vector? Does he know yet?"

"No. Birch went to go get him," Dave said, his eyes now on the box.

"What about Carrie's brothers?"

Dave looked at Numbers before leaning into Ben and murmuring, "We can't find them."

"What do you mean you can't find them?" Ben's voice was a strained whisper now.

"I mean we don't know where they are." Dave glanced over at Star who was still huddled next to Sarah. "Apparently, Star recently set her sights on Elton, that skinny triplet who gave you such a hard time when you first got here. Well, anyway, she went up to the entrance today to see him and this box was just sitting there. No Elton, no Steve, just this box."

"You mean no one was guarding the entrance?"

"Exactly."

Ben's eyes widened. "For how long?"

Dave cleared his throat. "We don't know."

DJ then spoke the words everyone standing around the box was thinking, "In other words, the Anti-Powers could be hiding somewhere inside the Misfit community even as we speak."

As that realization sunk into Ben's thoughts, a loud knock pounded on the community center's front door. "Dave? Petra? Open this blasted door and let me in!" Vector's voice burst through the bolted entrance. Dave nodded to DJ who quickly crossed the room and unlocked the door. An obviously frustrated Vector hobbled through the door with Birch on his arm. "What's going on? Birch won't tell me a thing! Just yanked me out of my lab with those elastic arms of hers like I'm some throw pillow. I was right in the middle of a training session and you know I don't like leaving my lab in the hands of those young interns. Now what in the blazes is so important?"

Numbers stepped forward. "Vector, something's happened. We…we have some bad news."

Vector stopped in his tracks and his eyes immediately flickered on the box. "What kind of bad news?"

Birch gently held Vector's arm tighter as Numbers placed his hand on the old man's shoulder. "It's Marshall. Vector, I'm sorry to have to tell you this, but Marshall…Marshall's dead."

Vector stumbled forward a few steps toward the box. "What? How?"

Dave stepped between Vector and the box. "We think the Anti-Powers did it."

"Did what?" Vector said as he took his cane and adrenaline and pushed Dave aside. The sight of Marshall's bloody head in the box caused him to clutch his chest. His eyes rolled back in his head as he stumbled back in obvious pain, unable to catch his breath. His head wobbled and his gasps filled the hall's silence as he struggled for air.

"Vector!" Birch yelled as her old friend collapsed on the floor right beside the box. "Dave, do something!" she cried. "He's having another heart attack!"

Dave and Numbers immediately knelt over Vector and began administering CPR. DJ and Ben just stood back in stunned silence, watching their old friend die right before their eyes. No one else in the great hall moved. They just looked on helplessly as DJ and Dave worked furiously over Vector's lifeless body.

After a few minutes that felt more like a hundred, Petra placed a soft hand on Dave's shoulder. "Sweetheart, you can stop now. I've seen the CPR isn't going to work. I'm certain of this." Petra's voice cracked. "There's nothing more you can do. He's gone. Let him go."

Dave and Numbers looked up at Petra and their rhythm of breaths and chest pumps began to slow as Vector's death pervaded the room.

"Are you absolutely certain?" Numbers' tearful eyes pleaded with Petra as he felt Vector's wrist for a pulse that was no longer there.

"Yes," she softly said. "The CPR does not bring him back. You need to let him go."

The stillness in the great hall was deafening. Ten hearts pounding like bass drums stood around the one heart they desperately wanted to hear. No one spoke, no one moved, no one breathed. Death's shroud blanketed the room and no one knew what to do.

Then, in the midst of the smothering stillness, as if suddenly shocked out of her death trance, Grace yelled through gritted teeth, "No! Not again!" and ran over to Vector. She knelt down and hugged the old man's frail, limp body to her chest, tears pouring from her swollen bloodshot eyes. "Please, no! Please, Vector, come back! Please! I don't want anyone else to die because of me! Please come back!" She sat there cradling Vector in her arms, rocking him back and forth with each desperate word. "Come back, Vector. Come on. Please come back," she loudly whispered with each back and forth motion.

Ben's eyes moistened to see Grace's vivid desperation and he knelt beside her. Just as he was about to pull Grace away from Vector's lifeless body, Ben heard the most wonderful sound.

In the middle of Grace's frantic rocking, Vector coughed.

It was a small cough, but one that grew louder and stronger with each back and forth motion of Grace's body until, finally, the coughs turned into breaths. They were sporadic breaths at first, but as Grace held Vector closer, pleading with the old man to take one more breath, then another, his breaths became deeper and deeper until finally, Vector opened his eyes and gasped, "Grace?"

"Yes! Yes, Vector!" Grace exclaimed. "I'm here! You're okay. You're going to be okay. Just keep breathing. That's it. Just keep breathing." Grace looked up at Ben. "He's…he's alive!"

Ben smiled at Grace with disbelief. He then looked up at Petra, questioningly. She shook her head and shrugged her shoulders at him in return. Ben quickly scanned the room and every face in there was filled with the same questions that swirled around in his own head.

Every face but one.

Dave stood directly across from Ben with wide eyes staring at Grace and Vector. His face held no questions but was a mixture of joy and vulnerability all at the same time. He staggered a few steps backwards and fell into a nearby chair.

Petra ran to him. "Dave?"

"I never imagined…I mean…it can't be. It's not possible." Dave stumbled over his words, his wide eyes never leaving Grace's face.

"What?" Petra leaned down and put her slender arm around her husband's broad shoulders. "What is it, dear?"

"It's Grace. She's not supposed to have any…but she does… she's…she's got the Gift," Dave stammered.

And with those words, Ben knew their lives had just gotten a lot more complicated.

Chapter Twenty-Three: Making Plans

The rocky precipice just inside the entrance to the Misfit community provided an expansive view of the valley below, but it was the underside of the precipice that was the more desirable location this night. Without the watchful eyes of the Boulder Triplets, the sharp ledge's underside provided a unique hiding place for unwanted visitors who needed to remain anonymous. As the wind from above whipped violently around the precipice, it brushed past the camouflaged soldier crouched below. The warm gush of air sent an odd shiver down the soldier's back as it ominously whistled through the rocks like a warning bell to stay hidden.

Huddled in the rocks, his eyes strained through the darkness, waiting to catch a glimpse of her. He had followed his leader's commands to the letter but he did not expect his contact to be so late. His patience was growing thin and he decided to give her five more minutes before reporting back to the princes. It was not his fault she had failed her part of the mission. Surely the princes would understand that. But, being understanding was not one of their virtues so, on second thought, perhaps the soldier should extend his wait to ten minutes. The five minutes more could be the difference between celebrating a successful mission and incurring the princes' wrath upon his return.

As he pondered his timing, he heard a branch crack a few yards away. He sat still, his trained breathing maintained his silence. If it was her, she would know where to find him.

Within seconds, she appeared at his side, breathless, with glowing aquamarine eyes even the darkness could not suppress. "Hey," was all she said.

"Did you deliver the package?" the soldier anxiously asked.

"Yes, but I wish you had told me what was in it."

"The younger Prince thought the surprise would help your credibility. How did they react?"

"Just as he thought they would. They have no idea what to do next."

"And the girl?"

"She's still here with Ben but I doubt they'll be here long. If you all are going to take her, it better be soon."

"I'll relay that to the princes." The soldier started to get up when she abruptly grabbed his arm.

"Please tell my brothers what I did. Please make sure they know I completed this part of the mission," she said, hanging onto his arm, waiting for his assurance.

"Of course. I'll tell them. Just make sure you're ready for your next part tomorrow morning," he nodded before disappearing into the night.

•••

The cabin's expansive great room felt small, crowded with the few Misfits that Petra and Dave had invited into their home. Word had spread quickly of Carrie and Marshall's demise but Vector's miraculous recovery remained a secret shared only by those in this room, along with Numbers and Birch who had taken the old man home to recover from his ordeal. While other Misfits boarded up their cabins and naively prepared to battle the Anti-Powers, Grace and her small circle of Misfit friends anxiously surrounded Dave and his large pile of antique books he had scattered on the wooden coffee table in front of the fireplace. Ben sat beside him on the overstuffed couch, knowing his own superhuman powers could not help Dave in his endeavor, but wanting to be close to him just the same.

"I just knew my father-in-law's old books would come in handy one day," Petra said to Rebecca in the kitchen as they fixed drinks and cake for the crowd. "Dave wanted to send them off to the Council library when his dad died, but I saw we were going to need them one day so I talked him into keeping them. At the time, I didn't see why they would be needed, just that they would be, but who cares so long as we have them here now."

"Shhh! Quiet, woman!" Dave yelled at Petra from the other room. "I'm trying to think in here!" He poured over the old, musty, leather-bound history books, releasing hundreds of years of dust with each page he turned. After what felt like an eternity, he finally looked up at Grace who sat beside Ben. "Your Highness, near as I can tell between these books and what I can see from the past, no one in the Family has ever had any powers."

Fully aware of all eyes in the room on her, Grace shifted slightly in her seat toward Ben.

"And on top of that," Dave continued, "no one has had the Gift since the 1300s and even then it was very, very rare."

Ben reached over and held Grace's hand with a reassuring smile.

"What exactly is the Gift again?" Grace asked hesitantly.

Dave took a deep breath and smiled, his eyes softening at the childlike naiveté Grace's question revealed. "Miss Grace, the Gift is the rare power to heal the injured or resurrect life with your touch. It is the greatest power our world has ever known…and you've got it."

Grace's fingers tingled as the image of the butterfly from the cabin's front porch railing floated through her head. Death did not work differently in the Misfit community. Death just worked differently for her.

"So what do we do now?" DJ looked at Ben.

"We get Grace back to the Council and away from the Anti-Powers immediately," Ben replied without hesitation or emotion.

"And how do we do that with the Anti-Powers obviously too close for comfort?" Rebecca asked as she carried in a tray full of drinks.

"I don't know yet. But I think we're going to need a lot more of that before the night is over," Ben half-smiled pointing to a soda can perched on the tray.

Petra placed a large pound cake next to the drinks. "I'll go make some sandwiches and get a pot of coffee brewing."

"Can I help?" Grace slowly stood and unsuccessfully tried to release Ben's hand.

"You need to stay here with me," Ben said still holding onto Grace's hand.

Grace wrenched her hand free. "Look, I've just been told I'm a freak even in your world. I need to do something normal and fixing a peanut butter and jelly sandwich is about as close to normal as I can get right now."

Ben looked at Petra, then at Grace. "Okay, but stay away from the windows and don't leave the cabin."

"I'll keep her in the kitchen," Petra said, patting Grace's hand and leading her out of the room filled with the staring eyes.

Once Grace was out of earshot, Dave looked to Ben and half-jokingly said, "Is there any way you could just speed back home and pick up some other full Powers on your way back? We sure could use some more like you right about now."

"I'm not leaving Grace." Ben's response sounded more like a military order than a statement. "She's a member of the Family and has the Gift and she just became a lot more valuable to the Anti-Powers, if that was even possible. Now it's way too risky for just the two of us to travel back home alone. They'd kill me and do who knows what to Grace. I'd need about five more full Powers with me to adequately protect Grace on that trip."

"I could go if you tell me where," DJ spoke up.

Ben looked at DJ questioningly. "You'd have to move so fast the Anti-Powers don't see you leave. And then you'd have to make it all the way to South Carolina, staying invisible the entire way. Think you can handle that?"

"Watch me," the tall lanky Misfit grinned. "I can try. It'll be nice to finally use my Power for something other than running the field in a ball game."

Ben started scribbling on a nearby scrap of paper. "Okay, here is my brother Tom's address. Don't use any phones. I still don't know how the Anti-Powers knew we were here and, while phones taps are a little old-fashioned, we can't take any chances. Get to him and he can get you to the Council. They'll be able to send full Power troops immediately."

"Your brother knows the Council?" asked Dave, raising his eyebrows.

"He does now that his younger brother is in so much trouble with them," said Ben.

DJ grabbed the paper and headed to the door, stopping only to hug Rebecca.

"Please be careful," Rebecca whispered.

DJ kissed her full on the lips. "You too," he winked at her and then disappeared out the door and into the night.

"Do you think he'll make it?" Ben asked Dave.

"He'll make it," Rebecca answered him assuredly.

Ben nodded at Rebecca before continuing, "Okay, now to strategy. What do we know?"

Dave walked over to a desk on the other side of the room. "Here's a map of our little community under the mountain." He moved aside his old books to spread the map across the coffee table. "Now we don't know for certain, but we can assume that Anti-Powers have breached our entrance and are hiding somewhere on this map."

Ben looked at the faces crowded around the map. "They wouldn't come here without some sort of plan. And we still don't know how many we're dealing with or what kind of powers they have." Ben rhythmically tapped his fingers on the map, analyzing the placement of each cabin on the broad canvas. "Do you have a list of everyone living here and their powers?"

"Right here," Sarah shoved a legal pad in Ben's face. "Star and I started working on this while you all were looking at those old books. We all want to help Grace if we can."

Ben took the legal pad and looked up at Sarah. "Thanks. This list will be a big help." Ben studied the list for a few minutes and, while he tried to hide it, his disappointment was evident to everyone in the room. "Is this everyone we've got? These are their powers?"

Dave sighed, "Ben, my son, there is a reason we're called Misfits."

"But surely there's more than this." Ben tossed the list down on the coffee table and slouched back on the couch. With this collection of practically useless half-Powers, his strategy had just changed from offense to defense. "Okay, then we just need to hold off the Anti-Powers until DJ reaches Tom and the Council sends back full Powers. Is Vector's the most secure cabin you've got?"

"Nope," beamed Dave proudly. "Mine is. We've got a secret basement. Only entrance is through the back bedroom. Petra saw we would need it one day so we designed it before we even thought about the rest of this cabin. Now, at least we finally know why we built it." He then scanned the collection of faces in the room and sheepishly added, "Well, it was a secret basement until just now."

"Okay, then that's where we'll hide Grace," Ben said just as Petra and Grace returned carrying sandwiches and coffee.

"So now you're hiding me?" Grace asked. "Don't I get any say in this?"

"No," Ben replied without looking up at her, his eyes still studying the map in front of him. "Petra, take Grace down to your basement and get her settled. I'll be down in a little while."

"Now, wait a second. What if I don't want to just sit in some basement? People are dying because of me! The least I can do is stay and help too." Grace stomped her foot, indicating a new mood swing. "I want to know what you're going to do. What are you going to do with me?"

Ben looked up at her, his blue eyes stern and emotionless. "I'm going to keep you alive, Grace. I'm going to keep you alive."

Chapter Twenty-Four: Prisoner

The bare wooden paneling lining the basement walls matched Grace's mood. It was dark and dismal and smothering. Even the basement air was dull and stale. And, but for the brightly quilted bed on which Grace sat, there was little furniture in the room and its starkness intentionally contributed to Grace feeling like a prisoner of war in a Nazi concentration camp.

Because that is what she was now. A prisoner of war. A pawn. A token to be taken home by the winner. No more blending in. No more staying on the sidelines. She was now the center of some strange world she knew nothing about, nor did she want to know.

"Here you are, Your Majesty," Petra sang out as she nimbly climbed down the ladder in the corner of the room. "I noticed the reading selection down here was a little old. I mean you probably weren't even born when most of these books were written. So I thought I'd bring you some newer books and the few magazines we have. You never know when you'll get out of here."

The pained look on Grace's face immediately made Petra regret her last words. "Can you see how long I'll be down here?" Grace asked.

"No, dear," Petra smiled. "Dave and I have tried all night to see anything that might help but we've only gotten bits and pieces. The only thing we know for sure is that the Anti-Powers will be here this morning. I saw them fighting our Misfits on the main road in front of the general store."

Grace looked at her watch. "But it's almost morning now."

Petra patted her hand. "And that's why I wanted to check on you this one last time to see if you need anything before I head out. Ben worked all night to plan out what each of us has to do and that includes me and Dave."

"So you're leaving?"

"Not for long and not very far. We're going to try to use our powers to help Ben's battle strategy. But don't worry, Dave and I know all our mountain's great hiding places. I promise we won't be in any danger. And neither will you with Ben here." Petra squeezed Grace's hand. "So, do you need anything before I leave?"

"No." Grace felt numb with her thoughts. "But when you saw the fight, were…were any of the Misfits hurt or…or you know?"

Petra responded slowly, "I did not see any faces, if that is what you are asking." She silently sat with Grace a few minutes before reaching into her pocket and pulling out a wadded up blue bandana. "One last thing. Last night I saw you were going to need this. I don't know why. I just know you do."

Grace unwrapped the blue bundle and nestled inside was an antique wooden hair clip. It was crescent-shaped with two sticks running through it to hold hair in place.

"I bought it from some guy selling them at one of the Grateful Dead concerts Dave and I went to. I loved the way the flowers were so intricately carved on that large curved piece. Even the wooden sticks are decorated," Petra said pointing to the clip's ornate design.

"Thank you," Grace said still looking at the clip.

"You're welcome. Why don't we try it in your hair, Your Highness?" Petra stood over Grace and pulled her hair back through the wooden clip into a ponytail. "You know, dear, I don't have any children, but if I had a daughter, I would want her to be just like you." Petra leaned down and gave Grace a hug.

Grace stood and hugged her back. "Thank you…for everything."

"This will be over before you know it," Petra said releasing Grace from her grasp.

"I hope so," sighed Grace.

At that moment, Ben flew down the ladder with his undetectable speed. "Petra, it's time."

Petra looked at Grace and smiled, "I'll see you later," before she glided up the stairs leaving Ben and Grace alone.

The two friends stood on opposite sides of the small room, their eyes not moving from one another.

Grace finally broke the silence. "When you said 'it's time,' does that mean they're here? Is the fight that Petra saw on the main road starting now?" she asked.

"Yes," Ben nodded.

"What are we supposed to do?" Grace still stood there.

"You're going to stay down here away from everyone and everything and I'm going to keep watch upstairs," Ben said matter-of-factly.

"So now you're in Guardian mode again?"

"Yes."

"And so we aren't…you know?"

Ben's eyes softened a little. "Gracie, you are always in my heart but when I am acting as your Guardian, I need my head to be in control, not my heart. Do you understand?"

Grace's nod was barely visible.

"I need to concentrate on what's going on out there so I can keep you safe in here. I mean, if anything ever happened to you because I was distracted by, well—" Ben shook his head as if shaking off a bad dream.

"I understand," Grace interrupted softly. "Isn't there anything I can do?"

"No. Not without putting yourself in danger and I can't allow that. I've thought of every possible scenario and everyone here is working to keep you alive. Even Rebecca has shape shifted to look like you and is running around acting as a decoy. The least you can do is try to stay out of the way so the rest of us can do our jobs," Ben stated bluntly.

"I'm sorry. I just thought if someone gets hurt or…you know, then maybe I could help with this Gift or whatever it is."

"No way, Grace. We can't risk the Anti-Powers finding out about your power. You just need to stay here for now. I'll be back to check on you in a little while."

"Where are you going?"

"I told you. I'll just be upstairs. Remember, sweetie, I won't ever leave you unless I know you are safe." And then Ben disappeared leaving Grace alone with her thoughts.

• • •

She waited for him. She knew what she had to do. And while it was uncomfortable watching her neighbors valiantly but uselessly fight the Anti-Powers on the road below, blood was thicker than water. So she hid beside the cabin watching the battle and waiting to play her part for the Anti-Powers. Her heart raced with the anticipation of seeing him again. Of seeing them all.

"Your obedience impresses me," a voice came up behind her.

Startled, she turned, almost stumbling over a rock. "You made it," she gushed.

"Of course. Did you doubt me?"

"No. I…I'm just glad to see you."

"And I you." The corner of his mouth curled up as if he was trying to smile but was unable. "Where is she?"

"In there." She pointed to the cabin, her aquamarine eyes now glowing with brighter tints of green. "In the basement."

"When did your eyes start to turn?"

"Right after I delivered the box to them." She could tell the prince was pleased.

"So, you are ready?"

"Yes." She looked at the battle scene below. The bloody bodies of her former friends were starting to pile up. When she saw Rebecca's lifeless body sprawled out on the side of the road near Ted's store, her friend's blue eyes vacant of any soul, she knew Ben's battle plans were starting to disintegrate. "You are taking me with you, aren't you? To see Father?"

"I said I would, didn't I?"

"Yes."

"Then my word should be good enough. Now, show me to Grace."

• • •

The stone floor was so cold, she felt its iciness creep through the thick soles of her tennis shoes. Her constant pacing did nothing to warm her, and Grace knew her chills were more likely generated by nerves and not necessarily by the frigid floor below. She had only been alone about an hour but Ben's absence made everything feel worse. Without him, she could not even think straight right now. Knowing what was happening on the main road below, knowing it was happening because of her, was too much. In her mind, the basement walls appeared to be moving inward, crowding her, seemingly crushing what little stale air remained in the room. She needed to get out of there. She needed Ben. And just when she thought she would smother in the room's oppressiveness, Ben slid down the ladder. He landed inches from her pacing path and his closeness immediately calmed her.

"Hey, came to che—," he stopped. "Grace? What's wrong?"

"Nothing. I just want to know what's going on out there. Is everyone okay? Are…are you okay?" Her nerves pushed out the words with rapid breaths.

"Yes. Everything seems to be going as expected…I mean, we're holding our own and I'm sure DJ will return soon with reinforcements." Ben paused. "Why are you trembling?"

"When you didn't come back…I thought…"

Ben shook his head and pulled her close. "Well, you need to stop thinking."

Grace closed her eyes and melted into Ben's arms. "I thought you were in Guardian mode."

"I am. But I can't have my assignment losing it on me, can I?"

"No. I'll be fine now. I just needed to know you were okay."

"I'm fine." Ben started to release his hold on her.

"No." Grace nuzzled her head closer into his chest. "Please just hold me a few minutes longer. I just need to feel us for a moment before you go back upstairs."

Ben kissed the top of Grace's head. "Just us," he whispered.

"Right," Grace sighed. "Just us."

They stood in each other's arms. Muffled battle cries from the road below attempted to invade their thoughts but the sounds barely passed through their moment. For that moment there was no battle, no Anti-Powers, no Family, no Gift. There was just Ben and Grace.

But unfortunately their moment was short-lived.

"Ben! Are you down there?" Star's frantic voice broke into their private thoughts.

Ben instantly released his hold on Grace and she saw in his face that he had reentered Guardian mode. "Yeah?" he shouted toward the stairs.

Star's face appeared in the shadow at the top of the stairs. "Ben, we need you! Dave's in trouble!"

"What? What do you mean Dave's in trouble?"

"He's hurt. Real bad. And they have him surrounded. We need you."

Ben looked at Grace.

"Go," was all she said.

Stay with Grace or save Dave. Ben's mind raced, looking for alternatives. There were none.

"Star," he directed. "You stay with Grace and if you see anything out of the ordinary, anything at all, you get on that front porch and glow like you've never glowed before. With my powers, I'll see you wherever I am. You got that?" His eyes were stern.

"Yeah, I got it. Please hurry. They have him at the community center and it looks like Dave's in a lot of pain."

Ben turned to Grace. "I promise I'll be back. Star will take care of you." He squeezed her hand and then disappeared up the ladder.

Grace looked up at Star who still stood at the top of the ladder. "Want to come down?"

Star glanced behind her before answering, "Sure. For a minute." She climbed down the ladder and surveyed the small bare room. "Real ritzy Waldorf-Astoria you got here," she smiled.

"Yeah," Grace smiled back. She could see why guys were attracted to Star. There was something about her that made you want to like her.

"I hear you're an orphan," Star stated abruptly. She stayed near the ladder, her face half hidden in the corner's shadows.

"Yeah. My parents and brothers were killed in a car wreck when I was four." *What a weird way to start a conversation*, Grace thought. "Do you have any family?"

"Yeah. But I haven't seen them in a while."

"Oh." Grace had no idea where this conversation was going but something in her gut told her it was going the wrong way. She casually stepped back, placing the bed between herself and Star.

"Obviously, the Misfits like to stay hidden so we don't get many visitors."

"Oh, yeah, right," Grace nodded.

"But luckily, one of my brothers has found his way here."

Grace crinkled her brow.

"Brother, dear! Come on down!" Star called to the top of the ladder.

Star's brother appeared on the ladder and Grace's gut lurched. She clutched the bed rail to steady herself.

"I think you two know each other," Star smiled as she stepped out of the shadows, her newly green eyes glowing.

"Grace, darling, where have you been?" Gregory's smile matched his sister's. "We've been looking everywhere for you."

Chapter Twenty-Five: Lost

Surveying the lanky man with the ponytail standing in front of him, Tom noted how low his apartment's ceiling hung. It was bare inches above the visitor's head and Tom was almost, but not quite, intimidated by the man's height.

"Are you sure about all this?" Tom asked. "I mean…how did the Anti-Powers know where you all were? The mountain's supposed to—"

"Cooper's dead." DJ's bluntness stemmed from his impatience, not out of any callousness. "On the way here I found him cut up on the floor of his store. Looked to be a couple of day's old."

"A couple of days?" Tom's voice cracked.

"Yeah, so I don't mean to be rude and all, but we really need to get going. Time is not our friend here."

Tom shook his head. "I told the Council that we needed to get up there and get them. All this could have been avoided! They gave some silly excuse about Misfit territory and passport documentation. Even the Council leader thought Grace would be safe there while they followed their stupid protocol. I mean I even gave the Council my dad's old map to the Misfits." Tom said mainly to himself.

"Look, I'm sorry they didn't listen to you then but do you think you could make them listen now?" DJ gestured to the front door.

"Yeah, we're going to make them listen." Tom waved his hand and the door instantly sprang open. "Come on. It's time I had another face-to-face with our stubborn Council leader."

. . .

Ben crouched behind a thick, old boxwood and pushed his back against the log wall. The community center's windows were slightly higher than most—something about the humidity controls for the artwork within—so Ben was hidden below the window listening, rather than watching, for any sign of Dave's struggle inside. But despite his superhuman hearing, Ben heard nothing. No voices. No scuffles. Nothing.

Just dead silence.

Staying low, Ben made his way around to the front of the community center and crept up to the front door. He listened again.

Still nothing.

Slowly, he cracked open the door and peeked into the dimly lit great hall. Not seeing anyone or anything, he slid through the door and braced himself, back against the wall. He scanned the large room and there, crouched down in the far corner, was Dave.

Ben glanced around again before stealthily skirting the perimeter walls of the room to reach his old friend. "Dave!" he whispered.

Dave looked up. "Benjamin! What are you doing here?" Ben noticed Dave did not bother to lower his voice.

"I thought you were hurt? I thought they had you surrounded?" Ben's instincts kicked into overdrive.

"Surrounded? What are you talking about?" Dave slowly stood up, rubbing his left shoulder. "I'm not hurt. Petra and I were up at the clearing trying to see like you wanted us to and I slipped, fell, and popped out my shoulder. No big deal. I've done it before. We got it popped back in and Petra went in the back here to get me some ice."

"So the Anti-Powers aren't here?"

"No! The only Anti-Powers I've seen were down on the main road."

"But Star—," Ben froze.

"Ben?"

But Ben had disappeared.

In an instant, he was rushing into Dave's cabin. "Grace!" Ben screamed. He flew down the ladder into the secret basement. It was empty. Cold and empty. Grace was gone. He had left her and now he had lost her.

Ben stood in the cold room. Still. Shock stealing the last of his breaths, his eyes unable to focus. He knew there was something he must do in this situation, something he had learned as part of his Guardian training. But his training had never taken into account his heart. It ached and the pain clouded his logic. So, he just stood there. Unable to move. Frozen to the cold stone floor.

"Ben!" Breathless, Dave stumbled down the ladder. He bent over, trying to catch his breath from his recent and rare run. "Ben!" Dave's panting voice was unable to penetrate Ben's shock. "Where's Grace?"

"Gone," Ben's voice was no more than a cracked whisper.

"Gone? What do you mean gone? What happened?" Dave's heaving voice escalated, still unable to pierce through the shock that paralyzed Ben's mind. He grabbed Ben's shoulders and shook him. "Snap out of it, son! Ben, answer me! Where's Grace?"

"Star." Ben mumbled.

"Star? What the—?" Dave shook Ben again. "What are you talking about? Benjamin, wake up boy! We need to find Grace! Can you hear me? Find Grace!"

Ben's eyes looked through Dave, still unable to focus. "She's gone. I left her and now she's gone," he whispered.

"Dang it, Ben! You are her Guardian! Get your head back in the game!" *Smack!* Dave reached across and slapped Ben's face as hard as he could.

Ben's eyes widened and finally focused on Dave. He rubbed his cheek and stepped back out of Dave's reach. "Oww."

"Sorry about that," said Dave, halfheartedly. "But I really need your focus right now. Forget you love her. What would her Guardian do? How would her Guardian find her?"

"Her Guardian—"

"Yes, you, her Guardian."

"She needs a Guardian now—"

"Benjamin, she needs you now."

Ben rubbed his eyes and took a deep breath, "Yeah, me. Her Guardian. Okay."

"Okay. Now, tell me what happened," prodded Dave.

But Ben was beyond that now. His brain was reviewing facts, assimilating data, determining next steps. The phrase *'Just be her Guardian'* kept playing over and over in the back of his mind like a theme song organizing his thoughts and canceling out his heart.

Eventually, his eyes cleared and he asked, "Where's the list?"

"What list?"

"You know. The list!" Ben called back to Dave as he bounded up the ladder.

Dave found him in the great room hunched over the coffee table. "Son, what are you doing?"

Ben did not look up. Finally, his finger smacked the yellow legal pad in front of him. "I knew I had seen him on Sarah's list. Who's Tracker? Tell me about Tracker?"

"Tracker? He's got a nose like a bloodhound but allergies that would kill an elephant."

"So that's why he lives here."

"Yeah. He's about as Misfit as they come. Why? What could… Oh!" Dave was now on the same page as Ben.

"Exactly. With his power, maybe he could lead me to Grace."

"Maybe. So long as his spring hay fever hasn't kicked in full throttle yet."

Ben and Dave zoomed out the cabin's front door to find Tracker but stopped suddenly when they reached the front porch railing. Below them, on the main road below, it was quiet. No screams, no sobs, no battle cries. No Anti-Powers. The fighting had ceased as quickly as it had begun. The Anti-Powers were gone leaving only mangled Misfit bodies in their wake. Some dead, some injured, but all being tended to by the few Misfits who had survived the short-lived attack.

"What the—?" asked Dave, relieved to see Petra among the caregivers.

"It's because they have Grace now. This fight was just a distraction until they got Grace." Ben's focus was clear now. He turned to Dave. "We need to find Tracker and pray he isn't one of those bloody bodies down there."

Chapter Twenty-Six: Found

They were over a mile from the Misfit community and Ben was growing impatient. He had decided to make this journey with Tracker alone, assuming two could travel the mountainous terrain faster than if Dave and the others had accompanied him. Unfortunately, his time estimations had not taken into account the limitations of Tracker's powers. Using Grace's old clothes, Tracker had easily picked up her scent leaving Dave's cabin and the Misfit community. But as they traveled deeper into the mountain's thick forest, pollen and spring's smells were taking their toll on Tracker and his sneezes began to outnumber his leads.

"Ah-choo!" Tracker sneezed for the umpteenth time. He awkwardly looked over at Ben. "Sorry about that."

"Just go on," Ben sighed and shook his head. He followed the diminutive balding man with the bulbous nose through a brier thicket and up a small hill. He wasn't used to being the follower and that, combined with Tracker's sneezes, was frustrating to the Council's preeminent Guardian. "Are you sure you know where you're going?" he asked impatiently.

"Her scent is getting stronger, sir. And since my allergic reactions are more prevalent here, her strong scent means we're close," Tracker stated assuredly as he reached the top of the hill.

Just as Tracker was about to start his descent down the hill's other side, Ben suddenly yanked the little man to the ground. "Get down!" he whispered and pointed to the bottom of the descent directly in front of them.

Tracker strained his eyes down to the bottom of the hill but all he could see were trees and the leaf-covered ground below them. "What?" he asked.

"There," Ben pointed to an area where the leaves on the ground appeared to be denser.

Tracker squinted even more. "But I don't see anything."

Ben sighed, "You may have the nose but I have the eyes. Trust me. I think it's a cabin, a well-camouflaged cabin, but it's a cabin."

Tracker's nose went up, aimed at the dense leaves. "She's in there. I can smell her."

"Okay. Go tell Dave. Tell him to wait until DJ comes back with the full Powers then bring them all here. I'll stay here and watch over Grace."

Tracker smiled and saluted, "Yes, sir," before turning to leave. He took a few steps back down the hill and then turned around. "Master Ben?"

"Yes," Ben whispered, his eyes never leaving the dense leaves.

"Thank you for allowing me to be of service to you."

Ben looked back at the humble little man, not realizing until that moment how much the Misfits simply wanted to be part of their world. To work as a Power. To be useful. "No problem, and thank you for your help," he smiled before refocusing his eyes on the dense leaves below.

With Tracker gone, the forest seemed quieter to Ben. No birds singing, no leaves rustling, no squirrels scampering. Just silent stillness feeding Ben's concentration on the hidden cabin below. In the forest's stillness, he tried to listen, but the cabin was silent as well. If she was in there, why couldn't he hear anything?

Ben's curiosity began to rip at his Guardian instincts and he decided to furtively make his way down the hill to the cabin. As quickly and as silently as he could, using all his Powers and skills, Ben inched down the hill, never making a sound, not even a ripple in the air. When he was closer, he could see the walls and roof of the cabin more distinctly and discovered two well-disguised windows facing out opposite sides of the cabin. He crouched below the closest window, listening for anything, and it was soon apparent to Ben that the cabin's walls and roof were soundproof, the intent of their design confirming Grace's presence within. But the window did not share that same feature and Ben's stomach turned when he heard the first sounds emanating from the cabin.

For in the middle of the forest's stillness, Gregory's voice etched up Ben's spine like fingernails on a chalkboard.

Ben's anger briefly derailed his focus and only when he heard Star's voice join in with Gregory's did he know what he had to do. She had taken advantage of him once but Ben had learned his lesson. He cautiously peered through a lower corner of the window and surveyed the inside of the hidden cabin.

On the opposite wall next to the other window was a door that presumably led outside. Star sat on a couch near the door, filing her nails as if waiting for her next salon appointment. The only other person Ben could see was Gregory, who was leaning against the wall beside Ben's window and talking to someone or something on his left. In the midst of his one-sided conversation, Gregory crossed to the other side of the cabin toward Star, leaving Ben a clear view of Gregory's conversation target.

Grace.

She sat in the far corner, hands and feet tied to a metal, ladder-back chair. She was in no obvious pain, but her blue eyes were anxiously wild and darting back and forth from Gregory to Star. Her face was dirty, hair disheveled and her shirt was torn, revealing a pale pink bra strap. Her darting eyes never left Gregory or Star and Ben thought he could actually see the wheels in her head trying to find a way to escape.

Ben stayed motionless, staring into Grace's prison while he weighed his options. He knew Star's glowing power was insignificant but her newly discovered deviousness needed to be considered. Gregory's strength would probably be a hindrance for Ben, and he was not sure what other powers his obvious nemesis possessed. As he pondered his situation, a familiar voice softly resonated in his ear.

"Hey," Tom whispered. "Need some help?"

Relief flooded over Ben at the sight of his older brother. "How did you—? Where are the others?"

"On their way," Tom said. "So what's the plan?"

"Still working on it. I was a little outnumbered until you got here."

Tom peered through the window. "Let's just take them. You can handle Gregory and I'll take Miss Glowworm."

"You remember her?"

"Uh…yeah. Who could forget Star?"

"But what about Gregory? Do you think he has any powers other than his strength?"

"Bro, you're doubting yourself again. You can take him." Tom slapped Ben on the back. "Come on."

Tom started around the cabin to the door. He stopped and motioned for Ben to join him. Ben shook his head but crawled near his brother anyway.

"I don't know about this. There are too many unknowns. We should just wait for the others," Ben urged.

"You saw the way Grace was in there. We don't have time to wait."

Ben looked at the door and then to his brother. "Okay," he said. "When you get in there, go left and take Star. Let me handle Gregory."

"Got it."

Ben took one last look at Tom before bursting through the cabin door.

Gregory looked up, not startled in the least. "Hey, Benny Boy. We've been expecting you."

Ben's eyes narrowed at Gregory's response and he glanced over at Grace. She sat motionless, her wide eyes staring at Tom who stood behind Ben.

Ben stepped to the side, placing his back against the wall. He looked over at Tom now standing beside Star.

"I believe you've met my sister, Star," Gregory smiled.

Star smiled at Ben and he instantly realized the resemblance to her despicable brother.

"And of course you already know my brother," Gregory pointed to Tom.

Ben stiffened at Gregory's perplexing introduction of his own brother. As Ben stared at his older brother with questioning eyes, Tom's form shifted into the young blonde teenager who tried to smear Grace with the white pickup truck that fateful day. Then, as soon as the blonde girl fully appeared, she transformed into the familiar, bulky boy whose green eyes Ben had learned to hate.

Andrew.

Ben's heart raced. It was not Tom outside the cabin just now. The full Powers were not already on their way. It was Andrew. That stupid shape shifter messed with Ben's odds. He had been outnumbered all along.

"So what now, Greg?" Ben asked. When in doubt, stall.

"Now, we wait for our father to arrive. You see, Grace is expected at our lab for some testing and we wouldn't want to make her late, now would we?" Gregory walked toward Ben.

Ben glanced over at Andrew before turning his steel blue eyes on Gregory. "You know I can't let you do that." Ben noticed his last words slurred slightly.

"Oh, Lover Boy, but you can and you will."

Gregory was so close now Ben could hear him breathe. He felt tired suddenly, his head swirled. He looked over at Grace and the last thing he remembered was hearing her scream, "Ben!" Then everything went black.

Chapter Twenty-Seven: Jamison Reich

Grace watched as Andrew threw Ben's limp body into the large square contraption of a chair. It had been hidden in the back corner of the cabin and, watching Andrew clamp the metal cuffs down over Ben's wrists, it reminded Grace of an executioner's electric chair. It had wires protruding from all sides like an electric chair but instead of being built from wood, however, the entire chair was made of some strange-colored metal that was not exactly shiny and not exactly dull and had a slightly reddish sheen to it. The chair was unlike anything Grace had ever seen and, while its harshness had scared Grace when she first entered the cabin, it was even more frightening with Ben's practically lifeless body lying across it.

"Don't move," Andrew smirked at Grace before flipping an ornate silver switch on the chair and heading outside to join Gregory and Star. Grace could see the three siblings through the nearest window. Lounging by a large oak that towered over the cabin, they did not look like they had a care in the world. They were laughing and smiling and were obviously not worried about the two prisoners they were supposed to be watching.

"Ben!" Grace whispered as loudly as she could. She was in the corner opposite him on the same side of the cabin and only had to move her chair a short distance to reach him. But if she did that, she would lose sight of the window and her captors outside. Torn, she opted to maintain her vigilance at the window. "Ben!" she repeated. "Please wake up!"

Ben's head bobbed and he mumbled something but whatever Gregory and his weird chair had done to him was too powerful and he remained semi-conscious. Grace studied the chair with its wires and weird metal and fancy switch.

The switch.

Grace glanced outside and the siblings were still beside the tree. Still tied to her own chair, it took Grace five large scoots across the cabin floor before she was beside Ben and his immobilizing apparatus. She maneuvered her chair sideways until her foot was beside the switch. Just as she was ready to flip off the switch with her foot, the cabin door opened and in walked Gregory.

"Tsk, tsk, Grace darling. Now, you should not mess with other people's property. You know better than that," he scolded. He waved his hand flamboyantly and Grace's chair, with Grace tied to it, instantly slammed back to its original place in the opposite corner. "Besides, even if you could get Benny Boy out of that chair, he would be useless to protect you. Just look at him. I have manipulated his mind into a stupor. That chair is just a little added bonus from my father to ensure he stays put."

Grace glared at her captor.

"You really have no clue about my many powers do you?" Gregory laughed. "Physical strength, intellectual powers beyond comprehension, and my rare ability to manipulate a person's mind and emotions. To make them feel whatever I want in their innermost soul."

That last power hit Grace hard and it showed.

Gregory snickered, "Oh, I hit a nerve, did I? You mean you actually thought I liked you? Silly human, of course not! How could you ever think you were worthy of me? Look at you and then look at me. There' is no comparison!"

Grace felt a lump in her throat looking at Gregory who was still the most gorgeous boy she had ever seen. Or was he manipulating her emotions again? Grace could not tell the difference between what she felt and what Gregory was making her feel.

"I was just doing my job, my dear. That's all you were. My assignment. Isn't that the term Benny Boy uses for you?" Gregory continued, moving closer to Grace. "Although, I particularly enjoyed our kisses. I'll give you that. You are quite a good kisser." Gregory's lips were close, his green eyes mesmerizing. "Perhaps we should show our friend Ben just how good."

Grace tried to turn her head away from Gregory's face but his pull was strong. She was unable to fight him now. Their lips met and she felt lost. Her head bobbed and her lips sensuously moved with his but somewhere in the background she heard Ben groaning.

Gregory briefly released his hold on her. "Sounds like Benny Boy doesn't like our kissing."

Grace looked over and, although Ben's eyes were barely open, they still bored into Gregory with a hatred she had never seen before. His head twitched and it was evident he was fighting whatever Gregory was doing to him.

Gregory walked over to Ben. "Give it up, Benny Boy. As long as I am here, there is nothing you can do for Grace," he laughed before turning back to her. "Now where were we?" He leaned in to Grace again and she began to feel relaxed. Too relaxed. He was close now. Her lips opened, waiting, wanting Gregory's lips.

"Gregory!" Jamison Reich's voice boomed at the cabin door.

Gregory stood straight up, releasing his hold on Grace. He wiped his mouth with his sleeve and winked at Grace. "Yes, Father."

"Stop toying with Miss MacKay. We need her at full strength for our tests." Mr. Reich walked over to Grace. "Hello, my dear. So glad you could finally join us. We have been waiting a long time for you."

Grace looked over at Ben whose eyes were slightly more open and now focused on Mr. Reich.

"It's nice to finally see Mr. Pickett where he belongs," Mr. Reich continued. "He and his family have been a thorn in my side for far too long." Mr. Reich concentrated on the metal cuffs around Ben's wrists and they visibly tightened, practically cutting off the young Guardian's circulation.

Ben grimaced and his half-opened eyes looked angry now.

"And you, my sweet Grace," Mr. Reich turned to his prize prisoner. "I know you will be worth all the trouble I've gone to. From the minute you survived your parent's car crash I knew you were special. I melted that car into such a large metal mess. But it did not affect you. Not a scratch on you. I knew then, you would play a part in the Anti-Powers' rise to greatness."

"You? You killed my parents?" Tears started welling in Grace's eyes.

"Of course. Who else would be so bold? I killed your parents and your brothers. Of course, I had the troops take care of your cousins and everyone else in the Family. I mean, why should I have to do everything when I really needed to concentrate all my efforts on you? When you survived that crash, I realized I only needed you and had to make sure the rest of your Family did not stay under Council control. It was quite a brilliant plan if I do say so."

At that moment, Star and Andrew reentered the cabin. But they were not alone. Between them stood Annie, expressionless and unmoving.

"Annie!" Grace cried out. "Oh no!" She looked at Mr. Reich. "Please let her go. She's not part of the Family. She's just my friend. Please don't hurt her. I'll do anything. Just please don't hurt her and Ben. Please!" Grace pleaded.

Mr. Reich just smiled.

"Annie," Grace turned to her old friend. "I'm so sorry they got you involved. You shouldn't be here. You shouldn't be part of this!"

"Gracie," Annie smiled. "But I am a part of this. I've been a part of this from the very beginning." And in Annie's smile, with her long blonde hair flowing around her face, Grace saw it.

The same look she saw in Star. And Andrew. And Gregory.

"No!" Grace shrieked.

"Oh, Gracie. Stop being so dramatic. So what if I'm an Anti-Power? We had some good times didn't we? I know I did. Well, except for wearing those stupid contacts. I'm so glad I'll never have to wear those again." Annie's green eyes glowed as she put her arm through Andrew's. "But my job is over now and it's time for me to be with my own kind." She patted Andrew's arm. "Besides, I've missed my family."

Grace's chest hurt and her stomach rolled. "But...but why?" she stammered.

"Because we couldn't allow the Council to be closer to you than we were," Mr. Reich said. "When we found out about Ben, we had to send my sweet Annie. You see it was easy for you to pick her as a best friend. That's one of her many powers. Annie can make anyone like her. Or as it was in your case, *need* her. And you needing your best friend these past few days really worked to our advantage. With all your desperate phone calls to Annie, we knew just where to find you."

Grace's entire body was numb and trembling all at the same time. Her best friends. The Three Amigos. It was all a lie.

And she had told Annie exactly where she was. Bess's Diner. Cooper's. Grace had led the Anti-Powers right to her.

"Now that we have you, it should be easy to dispose of the Council," Mr. Reich leered toward Grace. "With your genetic material, the Anti-Powers will be everywhere, out in the open, not hiding like some sniveling weaklings. So, before we go any further, I want to thank you, Miss MacKay. Thank you for helping me realize my father's dream." He brushed his hand across Grace's face and his fingers lingered on her lips. "I can see why my son enjoyed kissing you. You really are quite beautiful. Despite your dark hair and blue eyes, your genetic make-up and looks will fit in nicely with the rest of my family."

Grace pulled her head away from his hand and glowered at Mr. Reich.

"Oh, come now, dear," he smiled. "Look at the family I have arranged—Andrew, Annie, Gregory—magnificent creations if I do say so myself. Your genes will make excellent offspring for them."

Grace felt nauseated. She looked at Star who stood off to the side behind Gregory. "What about Star?"

Mr. Reich stood a little straighter and cleared his throat. "My daughter's glowing power did not exactly fit into my plans. I made sure the Misfits found her as a baby and I assume she has had a happy life." He looked at Star and smiled. "But thanks to your little visit to their community, Star has reclaimed a place in our family. She played her part beautifully and here you are."

Star arched her back and unintentionally glowed, her pride evident on her face. "Thank you, Father."

"Yes, yes. But try to control that glow of yours," he said brusquely with a wave of his hand. "We still need to stay concealed until we get out of these mountains and nasty trees. You know how I hate the woods. I don't want to spend any more time here than I have to."

Star's glow immediately disappeared and she sank back down onto the couch.

"So now," Mr. Reich looked to his other children, "it is time to move on. Please go get the Hummer ready. We have a long drive and the lab is waiting."

The three siblings nodded at their father and headed toward the door.

"You too, Star," Mr. Reich directed.

Star's face beamed as she popped up from the couch. "Oh yes, Father. Thank you, Father, thank you," she gushed before rushing outside to join her siblings.

"Andrew," Mr. Reich called after them. "Please take care of Ben after we leave. And try not to make too much of a mess. I don't want any evidence left behind."

"My pleasure," Andrew's eyes glowed red and he winked at Ben before he left the cabin.

Mr. Reich bent down and began to unlock Grace's restraints. "Time to go, my pet."

Grace looked over at Ben, whose eyes were now wide open as he struggled with his metal cuffs. "Stall," he mouthed to her.

"What about the Misfits? Aren't you afraid they'll find you?" Grace asked, wringing her one free arm out in relief. She glanced out the window and saw that the four siblings had their backs to the cabin, preparing to leave.

"Of course not," Mr. Reich laughed. "I went to training camp with that Dave and Petra and am fully aware of the Misfits' limitations. We'll be long gone before Petra can see anything."

Petra. Grace's eyes tried not to twinkle.

"So what are your great powers, Mr. Reich?" Grace said as she stretched her free arm up above her head.

"Mine? There are too numerous to mention, my dear. But as for my favorite, let's just say that I am partial to metal," Mr. Reich snickered as he leaned over Grace, working on the last of her restraints.

"So you really don't like wood!" With her one free arm, Grace grabbed one of the long wooden sticks from her hair clip and, with all she had left in her, thrust it deep into Mr. Reich's chest, piercing his heart through to the other side. His green eyes flew open and he fell back, gasping for air, unable to speak, the gurgle of blood being the only sound springing from his throat.

The clip banged to the floor and Grace's hair fell down into her face. For a moment she couldn't see. She just sat there dazed, trembling with heavy breaths, unable to move as she listened to Mr. Reich's bubbling throat.

It did not take long for Mr. Reich to die.

And with his last gurgling breath, the smell of burnt metal flooded the cabin as the few metal items in the cabin melted. Mr. Reich's power wafted from his lifeless body, attacking any metal it could find, even the massive chair imprisoning Ben.

"Grace!" Ben whispered to her. "We need to go!" Mr. Reich's dying power made the metal cuffs restraining Ben so pliable, he easily wriggled his hands and feet free. He stood up just as the chair became a metal mess pooling on the wooden floor.

The smell of the burnt metal goaded Grace out of her shock and, after struggling for just a moment, she was finally free of her last restraint. She pushed her hair away from her face and her eyes locked on Mr. Reich's bloody chest.

"Grace! Forget about him. We need to go now!"

Grace blinked her eyes and focused on Ben.

"Are you with me?" he asked.

Grace nodded, her eyes returning to the red ooze covering Mr. Reich's shirt.

"Okay, then come on!" Ben grabbed Grace's hand and pulled her toward the door. "But watch where you step. I don't need you stumbling over him and accidentally bringing the guy back to life."

Grace held onto Ben's hand as she sidestepped Mr. Reich's body, her eyes still fixated on his bloody chest. The blood was now spreading across the wooden floor and was hard to avoid as she crouched beside Ben underneath the window by the door.

Outside, a Hummer sat idling, aimed at the woods beyond. Star and Annie were in the backseat and Gregory sat in the driver's seat. Andrew leaned against the passenger door, laughing with his siblings inside.

"I don't think they know anything yet, but we can't stay in here forever." Ben said.

"So now what?" Grace's breathing was still heavy. She glanced at Mr. Reich's blood still streaming over the wooden floor and gripped Ben's hand tighter.

"I don't know. Let me think," Ben said, releasing Grace's hand. He had reentered Guardian mode.

Ben sat there, silently weighing his options and not too happy with his odds when all of a sudden, he saw Powers troops appear from the treetops. Dressed in camouflage, they flew down ropes, scrambled down tree trunks and glided in from the sky. Only seven or eight in number, they still outnumbered Gregory's entourage who looked around with shocked faces.

"Come on," Ben yanked Grace outside through the door. He turned and looked behind the cabin to the top of the hill. There stood Tracker and Dave grinning and waving.

Hearing the cabin door's wooden creak, Andrew spun around, his eyes meeting Ben's.

"Give it up," Ben yelled to him. "Daddy Dearest is dead."

Andrew stumbled back against the Hummer.

"Get in!" Gregory yelled to his brother.

Andrew's eyes narrowed at Grace before he jumped into the Hummer. The sibling Anti-Powers took off through the woods, the Hummer jostling over the rocky terrain. The Powers troops followed on foot, through the trees, and in the air.

Ben looked down at Grace and squeezed her hand. "Let's go home."

Chapter Twenty-Eight: First Kiss

The brick mansion was massive even by today's standards and the plantation was one of the few in South Carolina that survived the Civil War intact. The huge, white-columned front porch spanned the width of the entire house and the ornately carved front door was bordered on both sides by floor-to-ceiling, triple-sash windows. Inside, the foyer revealed a grand staircase that even Scarlett O'Hara would have envied. The mansion was palatial and filled with antiques and scared the life out of Grace.

She sat there in the cavernous foyer staring at the large double doors at the end of the long hall. Behind those doors sat the Council, discussing her fate, her life. Her Ben.

As if reading her mind, Ben reached over and softly held her hand. "Don't look so uptight. Everything will be okay."

"Can you promise me that?"

"No. But we can hope can't we?"

One of the doors cracked at the end of the hall and Dave poked his head out. "They're ready for you now." He half-smiled before closing the door again.

Ben and Grace stood and slowly walked the long hall toward the Council boardroom. The hall wasn't carpeted so their footsteps echoed loudly through the mansion. Grace didn't know which was louder, her footsteps or the heavy thumping of her heart.

"What do you think they will do?" Grace whispered over their footsteps.

"I don't know. Based on the Council code, their choices are limited. Execute me or send me off on a mission. Either way, I doubt they'll let us stay together."

"Do they always follow Council code?"

"Almost always. But we kind of have a special situation here with you being, well…you. So who knows what they'll do? We're kind of in uncharted territory here."

Grace's hand tightened around Ben's and she stopped right in front of the boardroom double doors. "Then it's now or never isn't it?"

Ben turned to face her and his face softened. "Absolutely."

Without hesitating, he wrapped Grace tenderly in his arms and their lips came together in a soft hungry kiss that had waited forever to be had. Sensual and desperate, their lips moved as if they were one. They explored each other as if touching for the first time. As if nothing else mattered but that gentle, wet kiss. The kiss that pressed their bodies together with a force only reserved for new lovers. The kiss that stirred their bodies to touch in unspeakable places, to move in breathless and uninhibited unison. It was a first kiss worth waiting for, worth devouring, worth savoring and in that kiss Grace finally felt safe. She felt like she belonged. She felt like she was home. In Ben's arms.

When Ben's lips finally released her, he still held her close, his fingers caressing her back in soft, firm waves. "Ready?" he whispered.

"No." She clutched Ben tighter and kissed his chest through his open collar. She let her lips linger on his skin to memorize his taste. She needed to feel him with every sense she had. To taste him, to smell him, to touch him as only his lover would. She needed more time. More time to experience Ben's arms, Ben's lips. Ben's everything.

But there was no time.

"I'm not ready either," he whispered, kissing her forehead delicately. "But that kiss was definitely worth the wait. Thank you for loving me." He looked down into her eyes one last time before he released her and slowly opened the doors to the Council boardroom.

Grace entered behind Ben, still gripping his hand, and nothing was as she expected. The room was a sea of faces, some of them familiar, most of them not, but all of them looking at her and only her. She was the center of their attention. Grace stood straighter, keeping her hold on Ben, his kiss empowering her to take whatever the Council dished out.

Dave walked over and gently guided them to the long table in the center of the room. "I believe you both know our Council leader, and my much older and wiser sister, Lady Covington."

Lady Covington sat at the head of the table and took her time looking them both over, but her eyes ultimately focused on Grace. "It is nice of you to join us…finally. We have been waiting longer than expected for you, Grace," she said.

Dave then gestured to the men sitting to the right and left of their Council leader. "And, of course, you know Julian, Lady Covington's lieutenant, and also Council member Carleton Hillary."

Grace smiled at the familiar faces but they did not smile back. She then glanced around the room and the only other person she recognized was Tom. He was standing across the room in the far corner staring at her, but when their eyes met, he awkwardly looked down and never looked back up.

"Well, Mr. Pickett," Lady Covington broke the room's heavy silence. "I hope you are ready to plead your case, young man, because you have quite a lot of explaining to do. And considering the special circumstances of this situation, we are all very eager to hear what you have to say. We appreciated the debriefing you gave Councilman Hillary on Gregory and his family. Your history with them should help our troops find the Reichs very soon. And your knowledge of the Anti-Powers will also go a long way in the defense of your case." Lady Covington paused and looked hard at Ben. "We are not your enemies, Mr. Pickett. You see, none of us want this to end badly, but we do still have our Council code to consider…as well as any supposed feelings you two may have for each other." She glanced at Dave who winked at her. "And while your feelings may be a factor in our decision on how to proceed in this matter, please know that this decision belongs to the Council and *only* the Council." She smiled and gestured to two empty chairs at the other end of the table. "So why don't you two have a seat and let's get started."

Ben looked down and leaned into Grace. "Remember, whatever they decide, we still have us," he whispered. "Just us."

Grace looked up at Ben and her blue eyes melted into his. "Yes. Just us."

More From This Author

(From *The Laws of Love*)

Her stomach knotted with the day's growing frustration.

"Where is that wire?" Livi yelled into her assistant's office. "The money was supposed to be here two hours ago!" The young attorney walked out of her office and plopped down in the small leather office chair across from her assistant's desk. "Are we sure the fax went through? Did they get our signatures?"

"Yes. Calm down," her assistant Nadine said as she turned away from her computer to face her irritated boss. "They received our signatures, the contract is fully executed, and they have our correct wire instructions. Accounting simply hasn't received the money yet. Don't worry. It'll get here."

"I know the money will get here eventually, but I told Robert the deal would close *today*," Livi said, as if Nadine did not know that fact already.

Her assistant's calmness did nothing to improve Livi's mood. Last night's blind date fiasco had reminded Livi once again that her monogram's initials were not going to change anytime soon and thus she had started this morning off in a bad mood only to have the day plummet downhill from there. It had taken a year to negotiate this fifty million dollar deal and now it came down to a silly computer dictating when Hampton Steel's money would be received. Livi was not handling the delay well.

As Assistant General Counsel, Livi Miller had closed more deals for Hampton Steel Incorporated than she cared to remember and waiting for the other company to wire the money into her company's account had always been the most aggravating part of these transactions. In this age of technology, Livi did not understand why the wire could not be here with a simple press of a button. However, transferring money from one multi-million dollar corporation to another was not easy, and the layers of approvals between corporations and banks had gotten thicker in recent years thanks to Wall Street's ethical shortcomings.

In her head, David Bowie and Freddie Mercury were loudly and repeatedly singing "Under Pressure." She needed this deal to close today. While her job did not depend on it, she wanted everything to run smoothly right now. With her boss, Robert, retiring soon, Livi was next in line to take his place as general counsel. It was not official but Robert had implied Livi's succession so many times that the entire company assumed she would get the job.

Despite her boss's implications, however, Livi still questioned the absolute certainty of her promotion. Robert's drinking had reached a point where his legal opinions bordered on malpractice thus intensifying Hampton Steel's need for his retirement to occur sooner rather than later. While Livi could usually cover for her boss and his alcohol-influenced legal opinions, her promotion was entirely in his hands. Having her deal close today would reinforce Livi's ability as the company's top lawyer and hopefully cement her succession in the sometimes cloudy mind of her boss.

Thinking of this deal's impact on her promotion prompted Livi to grab a hefty handful of M&Ms from the crystal bowl sitting on the corner of Nadine's desk.

"Are you that worried?" her assistant asked.

"No." Livi smiled. "But I appreciate you keeping this stash for me." Chocolate had always been her "go-to" vice whenever she was anxious.

Livi had known Nadine since high school. They had not been best friends at Millersville High—Nadine had been the social butterfly while Livi stuck with her boyfriend and the school library. But when Livi was hired by Hampton Steel a few years ago, she was pleasantly surprised to find Nadine's familiar face in the assistant's chair outside her new office, and they had worked together as a team ever since. Livi appreciated having an old high school acquaintance around and was always careful to call Nadine her "assistant" and not "secretary". She knew how valuable Nadine was to her and did not want to point out the obvious working hierarchy between them.

"Would you please call accounting and check again?" Livi sighed as she walked back into her office while finishing off her M&Ms and gulping her third Diet Coke of the afternoon. She did not care that the caffeine could intensify her soon-to-be-here migraine. She just knew it made her feel better now. She would worry about the migraine once it got here tonight.

Livi sat down at her desk and stared out her office window, irritated with both her failed blind date and the delay in today's deal closing. She knew she loved her job, but stressful times like these caused Livi to question why she had not just married right out of high school and taken a simpler and more traditional path for her life as most of her friends had. However, Livi had been anything but traditional growing up and this nonconformity allowed her to discover her life's goal in the law as early as junior high school.

She had just completed seventh grade and was volunteering as a summer tour guide for Millersville's historic courthouse. While other kids her age were riding bikes along rural trails or swimming the cool waters of the local lake and river, Livi intently watched Millersville's petty legal dramas unfold from the back row of the courtroom. The law excited the geek in her and she absorbed it with the intensity of someone twice her age.

As she grew older, nothing could extinguish her excitement, so it was a natural progression for Livi to eventually leave her hometown of Millersville for college and law school. The University of Virginia had not been easy. Its reputation had been right on the mark. But while she questioned her chosen career path at times, she never regretted it, despite the constant reminders of what she was missing in her social life.

"Liv," Nadine called from her outer office. "Your dad is on line one."

Livi immediately realized she had forgotten tonight's birthday dinner for her sister. "Hey, Dad," Livi tried to sound nonchalant over the phone. "What time is dinner?"

"You know darn well dinner's at six o'clock. That time hasn't changed since I left you all those messages on your cell, and at home, and at work," her dad sweetly bristled. "Don't ask me what time dinner is and don't be late. Elizabeth is looking forward to spending time with you and I know you can stop working long enough to celebrate her birthday."

Livi sighed. "Don't worry. I just have one more thing to close out and I'll be there with bells on."

"Well, I don't care what you're wearing. Just make sure you bring your undivided attention. And Livi…" Her dad paused.

"Yes, Dad," she said, anxious to get off the phone.

"I love you."

"I know, Dad. Love you too." Livi hung up the phone. "Nadine!" Livi called into her assistant's office. "What did accounting say?"

Nadine was already standing in Livi's doorway, her arms crossed and eyebrows raised in an I-told-you-so fashion. "You forgot your sister's birthday dinner, didn't you?" she said, ignoring Livi's question.

"Yes," Livi rolled her eyes.

"Well, today must be your lucky day," Nadine smiled. "Accounting just received the wire so the deal has officially closed.

You now have time to go downtown and get your sister something she actually wants—not whatever you can grab on the way like you usually do. So why don't you get out of here?"

With her multi-million dollar deal closed, Livi took a deep breath and finally relaxed. "Shopping is my thing." She beamed with an immediate mood change as she began packing up her briefcase. "Call me on my cell if anything comes up," she yelled to Nadine who had already retreated back to her office.

"I always do," said Nadine as she sat down in front of her computer again. "I'm just shocked you're actually leaving the office on time."

"Chalk it up to family guilt," Livi joked as she headed out the door.

• • •

Livi parked near her favorite store but decided to walk around downtown Millersville before hitting her beloved antique shop. A fall breeze helped push her along as she strolled, and while most of the trees had not yet reached their full color potential, Livi was already keyed up for the season to come. Fall was her favorite time of year, and she especially loved a Millersville fall. Set in the mountains of Virginia, Millersville was founded in the late 1800s by Livi's great-great grandfather, James Bradford Miller.

The town began as the only railway stop for miles, but GranPa Miller, as he was known, had positioned the town on the map when he established the first department store in the area. Even though any money her ancestors had was long gone, and Miller's Department Store closed in the 1960s, the Miller name was still prevalent throughout the area as evidenced by the faded paint on several downtown buildings. The Miller and Sons Dry Goods building now housed the local pub and Miller First National Bank had been remodeled into Nell's, Livi's favorite antique store.

In more recent years, a downtown resurgence had produced new, unique shops and restaurants, once again positioning Millersville as *the* place to be in the region. The town spent thousands of dollars on new sidewalks, lighting and landscaping in the downtown area, and today's busy streets were evidence of a successful investment. Tax breaks were granted to businesses that moved into town, and, thus, Hampton Steel, Livi's employer, made the astute decision to relocate its headquarters in Millersville.

These tax breaks, combined with the local non-union workforce, had helped the company become Millersville's primary employer as well as one of the top steel fabricating plants in the country. Hampton Steel's move also provided Livi the opportunity to practice what her father called "big city" corporate law while maintaining her hometown roots.

Olivia Grace "Livi" Miller was born and raised in Millersville and she loved everything about it. Familiarity of sidewalk smells and the knowledge that she recognized almost everyone in town gave her a comfort level living here on her own. Livi was fascinated with her hometown's history, and she had recently lucked into buying a home in the older, established section of town just blocks from where she was now walking. The home was not large, but it was not a cottage either and had enough room for her and her large mutt, Gatsby, to have their own space when needed. It had been built by some long-forgotten ancestor of Livi's and, overall, was still in fairly good shape. She was slowly filling it with the English antiques she loved and hoped to have her dining room complete in time to host her family's Christmas dinner.

After browsing a few of the other downtown stores, Livi finally found herself at Nell's. With her limited free time spent decorating, the antique store had become her new home away from home. She took a deep breath as she walked into the store and immediately began to forget today's stresses. She knew she would leave Nell's with more shopping bags than she needed, filled with more items for herself than for her sister.

The bank building's smell still permeated the shop's plastered walls and the dark hardwood floors creaked with history. Bank teller windows had been uniquely converted to display cases showcasing Nell's latest acquisitions from her contacts in the antiques world, and upon a quick review of today's displays, Livi immediately saw something she wanted for herself. There, propped up in the center teller window, was the most gorgeous Imari platter she had ever seen. The blue and orange details intricately woven on the large porcelain oval popped out at her screaming, *Take me home*—or so Livi envisioned until a little voice from the back of her head whispered, *Remember your sister.*

With one quick look at the price tag and a small choke as she realized her checkbook would not allow her this luxury right now, Livi began browsing for her sister's gift. The antique platter's perfect spot on her dining room wall would remain empty for now.

"I saw your heart flutter at that one." Nell Cooper Harris laughed as she came out of the back storeroom wiping sweat off her brow and hair out of her eyes with hands gloved in a workman's dirty suede. "I just got that in from Atlanta."

"Well, my heart may be fluttering but if I don't get Elizabeth's birthday present before six o'clock tonight, my butt will be burning with my dad's boot print. By the way, you look a mess," Livi joked as she headed to the next display case.

"Inventory." Nell sighed and smiled. "Did you have anything in mind?"

"No. You know Elizabeth. She's hard to buy for. She flits from one interest to another so it's hard to know what this week's passion is." Livi loved her younger sister but her own Type A personality never understood Elizabeth's artsy side.

Nell walked over to Livi and gave her the usual welcoming hug. "I think I might have just the thing for our Elizabeth," she said, motioning for Livi to follow her.

Like Livi, Nell had grown up in Millersville and moved away for college, but after graduating with a degree in art history, she and her college sweetheart had settled back into her familiar Millersville life. Nell's husband, Richard, was an entry-level bookkeeper at Hampton Steel, so Livi saw at least one of them almost every day and considered the couple two of her closest friends. Nell appeared to effectively balance her sole proprietor image with that of soccer mom to her three children, and, at times, Livi envied her. Nell had succeeded with the two-sided life Livi envisioned for herself, maintaining a career on one side and a family on the other. But being raised Baptist in a small southern town meant that before Livi could check "having children" off her Life List, she needed to check off "find true love and get married." So, while she had maintained control of the career side of her life, Livi had been unable to find the socially acceptable order of her life's personal side. Nevertheless, whenever she felt her envy of Nell creeping back in, Livi rationalized to herself that Nell was a few years older and had had more time to develop her perfect life. Livi liked to believe she still had a few more years for her Life List to establish its own proper order.

"What about this?" Nell said, holding up an antique brooch enameled in candy-apple red—an appropriate gift for an elementary school teacher.

"Perfect." Livi smiled.

As Nell wrapped the gift at the front counter, Livi's eyes glanced at the framed photo hanging over the cash register. It never failed. Every time she stood at that counter, her heart beat faster as she tried not to look at his green eyes. The photo showed Nell's younger brother, Jake, dressed in his desert camouflage posing with his friend, Ben, both grinning from ear to ear despite their obvious surroundings. The dust on Jake's face made the green of his eyes more intense and, although the photo appeared to be somewhat recent, Livi thought Jake's eyes looked just as they did in high school.

The military and rugged sands of Iraq had not dimmed the sparkle and mischief radiating from those eyes, and they still revealed an old soul that held a special place in Livi's heart. Today especially, with the barrage of reminders of what Livi's life lacked, these green eyes attacked Livi's heart more than usual and she allowed herself to wander through her minefield of memories while she waited on Elizabeth's gift to be wrapped.

By all accounts, Jake Cooper was Livi's first love, and except for a mistaken stint with a fellow law student that truly did not count, Livi probably considered Jake her only love. All of Livi's other beaus had been measured by her "Jake" standard and, unfortunately for them, none had ever reached Jake's level in Livi's heart. They began dating at the end of their sophomore year of high school, and the following summer taught Livi the joys of young, carefree love with a boy who admired her as much as he adored her. They spent that summer swimming in the lake, hiking the local hills and learning how to hold hands in a way that made Livi's heart take precedence over her mind's legal ambitions. Over time, Jake taught her to fly-fish and she taught him which fork to use with shrimp at her graduation dinner. For their senior prom, they even learned to dance the shag together just like Livi's parents used to dance on the Myrtle Beach boardwalk in their younger days.

The two teenagers made a beautiful couple. Livi had long, dark hair and "girl-next-door" looks. Jake was ruggedly handsome with his green eyes and tall, broad build. His obvious strength contrasted with the sweetness he showered on Livi, and her blue eyes melted whenever he gave her that special look. Their relationship was the envy of the high school gossip mill, for they met the clichéd definition of opposites attract. He was star player of the football team. She was star member of the debate team. While Jake spent his afternoons in the gym, Livi spent her time in the library. However, for whatever reason, when they were together it was as if heaven had thrown a star around the two of them and each one glowed brighter than when they were apart. The laughter they accumulated over the two and a half years they dated was immeasurable, and Livi's memories of their time together had become more romanticized in recent years, pushing aside the realities of why their time together had ended.

When all was said and done, Livi blamed herself for their break up. The summer after their high school graduation had been a confusing mix of plans and memories. Both fully intended to stay together but each knew that fall was closing in on them. As summer ended and Livi packed her bags for Charlottesville, she and Jake told each other that distance would not affect what they had.

However, time had different intentions and, while they tried to keep in touch, the calls and visits became fewer and fewer. Livi worked to maintain her grades and Jake searched for his lot in life assuming Livi was quickly leaving him behind. By the time her exams were over that first semester and she returned home for Christmas, Jake had already left for California with Ben. He had told her that he had a line on a great job but that he had to be out west before the first of December. Thus, Livi came home to an empty holiday realizing she and Jake had broken up without either really saying the words.

Deciding to ask the question that had never been asked in all her time spent in Nell's store, Livi's remembrances forced her to blurt out, "So, how's Jake?"

Nell stopped wrapping the gift and looked up with a grin that competed with the Cheshire Cat's. "Do you have ESP or something?" she said.

"No." Livi was confused.

"Then why don't you ask him yourself?" Nell loudly called out, "Jake!"

And with that one word, Livi turned to see her past rounding the corner out of the back storeroom and looking better than anything she had seen in quite a while.

About the Author

Lisa White was born in Kingsport, Tennessee and raised in Bristol, Virginia. After graduating from the University of Virginia with a degree in Italian language and literature, she obtained her law degree from the University of Richmond School of Law. She currently lives in Southwest Virginia with her husband and two children.

Please visit Lisa at:
www.lisawhiteauthor.com
Other books by Lisa
The Laws of Love (Crimson Romance 2012)